Visit us at www.boldstrokesbooks.com

By the Author

Hers to Protect

Secrets on the Clock

Shadows of a Dream

SHADOWS OF A DREAM

by
Nicole Disney

2019

SHADOWS OF A DREAM

ISBN 13: 978-1-63555-598-1

This Trade Paperback Original Is Published By
Bold Strokes Books, Inc.
P.O. Box 249
Valley Falls, NY 12185

First Edition: December 2019

CREDITS
Editor: Cindy Cresap
Production Design: Susan Ramundo
Cover Design By Tammy Seidick

Acknowledgments

As always, a big thank you to Bold Strokes Books. I am so honored and happy to be part of this group of incredibly talented and kind people. Thank you to Radclyffe for building this beautiful community and giving our stories a home.

Thank you so much to Sandy Lowe for being willing to take a chance and letting me push some edges with this one. Your thoughts and input made this story a better, stronger version of itself. You understood what I was going for right away and helped make it real.

Speaking of amazing editors, a big thank you also to Cindy Cresap for all your work, patience, advice, kindness, and the sharpest eye for detail I've ever seen. Thank you for always taking me up a level.

A huge thank you to my family. You are such a group of rock stars I can't even imagine living without. Mimi, Patty, Celena, Annalese, Larry, each of you have always been so supportive, and you all mean so much more to me than I can put into words.

A special thanks to my mom for all your support, belief, love, and always always having my back. Being your daughter is the luckiest thing that ever happened to me. There has never been a better mom.

And, of course, to the love of my life, Cassandra. I couldn't do any of it without you. Always my first reader, my guidance when I'm stuck, my reassurance when I'm full of doubt, my perspective when I'm hurt, and my best friend no matter what. I love you.

Dedication

For the lost ones

Author's Note

Hello and thank you for stepping into this novel with me. This story is one that has been in my heart for many years now, and I often say it is where I found myself as a writer. It was originally published in 2013 by JMS Books under the title *Dissonance in A Minor*. I was both sad and relieved when that contract came to an end, sad because this world and all of its characters mean so much to me, but relieved because I knew if I was given another shot at this story, it could be better.

Shadows of a Dream is a reworking of *Dissonance in A Minor*. In many ways, it is untouched, and in others, it is a completely different story. Deciding what to tinker with and what to preserve was a great challenge. There are parts of this story that sound young to my ears now, six years after publishing the original, but I remind myself it is indeed about a young woman finding her way, and the way it is written is what that sounds like, juxtaposed by some of the most adult situations a person can face. There are references to things like pay phones that aren't relevant today, but it felt wrong to rip these characters out of the world in which they lived to move them to current day. The pieces I did decide to change have all been in the effort of making the story more of what it was always supposed to be, not making it something else.

Love can be consuming, and that can sound romantic, but this story is about finding the wisdom and compassion to love yourself.

I hope you enjoy it.

Chapter One

Her lips are soft; I can tell just by looking. They're shameless but timid. They're waiting, begging for mine.

Wait, I need to back up.

There's this girl getting in my face, one with not nearly as attractive lips. "You rug lickin' dyke!"

Wait, wait, wait. That's still not the place to start. Okay, let's go to the beginning of that evening, the evening I met Jaselle.

I'm in my alley, passing the time by walking up and down the parking space line like I'm doing a roadside sobriety test. I'll do anything to take the focus off my ice cube limbs. The back door opens and Benny sticks his balding head out.

"Rainn, you only got fifteen minutes left. You know that, right?"

"I know, Benny. I know."

"Where are they then?"

"They're coming." God, I hope they're coming.

"I got people lined up after you, you know? You're going to throw my whole night off again." The door closes before I can say anything. Poor Benny. If he wasn't so attached to us losers, he'd have told us never to come back a long time ago. Although, I guess he does get us for a pretty good price: free.

Jayden swings wide around the corner in his beater pickup, the back of which is spilling over with drums, amplifiers, cords, and all kinds of other miscellaneous crap. Alex and Shiloh comprise part of the "miscellaneous crap," trying to keep everything balanced and nearly falling out themselves.

"You're late."

"We don't go on for fifteen minutes." Jayden slides out of the driver's seat, and I see the most probable reason they're late. His foot-tall Mohawk is in excellent condition and freshly dyed red.

"When's the last time you set up that fast?"

"Will you just grab the snare?"

We set up at Mach 3 and still don't even come close to being ready in time, but Benny is a pal, so the house music blares while we finish up and the band in the slot after us gets bumped. Not a good way to make friends.

We're regulars here, and so are the Chapel-rats, so we get some cheers when I finally lean in to the mic.

"We're the Suicidal Angels."

The music pulses through me so loud my teeth are rattling. I don't have to think about the words I'm singing anymore. They just come out. I try to think about them, though, to stay in the moment and feel every note, every syllable, every subtlety, to connect to those secrets woven beneath the surface that are so much more than the simple vibrations.

But every time I start to slip away into that erotic dimension of pain and instinct, I'm drawn back by Alex, who's wandering off the beat every eighth measure; Shiloh, who's jumping around with his bass like a lunatic, wrapping himself up in the cord to the point there's no way he won't eat shit; or Jayden, talented Jayden, who's not so much messing up as much as ignoring the song completely and playing whatever he damn well pleases.

And now I suck too because I'm not in the music anymore. Now I'm chewing Jayden out in my head, telling him how hard I slave writing this music, how many times I've begged him to help but he never does. No, he's not creative until he's on stage playing on a whim and sounding like hell because of it.

Still, the rats are jumping around in a state of intoxicated, brain cell stunted glee. It's all the same to them. "*I'm talking to myself again, echoes of insanity*," I sing.

Finally, the pain is over. The show is done, and it felt more like public humiliation than performing. We head to the bar for shots. It takes all of three seconds for Jayden to be in the center of an adoring circle of tramp stamp bearing underage females. He's always surrounded by girls. He's hot, I guess, if you like red Mohawks.

They're asking about the scar above his eye, which is a slash through his eyebrow where the hair won't grow back.

His story: "I was snowboarding in New Zealand with Shaun White. He dared me to hit this wicked rail. He was too chickenshit to do it 'cause it was getting icy. I was doing this sick tailslide and wiped out. Hit my face on the rail. Had a concussion. It knocked me out for five minutes. Shaun was flippin' out."

The girls ooh and ah, and he gets laid later.

Real story: Jayden, Alex, Shiloh, and I are piled in the pickup. Jayden finally caved and let Alex drive because only Alex knows where we're going. He has friends in the mountains having a party we can't miss.

The party has already started. We're all inebriated and far beyond responsible driving capabilities. We've each eaten a handful of mushrooms and are seeing things that aren't there.

The radio is blasting one of Alex's favorite songs. He gets so worked up in a drunken steering wheel drumming session that he mistakes the brake pedal for a kick drum. He slams the brakes so hard Jayden flies out of the passenger seat and smashes face-first into the windshield.

He does not have a concussion. He does not lose consciousness. No one is flipping out. Actually, we're all laughing hysterically.

The girls think he's a moron, and Alex and Shiloh get laid. Needless to say, Jayden tells his story.

"Look who's here." Alex nods at the door.

"Shit." It's this major pain in the neck named Bianca. Every time she's here she makes sure to come ruffle my feathers. I don't know how I got on her bad side, but she's relentless.

Like there's a Rainn detector in her brain, her eyes lock on to me. I already know there's no way to avoid the confrontation that's waltzing toward me on stilettos, freshly ripped out of a Jersey Shore episode.

"I thought I told you to quit coming in here," she says.

"Fuck you, bitch." Yes, I know, my wit is dazzling. We're close to a table where two women are just trying to enjoy a couple beers. I notice her immediately but am way too caught up in the Bianca situation.

Bianca shoves her whole body up against mine, our noses nearly touching. "Take your no-talent scrubs to another spot. We're tired of hearing your dumb asses." I laugh and give my friends a "what the hell is she doing" look.

"That's not sinking in for you, bitch? Listen, no one wants your disgusting fag ass in here." Yeah, we're up to speed. Bianca is the female with the not so attractive lips.

"You rug lickin' dyke!"

I'm not supposed to fight with the customers. I have to stay cool.

She spits in my face.

She spits in my face. (Just making sure you've got the picture) She spits a big ol' wad of saliva in my face.

My fist acts of its own accord. It winds back and swings without asking my permission. It lands with vicious force, not disrupted along the way by anything, no arms flying, no grazing off her because she managed to move a little, nothing. Pure connection.

It sends her to the ground. I'm on top of her before I know it, my knee in her chest, my fist beating her face repeatedly. Blood is coming from somewhere. Her entire face is covered with it. I swing again, but finally something prevents me from annihilating her.

A strong arm wraps around me and pulls. It's Jayden. He lifts me all the way to my feet and bouncers take over from there. They drag me, kicking and raging, to the door and give me a shove that knocks me to the gravel outside. The boys are already piling out after me laughing.

Then Benny comes out. "Settle down, girl."

They're high-fiving, nothing like a Friday night chick fight to paste smiles on their faces. I get up and dust myself off, then shove Benny.

"What's so fucking funny? How could you bounce me and not her?"

"Hey, she's not exactly in there drinking it up," he says. "She's trying to find her face, and then she'll be going to St. Joseph's to have them reattach it, okay?"

"Whatever."

"Look, someone is going to call the cops over this, and when they get here what am I supposed to say? That the chick on the floor with the crushed skull is to blame? She started it, Officer, I swear? It won't matter. You have to get out of here."

"But, Benny—"

"I know. I heard what she said. I saw her spit at you, okay? I know, babe. And I'm glad you did what you did. I just don't want you getting in trouble." He slaps me on the back like he's a coach.

"Go on, get. Take that bloody shirt off too." He tosses me his T-shirt, which leaves him in his undershirt, round belly bulging. I change right there in the street and get a whistle from Shiloh.

"Fuck off."

Jayden comes and gives me a hug. "You need a ride?"

I can't help but laugh a little. "Who needs a ride to nowhere?"

He smiles and gives me a punch on the arm before he turns to go back inside. It's times like this I wish I did have a place, times like this when the romanticized image of the struggling musician from the back alley turns into the idiot bum who should have at least picked a fuckin' beach to be homeless on, not cold ass Denver.

I go around the building to retrieve my coat from the alley. I crouch down and start digging in the small storage space that contains all my possessions. I hear music spill out of the Chapel behind me. People aren't supposed to come out the back door, and since the back door leads to my domain, I find it more irritating than most people expect. But when I turn around to chew out the offender, I stop short.

She's stunning. She has tattoos covering the majority of both of her arms, not sleeves though, individual tattoos. And she has dreadlocks. Long, dark, perfect dreadlocks, if there is such a thing as perfect dreadlocks. If you asked me five minutes ago to conjure up my ideal female, it would not have sounded like this, but I'm not sure I've ever been so attracted to someone. And the second I see her I know with absolute certainty she is about to change my life.

"Can I help you?" My voice comes out sharper than I wanted, residual effects of my initial irritation.

She shakes her head only once and digs in her pockets. She finds what she's after and emerges with cigarettes. She lights one with a match. The orange glow reflects in her eyes. She shakes the match out and exhales.

"Need one?" I notice the word "need" immediately. She didn't say "want one," but why? Because my shoe sole is a free hanging flap and she assumes I can't afford my own? I take the cigarette she's offering and lean into the match she lights. As I lean toward her, I catch a whiff of a heart-stopping scent, strong, smooth, warm. I'm halfway through a Newport before I remember I don't smoke.

I allow myself to drift away for a moment before a faint but unmistakable sound disturbs the air. Sirens. And I know they'll only get closer. I sigh loudly and turn to tell her I have to go, but when my eyes make it to hers, she smiles just a little and nudges her head toward the front of the building.

"You need a place to crash?" I force a smile. There's that word again. I want to go so bad, but not like that. "I got some wine at home," she adds.

I return my smelly coat to the storage space and stand up with a grin. She smiles. It's over when she smiles. She leads me back around front to the parking lot.

My stomach lurches when two cop cars pull up as we're walking away, but she appears to be unperturbed. She puts her cigarette between her lips as she opens the door to a ninety-something Toyota Celica and slips inside. She leans across the car and unlocks the passenger door for me. I take a last look at the Chapel, the flashing red and blue lights, flick away my cigarette, and sink into the passenger seat.

Inside the car, it seems like a different world. Yes, the lights are still flashing behind us, but I'm no longer vulnerable to them. It's all a big joke now. The only thing to remind me it even happened is my torn and bloody knuckles, throbbing deliciously.

She pulls out of the Chapel's parking lot. Her Celica jerks eagerly. She's so relaxed I wonder for an instant if she realizes they were there for me. Of course, she does. Aside from the knowing look when the sirens were closing in, we'd crashed into her table for Christ's sake. That reminds me, she'd been there with a chick.

I steal a glance. She's so friggin' beautiful I still haven't gotten over the awe factor.

"So, where'd your girl go?" I ask.

"She wasn't my girl, and I imagine she probably went home." I try to stop myself from smiling but can't.

I catch myself zoning out watching the road zip by. I try to pay attention to where we're going and am vaguely aware we're heading over the borders of my part of town. I can breathe easier here.

When she parks, I feel like I'm waking up from a nap. She's stopped in front of a cozy looking five-story building. I get out and follow her up the stairs, admiring the stone lions on either side as I pass.

We're uptown now, not in the richest of neighborhoods, but a few steps over the Chapel for sure. She appears beside me and finds her key. Again, her warm smell overwhelms me.

"Well?" she asks. I step inside. Where does she live? Top floor? First? She leads me around the corner and starts down some stairs. Basement. I follow along behind her. She stops in front of a door at the end of the hall.

"I should probably warn you, I have a roommate." Her face tightens with anxiety as she says it.

"Okay. That's cool." I don't have to tell you I'd rather be alone with her, but I smile anyway and try to seem nonchalant.

She turns the key and creaks the door open. She steps in so quietly it feels like we're sneaking in. I guess we might be.

"Jaselle?" It's a man's voice from another room. She sighs and looks at me apologetically before answering.

"Yeah, it's me." There's a short hallway that is the entrance into the place, and to the left an open door reveals a room in disarray. There's a mattress on the floor, One Love posters on the walls, clothes everywhere, and dishes littering the ground. I know instantly this is the roommate's room. It has man written all over it. Around the corner to the right, the place opens up into a much bigger living space than I would have guessed.

The most conspicuous thing in this room is the man lying stretched across a brown couch in a torn, fringed, and faded bathrobe far beyond its lifespan. He's already starting to sit up when we come in, but when he sees me he shoots to attention.

"Who the fuck is that?" He flings his arm my way.

"This is, uh—"

"Rainn," I say. Nice, she doesn't even know my name.

"*Rainn*? Damn it, Jaselle, you can't just bring home any trash you want. What's the matter with you? Where did you get her?"

"She's not a stray dog, Noah, she's a friend. Relax."

"Who do you think you're fooling?"

Jaselle stares him down, grabs my arm, and pulls me into the kitchen. "Here, sit." She pats the counter, then goes to work running my bloody hand under the faucet.

"You don't have to do that," I say.

She looks at me. "Hey, don't worry about him. He's an idiot."

"I can hear you," Noah says from the couch.

"He can't help it," Jaselle continues with a grin. "Dementia runs in his family."

Noah appears from around the corner. "I'm not crazy. I'm enlightened." He comes to get a closer look. "Oh, that's wonderful, she's getting blood everywhere."

"Shut up already, Noah, Jesus. She got in a fight."

"How barbaric."

"It's not like I started it," I say.

"Are you really that weak-minded? Violence is ignorant. Reverting to the ways of the caveman."

"I told you, I didn't start it."

"What difference does that make? Thank God you'll never be president. Every time someone pisses you off you'd just nuke them."

"I hardly think that's the—"

"She's a savage, Jaselle. Look at her."

"I was there. The bitch got what was coming to her." Jaselle turns the water off and pours two glasses of the promised red wine.

"You're both savages," Noah says.

"Well, we savages are going to bed." Jaselle hands me a glass, grabs my free hand, and guides me out of the kitchen. We turn the corner to the hall I had already predicted to be Jaselle's section of the apartment. It's like a different universe from the hall we entered through.

There are paintings covering every inch of wall from the hallway all the way into her bedroom, hundreds of them, big and small, hung and stacked and leaning.

"Wow. What are all these?"

"They're mine. I can't afford a studio for all this right now. Sorry about the clutter."

"Sorry? They're amazing. You painted these?"

"Yeah, but trust me, I'd rather they weren't here. I need to sell them."

I'm aware of Jaselle shuffling things around behind me, doing I'm not sure what, but I'm preoccupied with browsing the walls. The colors are striking. The scenes are somehow sad. I feel like I just dropped into Wonderland.

"They're beautiful." Jaselle doesn't seem to mind when I leave her room again to look at the paintings in the hall. Each is more intriguing than the last. They pull me farther and farther down the hallway until I'm at a second door. It's open just a little, and through the crack of space I catch a glimpse of it, a grand piano, cherry wood finish, curved legs, intricate hand carvings. I'm craning my neck for a better look when Jaselle startles the stealth right out of me.

"Go on in."

"You sure?"

"Yeah, come on."

I circle the flawless piano, afraid to touch it, certain I'm imagining it. "Do you play?" I ask.

"Nope. My grandmother left it to me."

"It's spectacular."

She must notice I'm salivating over it. "I'm told it has a beautiful sound," she says. Instinctively, I go to it and hold my fingers over the keys.

"Play something," Jaselle says.

"You sure? It won't irritate your roommate?"

"I'm sure it will, but if we live in accordance with Noah we won't be allowed to do anything but smoke weed and draw peace signs."

I sit down and take a deep breath. I'm nervous. It's been a while since I could say that. Besides the fact that I have a gorgeous woman watching me, I'm unsure of my abilities. Back in my little alley, all I have to work with is a not so glorious hundred-dollar keyboard I can only power by jacking Benny's electricity. And here I have the most beautiful antique grand piano I've ever seen. Completely different animals. The keys of a piano are heavier and a little wider. Aside from aesthetics the differences are subtle, but can still spell catastrophe for muscle memory.

I decide something short, slow, and pretty is a good way to go, so I start playing Chopin's Prelude Op. 28 No. 2, one of my favorites. Once I'm past the first measure my fingers take over, and the rest of the room melts away.

Then I feel her arms slip around me, her breath in my hair. I press the last note and spin around on the bench.

She doesn't back away. "You're really good."

Her lips are soft, I can tell just by looking. They're shameless but timid. They're waiting, begging for mine.

Chapter Two

Something about not being on my own, well, pavement, keeps me half-awake all night. The soft pastels of sunrise are only just creeping in, and I'm staring at the ceiling with a titanic knot in my stomach. I can hear Jaselle breathing next to me though I refuse to look at her.

Instead, I look out her window, which is three-quarters of the way up the wall since we're in the basement. It feels like it's a mile away. The view is overgrown weeds and some kid's bicycle wheel.

I sit up slowly, in microscopic increments so as not to wake her. Once I'm up, I notice the weakness and dehydration that comes from drinking. I don't have a headache, though. I didn't drink nearly enough to get sick, and still there's this nauseous squeezing in my throat. What have I done?

The night comes back to me in flashes, Bianca's spit landing on my cheek, the moldy pizza on Noah's floor, Jaselle's breath in my ear, her thighs around my neck, the warmth of her kiss. Too warm. Way too warm. I have to get out of here.

I ease out of bed and start putting on my clothes. My heart is pounding like waking her will detonate every nuclear missile in the world. I'm missing a sock and using every ounce of my energy to calm my frantic search. I'm certain I'm going to wake her up. Finally, I say screw the sock and put my shoe on without it.

I stand in the doorway for a minute, looking at her finally. Something about her pulls me toward her in a way I've never felt. She's a magnet, and I'm metal. I'm certain it must be exactly that, not the other way around.

I roll my eyes when I notice the wood floors. Last night they looked nice, but now they look like a never-ending death trap. No matter how slow and careful I step, I can still hear the tap of my shoe, and as I shift my weight there's a steady groan. It takes me ten minutes to cross the living room.

I feel that thunder in my chest again as I turn the corner. Noah's bedroom stands between me and freedom. I take long, painstaking strides past his open door. He's facedown on his mattress. His muffled snores are steady.

I put my hand on the doorknob, squeeze my eyes shut, and turn it. It sounds like someone crumpling up a newspaper. Noah stops snoring. I stop moving, frozen, petrified. Then he starts again. I let out a huge breath of relief and cram myself out the tiny opening I've made.

Outside, the wind is blowing, making what should have been a warm day sharp and cold. I curse myself for not bringing my stupid coat. So what if it's dirty and ripped?

I walk fast like she's going to come get me until I'm off her street. Then I start laughing like a crazy person. I can't stop. What an absurd fear, that someone's going to come after me. Then the tears come. I can't put my finger on what it is, that she's going to wake up and think I played her, that I'm running from something I should want, or the irrational terror that she's actually going to chase me. No one is chasing you, Rainn. No one will ever chase you.

I take a deep breath and wipe my face, then turn my attention to figuring out where I am and how to get home. Why didn't I pay better attention on the way here? I pick a direction and walk, hoping something along the way will jog my memory. I call this psychic walking, letting intuition take over and hoping for the best. It usually works out.

But today it doesn't, of course. I'm walking and walking and nothing seems familiar. Eventually, I do what I should have done from the beginning and stop at a gas station to ask for directions. The relief of walking inside makes me want to just curl up and stay here. My hands and arms have this nice pattern of purple going on, like the shadow of water. My knuckles have cracked back open and are bleeding again.

I walk around like I'm doing something for a minute, stalling so I can warm up. The cashier is eyeing me. I don't know how people know you don't belong, but they always do.

I go up to him. "Hey, I'm trying to get downtown, 20th and Welton-ish."

He smirks at me. "Well, you're all fucked up then." He rolls out some blank receipt paper and goes to work drawing a map. It's never a good sign when the directions are so extensive they need to draw. He turns it around for me to examine and starts going over all the different ways I might choose to go. They all boil down to one thing: you should have found your sock.

I thank him and take the map. Outside again, I notice a pay phone and think really hard about calling Jayden to ask for a rescue. I despise doing that, though, and the sun is starting to get higher, so it should be warming up. One day in the dead of winter I'll need that call more, and I'm mad at him about last night still anyway, so I start walking again.

Three hours later, I can see the beat-up sign that reads "Blue Moon" with a cheesy crescent moon shaping the second o, which doesn't even make sense. That's what the bar is really called. Only the guys and I call it the Chapel. I said it one day and it just stuck. It always seemed so much more appropriate.

Jayden's pickup is parked in front. I close those last few yards to the bar, take out my key, and let myself in. Benny and the band are all here. They're on their feet and all over me the second I step inside.

"Rainn!" "Where have you been?" "Where did you go?" The questions are a barrage. Benny seems genuinely concerned while the others are more curious than anything.

"I need a drink." My throat is on fire from the walk and the dry, chilled air. I meant water, but Benny slips a rum and Coke in my hand. I take a sip. The warmth of the rum runs down my arms while the Coke is the most refreshing thing I've ever tasted. Brilliant bartender, Benny.

They're already set up for practice. I must be really late. I go grab Jayden's guitar, sit on the stool in front of the mic, and absentmindedly start tuning it for him.

"Heeel-looo," Alex draws it forever. "Rainn, what happened?"

"I went home with some girl." I try to sound as casual as possible, hoping if I sound like it's not worth talking about, they won't drill me. Alex and Shiloh start whooping like third graders.

"Ohhhh, some girl, huh? Which one, player?" Shiloh says.

"The one with the dreads."

"Oh, yeah? She was hot. How come you get better pussy than I do?"

"Who says I got any?" Alex and Shiloh look at each other for half a second and then burst out laughing.

"Come on, tell us what happened. Was it good? We want to know!"

"No, no, no. We've got work to do, guys, come on. Get your shit." They moan and groan but eventually move to their instruments. Jayden is still sitting at the bar, unusually quiet. I go over and give him his guitar.

"Let's go. Only a month 'til Brad comes in."

He takes his guitar from me reluctantly. "I think we're ready," he says.

"I don't."

"You never do."

"Last night sucked. You know that."

"I was just trying something new. That's what artists do, not stick to some rigid formula like a paint-by-numbers."

"The stage is not the place to be creative, practice is. When we're on stage we need to be on it," I say.

"The show needs some life. You can't just stand there and deliver the same crap the exact same way all the time. No wonder we aren't getting anywhere. I'm bored by us, and I'm in the band."

"People want to hear good music, Jayden. Jumping around and acting crazy is great if you can do it and still sound good. New music is fantastic, but we *all* have to be playing it, not just you."

Jayden rolls his eyes.

"This guy knows everyone, Jay. I just want us to sound good when he comes to see us."

"Mm-hmm."

"So, fluff up your Mohawk and let's go." I flash him my biggest smile, begging with my teeth for cooperation. He glares at me but moves to his place.

The guys all have short attention spans on stage. Take away the audience and it's hard to get them through a single song without someone screwing around, but today they're on their best behavior. Jayden sulks his way through practice, playing everything exactly as it's written, offering no feedback. I know he's trying to make a point of how lame and boring that is, but he sounds fantastic, so the effect is lost on me. I don't let myself get irritated that now is the time I want him to share his ideas and be free, yet he refuses once again.

Alex and Shiloh tend to take their lead from Jayden, so when he stops with the antics and just plays, they do the same, and the music comes alive. This is what gives me hope, these small little moments. They keep me playing, keep me nagging and pushing for perfection. They keep me banging down Brad Schafer's door even though he's failed to appear the last two times he's promised to come see us.

The music industry is brutal, though, and I figure if he didn't want to see us he'd have no reason not to just say so. No one tiptoes around feelings in this business, so he must want to come see us. We're obviously not on the top of his priority list, but he wants to see us. I know it.

We barely get to practice since I was late. The bar opens at four o'clock, and we have to get our stuff out of the way so the band that performs tonight can have time to set up.

The guys have their hoodies on and are about to leave for the night. All three of them live in a one-bedroom apartment together. I say good-bye and spend the last hour before it gets busy hanging out at the bar with Benny. Then I head out the back door to the alley.

It's not too cold yet. I flip down the door to the little storage unit in the wall. It's a ground level, two-by-five-by-two hole in the wall by the dumpster with a thin metal flip door. It's probably intended for tools or something, but I use it to hold my few belongings.

I have three good blankets inside, my coat, a few changes of clothes, a couple books, notebooks, my keyboard, and the foldable stand and seat that go with it. I pull out my keyboard and set up my little music station. I use headphones and keep myself tucked away behind the dumpster so no one bothers me. Bad headphones though, really bad, bad on purpose so no one gets interested in stealing them.

And then I play. I start with the music before I worry about lyrics. It always happens a little different. Sometimes it's a beat, other times it's a melody, a chord progression, but there's always something rattling around in my head, and I just play until it sounds right. Then I add another layer, and another, and another. Then maybe I'll move things around, go up or down an octave, push a handy little button on my keyboard and see what it sounds like with a violin thrown in. We don't have a violin, or a violinist for that matter, but it's all about the creative process.

I'm deep in my mode when the back door of the Chapel opens and Benny steps out with a cigarette in his mouth, a plate in one hand, and a cup in the other.

"Hey," he says. I smile at him and accept the opportunity for a break. It's two o'clock in the morning. Benny always comes out for his last cigarette after the bar closes, which is two a.m. tonight. I sit on the step with him. He plops the plate on my knees.

"Benny, you—"

"Shut up and eat it. You haven't had anything since breakfast. I'm hoping that girl gave you breakfast."

I take a long look at the turkey sandwich on the plate. I can tell the bread is soggy without touching it. José must have made it. He's Benny's main cook, and he's not what you'd call a gourmet chef.

I pick it up and take a bite, for Benny's sake. He's such a worrier.

"So?" he says.

"So…"

"Did she feed you or what?"

"Sorry, I didn't realize that was a question."

"Did she?"

"She probably would have," I say.

"What's that mean?" He hands me the cup he's been holding, coffee. I take that a little more enthusiastically.

"I left before she woke up."

Benny stares blankly at me for a while and then starts chuckling. He takes a long drag off his cigarette before he speaks. "You're a piece of work, kid."

"That's what they tell me." I take another sip of coffee.

"Was it that bad?" he asks.

"No. It was that good."

Benny nods emphatically, like what just came out of my mouth could not have possibly made more sense. I love that about him.

"I think you could use something good," he finally says. I know what he's thinking about, but I'm not about to invite him to bring it up. "You have to quit punishing yourself someday. You deserve something good."

"No, I'm much happier depressed."

He begrudgingly chuckles, that big-bellied bear chuckle of his. "Seriously, Rainn. It's been, what? Two, three years since Michael?"

"Come on, Benny, I don't want to talk about that."

"All right, all right." He sighs. "I'll shut up. Sweet dreams, kid." He messes up my hair and takes my plate and cup back inside.

I flip down the storage door and drag out my blankets, then put my keyboard back inside. I put one blanket flat on the ground, then cocoon myself up in the other two. Benny's light flicks on upstairs, and I see his silhouette in the window. He's there looking down on me for a long time. Finally, the light flicks back off. I wonder if he's still standing there.

I stare at the dumpster wheel that's two feet away, at my eye level. It smells like rotting food and sour milk. That's probably exactly what it is.

Better than butane.

Chapter Three

I shouldn't have snuck out, huh?" It's been a month and I'm still talking to the graffiti cat I like to call Libido about Jaselle. His smirk has continually changing meaning to me. He's kind of like the Mona Lisa of back alley spray paint art, I guess. Today Libido is telling me I'm a moron. He's telling me that leaving was a chicken move, that I'm always in too much of a hurry, that I could have left any time if things went bad, but I can never go back and see if they would have.

"You weren't there. You don't get it," I tell him, but that blue smirk of his is unconvinced. "Regret is useless anyway. What a waste of emotion. Even if I wanted to do something about it, I can't. I don't have her number. I don't know how to get back to her apartment, and even if I did she'd probably shut the door in my face. So, stop bothering me about it."

Libido's expression refuses to morph today. Usually, I just tell him to change and he does. I'll notice some feature I've never paid attention to before, the friendly orientation of his ears telling me he's not judging me, or the curious tilt of his head saying he wants to understand. All I can get from him now is unrelenting skepticism.

"I should have let Benny paint over you months ago." I open the back door to the Chapel. I have better things to do than talk to a spray paint cat anyway. Brad is supposed to come see us perform tonight.

Backstage, Jayden looks like he's going to puke. I'm the only one who sees that, though. Everyone else sees the same old smooth, carefree, punk rocker.

"You ready?" I ask. All he can muster is a nod.

We spend our limited extra time peeking at the bar, hoping to see Brad, but before long the lights go out like we're doing a real concert, compliments of Benny, and it's time to take the stage.

I hear Benny doing our intro, but it's just a distant sound, taking a back seat to the twinge in my stomach. I clear my throat a little and pat my chest, nervous tics with no real function. Jayden's face is shiny with anxiety sweat, but there's no time to try to comfort him.

Benny's voice booms through the bar. "The Suicidal Angels!" The red lights by my feet and above my head paint me in time with Shiloh's pulsing bass intro. The sound is so strong and sensual it overflows me with energy. Then the drums thicken the sound. Jayden's guitar over the top, screeching heartache.

"*Calling up the dead. Awakening the sickness in my head...*" I sing with everything inside me. I scream until I'm raw. I feel.

"*You're alive somewhere, but you weren't there, you weren't there...*" I pull away from the mic so hard my sweaty hair flies away from my face. The lights beat down hot and smothering.

Ecstasy.

I try to penetrate the black wall the bright lights in my face have thrown up, but I can't. I want to know where Brad is. I want to sing to him personally. There's just no way for me to know, though, so I pour my soul into the entire room.

The end is coming. "*I have a confession for you, since we're alone. I think I want to die tonight. I think this might be it tonight.*"

Alex goes into his drum solo that caps off the performance. With his last powerful blast to the symbols I scream, "We are the Suicidal Angels. Thank you and good night!" It's cliché, I know, but I've always wanted to do it. We take a bow to the wild applause and buzzed roars.

There's a knot in my throat from the happiness. We've never performed so well, ever, and what a night to pull it together. I blow kisses to the crowd as we make our way off stage, fulfilling every cheesy whim.

The overhead lights come back on and the house music returns, quiet compared to us. The next band, Travesty, goes to work preparing their set. Benny is waiting to the side and spreads his arms wide for me. I fall into the bear hug.

"You guys were great!" He grabs my head and jostles me around. The guys come in for a group hug, smiles bursting off their faces. People are fist bumping the guys. Girls are coming up to compliment me. One person even asks for autographs. We're mini-celebrities.

I crane my neck to try to catch sight of Brad without being too obvious I'm doing so. He'll find us, so the guys and I go to the bar and get drinks. I turn on the stool so my elbows are resting on the bar and I have a view of the tables, dance floor, and stage. Brad. Where's Brad?

It's crowded and visibility is limited. I wait. He's here somewhere. I wait and wait. Benny keeps the drinks coming with added potency every time. Travesty gets further and further into their performance. It's been an hour and a half. The crowds are starting to clear. There are fewer and fewer nooks I can't see.

He's not here. He wanted to see us, had to see us. He promised, but he's not here. We gave the ultimate performance, technically and emotionally. He didn't see it. I turn back to the bar and take a shot.

"Easy, tiger." Shiloh rubs my shoulders. "It was still a great night. You know Brad. We should have seen this coming."

Well, he's right about that. This is, after all, the third time Brad's stood us up. I just thought for sure this time he was serious, that he'd be here. I always think I've learned my lesson about counting on people, but then something happens to make me realize I haven't. I genuinely thought he was going to come tonight, because he said he would. I take a shot.

We were supposed to be on the cusp of victory. We were supposed to have a real opportunity in our hands, but we're no closer than we've ever been. We're still street rats making noise in the local bar. We're still nothing.

"Hey." Benny breaks into my thoughts. I look up. "Fuck him. You guys are amazing. Talent like that doesn't stay in a dump like this for long." I smile for his benefit. We've been here for two years, so apparently it does. I take a shot.

A cloud of sweetness takes me, the smoothest, warmest smell. I glance over my right shoulder and there, so close the loose fabric of her shirt is brushing my arm, Jaselle. My chest tightens with fear, relief, desire, need. I look into my empty shot glass, only allowing myself to watch her through my peripheral vision.

There's a glow to her skin, a luminescence to her eyes, bone structure to make a sculptor drool. If she knows I'm sitting here she shows no sign of it.

"Two Coronas." She tosses a ten on the bar. Benny gets her the beers, but he's looking at me the whole time he does it. His face looks like his brain is busy trying to assess what's happening. She turns and walks away, returning to a table with a woman, a different one than the night we met.

Benny stares me down, hard. Then he nudges his head toward her sternly. He knows how much time I've spent thinking about her, and he was the one who planted the idea that I messed up "something good" to begin with.

I inhale deeply and stand up from my stool. I notice for the first time my level of intoxication, higher than I thought. I'm not trashed, but there's a little sway to my step, for sure, if only in my mind.

Each step I take presents a new fear. What if she cusses me out for leaving? Step. What if she won't acknowledge me at all? Step. What if she looks at me like I'm crazy for having spent any of my time thinking about it? What if she expected and wanted me to leave immediately? What if she wasn't even asleep, but pretending to be until I left to save herself the awkward conversation of kicking the homeless one-night toy to the curb? Step. Step. Step.

I'm standing at her tall table with my hands resting on the back of the empty seat before she looks at me. My stomach clenches.

"Hey," I say.

"Hey." She smiles. I try to resist the instant infatuation that happens when she does that. I toss a rudely disregarding and unconcerned glance at the woman she's with, then scratch the back of my head.

"I just wanted to—"

"We loved your show," the other girl blurts. "You guys were incredible. I had no idea you know her, that's so cool!" she directs the last at Jaselle. Jaselle just smiles subtly and sips her beer.

I stand, awkwardly shifting my weight, trying to think of what to say, if I'm welcome, whether or not I've just walked in on a date.

"You just wanted to..." Jaselle says.

"Uh," my voice gets stuck in my throat. "Just say hi, I guess."

"Here, sit down! I'm Shelby." Shelby hastily goes to work clearing the extra chair of her purse and coat so I can sit. Jaselle is still leaning far back in her chair, silently watching.

"No, no. Thanks, but that's okay. I'm interrupting. I just came to say hi." I can feel my cheeks getting red. I wave at Shelby like a moron and start to turn.

"Sit."

I look back and examine Jaselle's face. "Sit," she says again. I slip into the chair, holding eye contact with her as I do, trying to say everything I need to say by staring it into her. *I'm sorry. You're so beautiful. I was scared.* I can't tell if she's seeing me or not.

"So who came up with your band name?" Shelby asks. I feel the seconds passing in silence while I stare at Jaselle. Shelby clears her throat to draw me back.

"Oh, uh, I did."

"What's it mean?"

"It means some people aren't here to stay." Jaselle leans forward and stares into me while she answers. "It means that sometimes, even the best of us, even ones chosen by God, still will self-destruct. There's a darkness inside that will never go away, and it's always calling. There's nothing that can fix it. They touch our lives and then they're gone, looking over us. Angels."

Her eyes are blue-gray and stormy. I take a deep breath and look back to Shelby.

"Well, there you go," I say.

Shelby looks uncomfortable suddenly, her peppy disposition interrupted. She blabs on about something, obviously not picking up the tension between Jaselle and me.

"Let's get out of here," she finally says. I nod my head and prepare to take my leave, but Shelby reaches out and squeezes my arm. "You're coming, right?"

"Where?" I look Jaselle's way again, feeling incredibly anxious that I'm unwanted, guilty that Shelby is dragging me along.

"We're going back to Jaselle's. We got some boomers we're going to do."

"Boomers?"

"Yeah, you know, mushrooms."

I chuckle a little. "Yeah, I know."

"You ever done them before?" Shelby leans closer.

"Once or twice."

"We have plenty. Come with us."

I turn to Jaselle again. I wonder why it's not occurring to Shelby to run any of this by her. I keep silently asking permission for her. Jaselle gulps down the rest of her beer.

"Let's go then," she says. We all get up and head for the door. I notice the guys watching and nod my good-bye. Benny does a silly little salute.

I somehow end up in the front seat with Jaselle. Shelby volunteered for the back. I haven't quite figured her out yet. She breaks out the 'shrooms immediately. My buzz from the shots is starting to wear off a little already, a fact I'm grateful for as I pop the mushrooms in my mouth. I muscle through the familiar unpleasant taste. It'd be easier to just swallow them, but instead I chew and chew. Jayden taught me that chewing makes them affect you sooner. I don't even know if that's true, or why it would be so important to make them kick in fifteen minutes earlier anyway. It's one of those things you just do. Jaselle takes the bag next and puts a couple in her mouth, breaking the long stems so they're more manageable.

We're parked in front of Jaselle's building before any of us are feeling anything. I'm starting to get queasy from the mushrooms though. We head down the stairs, and Jaselle opens the door. I listen for Noah, expecting him to come chew us out, but he doesn't.

Shelby starts laughing beside me. I look over at her for the explanation, but there isn't one. Her smile is about to bust her cheeks right open. My stomach is starting to feel warm. Any minute now. She must be a little ahead of me.

We settle down in front of the TV and watch *South Park*. We're laughing hysterically within ten minutes. Shelby keeps falling all over me, making sure some part of our bodies is constantly touching. I figure she's just high.

"Hey!" she says abruptly. "Hey! You know what song I really like?"

"What?" I try to focus, but her arms are rippling like little sound waves and I keep chuckling, then trying to stifle it.

"Oh, man, what's it called? That one that goes *'you're my forever, I'm your first drink,'*" She sings a terrible rendition of one of our songs.

"Yeah? Cool." I'm no good with compliments.

"Oh, and the one that goes, *'drown me in the blood of yesterday's heartache.'*"

I just smile.

"Do you write the lyrics?"

"Yeah."

"I love them. I get them, you know? I feel like I already know you."

She springs to her feet before I have to answer and heads to the kitchen. I look over at Jaselle. She's smoking a cigarette and staring hypnotically into her swirling exhale, seemingly detached from us.

Shelby returns with three beers. The mushrooms are really starting to take me now. I'm getting a strong body high and I just feel good, about everything. And I want to touch.

Jaselle finally speaks, but it's a whisper, so quiet I barely hear. *"Drown me in the blood of yesterday's heartache. I am tomorrow's tragedy."* She hums my song. I close my eyes and listen. I want to reach out and hold her.

"That's a fucked up image, actually!" Shelby blurts. Jaselle and I both look at her, both obviously irritated.

"Seriously, have you thought about that? Drowning in blood?"

Once or twice, Shelby, it's my song, you idiot. "I guess."

"I don't think I like it anymore." I don't bother answering. I zone out for a minute, and then I hear a strange wind behind me. No, not wind. Something swirling? I look over. Shelby is holding her chest and breathing weird. In in oooooout. In out in innnn.

"Are you okay?" Jaselle asks. She just keeps breathing like that, holding her chest, turning pale.

"Shelby?" I say. "Dude, are you all right?"

"I'm freaking out, man. I don't feel good."

Jaselle sits up and puts her hand on Shelby's back. "What's happening? How do you feel?"

"The walls are red. Everything is blood. I don't want to be high anymore. I don't like this. I want to come down!"

I kneel down in front of her. "Look at me," I say. It takes her a long time to do so. "Look at me. It's going to be fine. You've got at least three hours to go, okay? But it will stop. Don't try to fight it, you're making it worse. Let's go outside for a minute, okay?"

In in oooooooout. In out innnnn.

"You're making the trip go bad. Stop freaking out," Jaselle says. Shelby can't answer. She's just busy breathing weird with wide eyes. I wonder what she's seeing now. Out of nowhere, she screams, loud. It makes Jaselle and me both jump.

"I don't want to die! I don't want to die!"

"Come on, honey. Let's go outside." Jaselle starts trying to pull her up.

Suddenly, trying to handle this is demanding too much thought, too much control. My trip starts trying to turn on me. I see the hallway that goes to Jaselle's room and it's too dark, dangerous. It turns into a mouth. Then it's just a gaping hole in the house, a cold vacuum that's trying to swallow my soul. It's evil. I'm certain there's a thousand bats and Satan himself in the shadows. Everything is collapsing on itself.

Stop. Change the scenery; that's the fastest way out of a bad trip.

"Shelby, get the fuck up!"

The sooner I get her to relax, the sooner I can. Stop resisting the high. It's the first thing you want to do when things aren't going right, get sober, stop seeing bad things. But that only makes it worse. Give yourself to the drug.

Finally, we tug Shelby up. We burst out the front door, where I've convinced myself the shadows can't get me. The nature of all my hallucinations changes. Now I'm in a Super Mario Brothers game. The sky is purple. The trees reach out forever.

Shelby has quieted down a little too.

"Shel, look," Jaselle says, pointing to some falling leaves. They leave trails of color behind them, so bright and beautiful. That takes care of it. Shelby starts giggling, then laughing.

We're out there for over an hour before we're comfortable coming back in. Shelby is sloppy and continuously erupting into hysterical laughter, falling all over me again. "You're really pretty." I wonder if she's ever done 'shrooms before.

When we come back in, Noah is in his room. He doesn't say anything to us, thank God. We settle back down in the living room. Shelby goes to get us more beer. When she tries to hand me mine, she trips and spills it all over me. She starts laughing until she falls on the floor. The anger threatens to turn my trip again, so I force myself to let it go.

Being high with this girl is exhausting and infuriating. Jaselle is beautiful though, soothing, like a river. I want to hold her.

"Come on." Jaselle is staring at me, and I realize I just went through a time warp and missed the last ten seconds or so.

"Huh?"

"You can wear one of my shirts."

Right, the beer. I forgot already. I follow her into her room. She's sliding the hangers over one by one, selecting something for me. She eventually pulls out a Grateful Dead shirt, tie-dye with the bears, perfect choice for the evening's extracurricular activities.

She doesn't make a move to leave, so I take off my Corona-soaked shirt right there, turning away shyly. I laugh to myself. She knows what I look like already, what am I hiding? It feels like she doesn't though, like that night never happened. She's so relaxed, like there isn't a huge question hanging in the air. I'm dying to answer it, but I want her to ask first.

"What's this?" She's pointing at one of my tattoos. It's a staff of music starting on the back of my shoulder, winding down my ribs, and ending by my hip.

"It's a song," I say.

"Well, duh, smart-ass. Which one?"

"You've never heard it." I hate the cold way it comes out, but she seems not to notice.

"How do you know?"

"Because my brother wrote it."

"He's a musician too?" She gently traces her finger along it. I shake with desire.

"He was incredible. Incredible," I say.

She doesn't dwell on the "was," just nods. "Will you play it for me sometime?"

I look into her eyes. My throat hurts just at the idea of it. I haven't been able to play it since he died. It's just too hard, to hear something that beautiful and know that it's all that's left of its creator. I'm too choked up to answer.

"Do you not want to talk about him?"

Again, my voice gets stuck. Jaselle is so gentle and soft about it I don't want to deny her, yet talking about him, well, I've never been any good at it.

"How about just one question, then," she says. "Nothing major, I promise."

I smile. "Okay."

She thinks for a minute, choosing her question. "What did he play?"

"Violin. And drums." Jaselle opens her mouth, then closes it again. I telepathically know it was another question she had to stifle.

"He loved the drums. Mom made him play the violin, the way she made me play piano."

"You didn't like playing piano?"

"No, I did. I always loved it. I just mean it was important to her that we both learn to play classical music. But Michael hated violin. He was just so good…" I can hear the soft notes in my ear. "I don't blame her for making him play. It was the most gorgeous thing you've ever heard." If tears have a sound, he knew what it was. That song, the one I have tattooed, it never fades. I can always hear him playing it. It's immortal the way nothing else can be. Even his face, his laugh, our last conversation, all those things blur, though I hate to admit it. But that song, that's him, and it's always there, fresh and alive.

"But I *haven't* heard it," Jaselle says. She looks ever so slightly toward the room that houses that dazzling piano. My eyes fill to the brim.

"Another time, maybe," I say. She doesn't press. We stand there just looking at each other. Ask me. Let me tell you. Why did I leave?

"Come on," she says and leads me back to the living room. Shelby is crashed out on the floor. We each take a huge sigh of relief, then laugh as we catch each other.

Jaselle lies down on the couch. I settle down between the couch and the coffee table, which puts me right by Jaselle, but two feet lower.

"Can I ask you one question now?" I say.

"You can ask me however many questions you want to, darlin'."

A wave of warmth goes through me. "Do you really like her?" I nod at Shelby.

"Nah, she sure likes you though."

"She's just high," I say.

"No, really, she was going on about how beautiful and sexy and talented you are before you even came over."

"Shut up." I fidget uncomfortably.

"She's right, you know, but in all the wrong ways."

I just let that hang in the air for a while. I can't think of anything to say that won't come out weird.

"Hey," Jaselle says, soft because she's falling asleep.

"Yeah?"

"Be here in the morning, okay?"

My insides melt. "I will."

CHAPTER FOUR

It takes me half an hour to scrounge up the change I need for the bus. I check the change returns in all the pay phones and soda machines I can find. I scour the floor by the self-checkout in the grocery store. Finally, I hit the jackpot by the window in the Burger King drive through.

An hour later, I'm sitting at the bar at the Cuff Link. The bartender's name is Jimmy. I know this because he tells me so every time I come in here. Apparently, I do not have a memorable face.

"Is Brad here?" I ask.

"Maybe," Jimmy says. "Maybe not. Who's asking?"

"Just get him out here, please."

Jimmy disappears for a long time, so long people at the bar are getting frustrated. When he returns, he's Brad-less.

"He's busy."

"Come on, man. Get him out here."

"Sorry."

I get up from the bar and crane my neck to see in the back room. "Brad!" Once I've made eye contact he smiles and gets up. I shoot Jimmy a dirty look. Jerk, must have described me as a greasy homeless girl who's taking up space at his bar just drinking water.

"Hey, Rainn!" Brad's smile is warm. All the lecturing I was prepared to do feels wrong now.

"Hey, Brad." I just stare at him. He obviously doesn't remember he was supposed to see us last night at all, but I just stand there staring until finally:

"Oh, shoot! I'm so sorry, girl! I missed your show, didn't I?"

"You sure did." The anger is coming back. Give it another second and I can proceed with lecturing.

"Gosh, it's just been so busy down here. Last night was ridiculous, and I had this new band I just picked up going on for the first time. Had a stage fright episode and next thing you know, completely spaced it. I'm sorry."

"It's okay." How mad can I really be at someone who's doing me a favor to begin with? It's like trying to yell at your boss, not an option, no matter how sweet the fantasies are.

"We'll reschedule, okay?"

I smile weakly, another reschedule. I guess I should be glad, but I just keep wondering if he's doing this because he's really interested or just to shut me up.

"Are you ever going to come see us?" I ask. My stomach turns with the anticipation of his answer. I've been too afraid to ask for so long. Maybe I don't want to know. "Just be real with me. Don't make me keep coming down here if you're not serious." Since it takes me forever and all. I remind myself that's not his problem.

His smile turns to a sneer. "Look, kid, I'm trying to be nice to you. I don't need you busting my balls. I've got a lot of shit on my plate, all right?"

"I'm sure you—"

"I'll get down there when I get down there."

"I—"

"People kill to get on my stage, you know. I don't need you. You need me."

"Trust me, I know I'm the one who needs you. I just don't want to be humored. If you're standing there knowing damn well you're never coming to see us don't keep telling me you are." I don't mean to raise my voice, but I must be because the whole room goes silent. "You don't have to lecture me about how important you are. Why do you think I keep coming down here? Trust me, I get it, but that doesn't mean that you don't need me too. We're the best."

"All you musicians think you're the best."

"Yeah, but we are. We can prove it to you if you let us. Let us play here if it's too much trouble to come down."

"Don't act stupid. You can't get on my stage until I know you're good. I won't know you're good until I come see you, and I can't come see you on just any Saturday night. I'm busy!"

"You picked the Saturday."

"Shit happens!"

"Shit happens?"

"That's right. Shit happens. Deal with it."

I just stand there, defeated. "Okay. You know where we are then, I guess." I turn to walk away. He's never coming. I've suspected this for a while, so why does it hurt so much?

"Rainn?" he says. I turn back reluctantly. "Come here," he says, gesturing wildly for me to come back over. My legs don't want to move. They're dead from discouragement, but he just keeps waving, so after a few lifeless seconds I obey.

"Look, the fact that you're willing to tell me off and walk away says one of two things. Either you're a little punk that's going to throw that attitude crap at me constantly or you're actually talented and you know you'll find someone else if it isn't me. Now for whatever reason my instincts are telling me you're actually talented. They've always told me that." Brad pauses long enough to grab the drink Jimmy is handing him. "So, what I need you to do is calm down, relax."

"This isn't as relaxing of a situation for me as it is for you. This is the only thing I've ever wanted. I know you have a million things to think about, but I don't. I've just got this."

"I'm not telling you to want it any less, Rainn," Brad says. "I'm just asking you to be patient. You wanted to know if I'm really going to come see you guys play, and I'm telling you I do want to. But you're asking me for honesty, and if I'm being honest, it's going to take me a while."

"A while?"

"How about if we just give it a few months? Let things settle."

"A few *months*?" I blurt.

He turns to the calendar on the wall behind him and starts flipping pages. "We'll shoot for, uh, the fifteenth, okay?"

"Sure, Brad. Whatever."

"I'm serious. The fifteenth of January."

"Mm-hmm." It's so far away it's comical to think he'll remember. I stand up and start heading for the door.

"The fifteenth, Rainn, I'm writing it down!"

I flash the horns at him and step outside.

I decide to go see the guys. I can take the bus if I want to look for change some more, but I can probably walk there faster than I can find the money. Their apartment is only forty-five minutes from here on foot; the Chapel is about the same from there. It's easier to do it in stages.

The outside door to their apartment building is broken and covered in graffiti. The speaker box people are supposed to use to get inside only works about half the time. They worry about me in the alley. I worry about them here. They've been here for years now, though, and so far without incident.

When I get to their apartment door, I can hear saxophone. I listen outside for a minute. It's beautiful, Shiloh. I know he plays, but only in a distant, vague, sort of way. He's embarrassed about it for some reason. I guess it doesn't fit with his bassist persona, only it totally does. Eventually, I knock. The sax stops immediately, and I hear him unchaining the door.

"Hey, you," he says when he opens it.

"Hey. You're tearing it up in there."

The tops of his ears turn red. "Just messing around." He closes the door behind me. "Jay and Alex went for beer."

We settle down on the couch, which is three feet away from the TV because the screen is so tiny. Behind the TV is a small open space where they've jammed all their music stuff, including a synthetic drum kit for Alex. There used to be real drums there, but now we pretty much leave them at the Chapel. There's a hole behind the drums from where I put Alex's head through the drywall two years ago.

I hear the front door open and Jayden and Alex laughing about something as they come in. They turn the corner, two twelve-packs in hand.

"Hey!" Alex runs and jumps on me. "Check you out, got your chick back, huh?"

I try to ignore him, but the smile I can't control says it all.

"She's your girl now?" Shiloh asks.

"I don't know about that. We just partied together."

"You guys hook up?" Alex asks.

"Of course, they did," Jayden says from the refrigerator, where he's putting the twenty-four beers away one by one.

"No, actually, we didn't." I scowl at him. He tosses beers across the room at the guys. I hold up my hand to say no.

"When do we get to meet her?" Alex asks.

Jayden sits by me on the couch. "Yeah, when do we get to check out your new piece of ass?"

My ears get hot. My chest is boiling.

"Aw, come on, Jay," Alex says. Shiloh and Alex both are watching. My reaction must be obvious. I just sit, waiting, fuming, unsure why it's ticking me off to this extent. She really isn't my girl, after all.

"I'm sorry, okay?" Jayden says. "What do you want me to call her?"

"Jaselle."

"When do we get to meet Jaselle?"

"Never if you're going to behave like that," I say. "I'll take that beer now."

"I got laid last night too, if anyone's interested," Alex blurts to ease the tension. I don't bother reminding them I didn't "get laid."

"Yeah, by a chipmunk," Jayden says.

"Guess we know who didn't get laid last night," Shiloh interrupts.

Alex points at Jayden and laughs in his face. "He gets grumpy when he's backed up." He hands me my beer.

"Hey, you can act like you don't know what I'm talking about, but you saw those cheeks. Chipmunk."

"Shut up, dude." Alex punches him in the arm.

"Get some females in here already, then."

"You guys are idiots," I say, but Alex is already dialing from his list of skanks.

I tell them about Brad while we're waiting for the girls. Shiloh and Alex are optimistic as usual. Jayden is more on the negative side with me. I can hear the girls giggling in the hallway outside, trying to figure out which door they're looking for. I decide it's time to go.

I point them in the right direction as I leave and overhear them arguing over who gets Jayden as I start down the stairs.

I go straight to the alley when I get to the Chapel. I don't want to talk to Benny and go through the whole not hooking up, she's not my girl crap again. I slide down against the dumpster so that I can see Libido on the brick wall. The blue spray paint he's made of is so bright he almost glows in the dark.

I notice the phone number on my hand, blue Sharpie. It's Shelby's cell, written in that loopy, girly handwriting. "It's not like I asked for her number," I tell Libido. Shelby was all upset when I left. She had the whole day planned out, breakfast, walking around downtown. Walking around aimlessly is just about the last thing I consider when I'm trying to make plans. I walk enough.

I keep catching the briefest hint of Jaselle's scent. Then I remember I'm still wearing her shirt. I pull it to my nose and breathe in deep. "Is it rude of me to keep it?" Libido's smirk has more life to it than the last time we talked. Now he's playful, saying, "Yes, it's rude, but you know damn well you're keeping it anyway."

"No. Cut it out." I point my finger at him. "I don't need or want a girlfriend. That just makes things complicated." But I keep catching myself thinking about her. It's too much. I feel like I'm violating her in some way, thinking about her like this. "I can be her friend. That's it. Her friend."

Now he's back to that skeptical look. The one that says, "Good luck with that," while chuckling in delight.

I've always said that some of our greatest moments of clarity come immediately after orgasm, once our heads are finally free of all that lust, the games, the facade you throw up over yourself that you think makes you attractive. We all have one, even if you consider yourself "real." We all modify ourselves, tweak our natural behavior just a little to fit with that person we're leaning into.

But once you orgasm, well, then you can relax. Not for long, just long enough to figure out if you feel like you're in the right place or not. Do you want to reach over and squeeze them as hard as you can? Don't let me go. Or do you feel guilty and wrong?

I don't remember what I felt after Jaselle. I just remember waking up six hours later and running for my life, but that doesn't count.

Libido leers devilishly down at me saying, "I guess there's only one way to find out now, isn't there?"

"Stop it. You're such an asshole, cat." I try to convince myself I'm actually talking to the cat, like some inanimate drawing is responsible for any of this.

"I should have gotten her number," I finally tell him. "I'm such an idiot." She was just standing there, looking at me with that serene stare, those stormy eyes. What's your number? That's all I had to say. Can I call you sometime?

"Coward," Libido says. His eyes were sprayed way too long and are darker than the rest of him, with small drips from the paint buildup that could be interpreted as tears at the right moment. This is not the right moment. He looks mad right now, reminding me that at least Shelby had the guts to come prancing across the room in gazelle strides. "You don't have a phone, huh?" she said. "Here! Take my number, we'll hang out sometime!"

It's that simple, Rainn. Shelby isn't such a moron after all.

CHAPTER FIVE

Three days of nothing, and then, "Rainn, you got a phone call." The heavy back door of the Chapel closes. I slowly emerge from my blankets. I've wrapped myself up so tightly inside it's a task to peel myself out. I finally stumble sleepily inside. Benny is standing behind the bar, receiver in hand, waiting for me.

"It's her," he mouths it even though he's carefully air locked the speaker off with his palm. I roll my eyes at him and hold out my hand for it.

"Hello?"

"So I guess this is how I get a hold of you, huh?"

"Yeah, I guess so. What's up?" I ask. Benny starts waving his hand at me like that was the wrong thing to say. He's swatting at me. I'm swatting at him. I miss what Jaselle says.

"What? Hang on." I smack Benny's arm as hard as I can. "Sorry," I say into the phone.

"Um, it's okay. So, can you come?"

"Yeah. Where?"

"Over here. I need inspiration."

"I'll be there in an hour." I give Benny the phone back and try to avoid his stare.

"You gave out the bar number?" he asks.

"Nope. She must have looked it up or something."

Benny's smile stretches. "You're lucky she's persistent."

"What do you mean?"

"Most girls would have never set foot in this bar again after you snuck out. Now she's going through the trouble to look up your number because you were too chicken to get hers? You worked some magic on this one."

I just shrug. "I have to go."

"You coming back tonight?"

"I don't know, Dad, we'll see." Benny hands me a few dollars I haven't asked for. He hates it when I walk a long way, or at all in the dark, really. I take the money guiltily and give him a man hug.

It takes more than my estimated hour to get there. The whole time I'm sitting there, bouncing up and down on the cracks in the road, leaning imperceptibly away from the gray homeless guy that smells like his own defecation, I'm focusing on one thing. Friends. You can be friends.

"The return of the brute." That's Noah's greeting when Jaselle lets me in.

"Actually, it was savage, if you don't mind," I say.

"More and more of one every day. Now you like to fuck and run?"

"Noah!" Jaselle's shocked protest sounds far away even though she's right there. He doesn't even look at her, just keeps staring at me. My skin is hot, battery acid, rippling under sound. My ears are pulsing. His ice blue eyes are hard, lacking that sense of depth that usually comes with light irises. I take a deep breath.

"So, this is your house, huh?" I finally say. I don't know where it comes from. It just comes out.

"That's right, Savage. This is my house." The intensity thickens the air between us. He doesn't have to say anything else. This house is mine. Jaselle is mine. I don't want you here. So far you have proved yourself to be exactly as worthless as I said when you first walked in. The animosity is suffocating. Because he's right. I left.

Jaselle is still standing there, watching, paralyzed. I wish she'd leave the room all of a sudden, but I'm still glued to Noah's judging eyes. I stop crumbling under them and straighten up.

"I will never do that again." I say it with a sincerity I know he can feel, no matter how he hates me. "Ever."

"We'll see."

I turn away and catch Jaselle and Noah making an animated silent exchange out of the corner of my eye. Then she's by my side going to her bedroom with me. She closes her door slowly like she doesn't want to make any noise. She turns and softly pads to the bed and sits down on the corner.

It takes me a while to notice she's staring at me. Once again, I'm lost in her paintings. I'm fighting embarrassment when I turn and see her. I put my hands sheepishly in my pockets.

"I want to paint you," she finally says.

"Why would you want to do that?"

"There's something about you I'd like to capture."

"Poverty?" I laugh a little.

"No. Humility maybe. Timidity. Understated passion."

I mull over the words. I have a hard time identifying the quality. Most people think I'm exactly the opposite. I tell her so.

"Well, I've never been any good at explaining. That's why I need to paint it. Is that okay?"

"I guess. What do I have to do?" The *Titanic* scene boldly seizes my mind, the couch, the diamond, Leonardo and his pencils.

"Nothing. Just sit where I tell you to and be patient."

I nod. She smiles and grabs my hand, then guides me out of the room. "Oh God, we're not going outside or anything are we?" I ask.

She doesn't answer, just turns the corner. I figure out we're going to the piano. Now there's something worth painting. I don't know why I have to be involved, but I don't say that. No one likes a self-deprecating model.

"Sit like you're about to play something," she commands. I do. The next several minutes she's on a nonstop round trip to and from her bedroom getting all her stuff. She sets up the canvas right behind the curve of the piano, so she's looking over the keys, facing me.

Then she goes to work on me, pushing my shoulder just a little to get the angle she wants, making my hair fall where she wants it, giving my shirt a little tug.

"Okay, now put your hands over the keys. Be natural."

I chuckle a little. "You've just arranged everything about me, what do you mean be natural?"

"Put your hands on the keys like you're playing, not like you're pretending to play."

"But I am pretending to play."

"You said you were going to cooperate."

I smile and put my hands where I'd put them were I starting to play Michael's song. She doesn't know it, but I'm taking a brick from my wall.

"Breathe," she says. "You look stiff."

"I'm supposed to." Mom used to make me practice with a board attached to my back with a belt to keep my posture right. Now I'm stiff, says the artist. Mom would be satisfied. Elbows slightly higher than the keys, back straight, wrists soft but not sagging. "Have you ever seen a hunchback pianist?"

"Just breathe." Jaselle's eyes are so warm they force me to obey. Breathe. At first, it's awkward, watching her take those first few strokes. My stomach flutters every time I catch her eyes wandering over me. I wait and wait. It takes forever. What does she see when she looks at me?

"You ready?" She's still looking at her work while she says it.

"Really?"

It takes her another thirty seconds to finally look up. "Yep." I get up and walk over. She backs away from it to look from a distance. When I see it, my brain goes quiet. It's a hundred times better than I expected. My Nirvana shirt is exact, down to the tear in my sleeve. The scratches on my knuckles give the impression of healing. The ivory keys are exquisite, spaced perfectly like she used a ruler. The propped-up lid of the piano frames me.

And my face. It's me. There's something gentle and thoughtful to my eyebrows, something churning in my eyes. I'm not sure it's accurate; I've never seen that in the mirror before. But it is deep, and probably the quality she was after.

I don't notice her standing over my shoulder at first. "Do you like it?"

I turn and face her. "Of course, I do. I don't know how you did this." I feel my heart in my chest. I want to touch her face, pull her to my lips, taste her burning kiss. She lifts her hand. I turn back to the painting abruptly. I see her drop her hand back to her side. I shiver sickly.

I hear a couple girls talking, in the house. I look to Jaselle.

"Noah has company." She nudges her head toward the door and we go out. From the hall I have a pretty good shot of the coffee table, Noah, and one girl's back. A tidal wave of marijuana smell blasts me. There's at least a pound of it sitting casually on the table. I want to examine the situation more, but Jaselle dips into the bedroom, so I figure I'd better follow.

"Good Lord," I say. "He's a dealer?"

"How do you think he pays for this place? He certainly can't hold down a real job."

"Nice. Bet you get all the weed you ever want then, huh?" I wish it didn't come out the instant I say it. I don't want her to think I'm after free weed.

"Yeah, most of the time." She doesn't miss a beat. "I wish he'd step his game up though, sell some coke or meth or something."

I blink a couple times while I catch up with that. I try to cover the surprise. "You into that stuff?"

"Oh, you know, every now and then. But I meant so he can make more money. He has to scrape by with the weed 'cause he smokes so damn much of it."

"Oh." I blush at the misunderstanding.

"You like anything other than mushrooms?" She smiles at me like she finds my discomfort entertaining.

"I don't know. I like weed. Acid was okay. I only did coke once. I wasn't really into it."

"Well, hell, let's smoke some weed then." She gets up and leaves the room. I hear a muffled scuffle between her and Noah, but she returns like nothing happened with a respectable nug of weed between her fingers.

It's strong. Only two hits out of Jaselle's swirling blue and purple pipe and my temples are tingling. We settle in on the bed. She has a small TV on the dresser but informs me it doesn't get cable. She has DVDs of *South Park, Family Guy, The Simpsons*, she says because it makes her feel like she's watching TV even though she's not.

The conversation is slow and awkward. I'm pretty sure that's my fault, since I'm more focused on her bare legs than what she's saying. Does wearing shorts qualify as flirting? Stop it.

"Where'd you go?" she asks.

"Hmm?"

"You're somewhere else."

"I'm nowhere," I say.

She smiles. "You need alcohol." Like magic, glasses, vodka, and cranberry juice appear from the side of her bed. I chuckle past the knot in my stomach and take the ice-less drink.

She watches me take a sip and waits for a while, like she's considering whether or not to say anything. Finally, "I'd like to put the painting in my next show, if you're okay with that." I imagine the canvas still set up in the piano room, paint drying.

"It's your painting. You can do whatever you want with it." Damn it, Rainn, why is it so difficult not to constantly be salivating over her or cold with her? Friends. I look over and her eyes are waiting, pulling, dragging me out of this shell I cower in.

"Once, when I was little I thought I'd be able to fly on Halloween night," she says. I blink a couple times, trying to digest the subject change. "Because my costume had wings," she explains.

I can't help but smile. "What was your costume?"

"An angel." She smirks. I can see her falling back through the years. "All white, obviously, with tons of glitter, a halo, and wings."

"What happened?"

"Well, I'd been going around talking about how excited I was that I'd be able to fly soon. So, Halloween evening, right before I was going to get dressed my mom sat me down and told me I wasn't going to be able to fly." She stops for a second, grabs the pipe, and takes a long, steady toke. She starts talking again, choked as she holds the inhale. "I guess she just didn't want me trying to jump off a roof or anything." She lets it go. I watch the smoke hang in the air between us.

"How'd you take it?"

"I told her I already knew that. I really sold it, told her I was just pretending." She looks up at me again, storms raging in those eyes. "It pissed me off though. What was I getting all dressed up like an idiot for if not to fly? To transform?"

"Candy?" I smirk.

"You have to know sparkles were not my thing, either. I did it for the wings. I could have gotten candy in the evil jester costume I wanted."

"A clown?" I ask. "That doesn't sound like you either."

"No, a jester. Like a joker out of a deck of cards. Pointy hat with bells…"

I start to laugh. "I can't see you in a pointy hat with bells, sorry. I figured you for more of a grim reaper type."

She sighs, quieting my laughter, then pulls up her sleeve, revealing a tattoo of a jester on the inside of her left bicep, juggling a flame, a four leaf clover, and a dove, presumably, but the dove is at the height of the juggle and is flying away. I stare at it for a long time, wanting to understand it all without being told. She knows I can't and explains.

"A clown is a victim. He's usually stupid and weak, existing to be mocked. A clown *is* the joke."

"And a jester?"

"To a jester, *you* are the joke. The world is the joke. He says what others won't, sees through all the show to the core, the simple underlying truth. He plays the part of the fool, but really he's the only one who sees things clearly."

"I wanted to be a vampire because the teeth were cool," I say, feeling inadequate next to her. We both start laughing.

"Yeah, I don't think I cared about all that at the time. That sort of developed later," she confesses. "I'm just saying, I wouldn't have been an angel."

We just stare at each other for a few minutes, trying to make a moment, or resist one, I'm not sure which.

"Your turn," she finally says.

"For what?"

"To tell me something."

"What do you want to know?"

She leans forward a little, staring intensely, like she's looking for something. *Family Guy* voices in the background suddenly are driving me crazy. I keep realizing how high I am, then it fades from my consciousness. My head feels heavy. It wants to collapse onto Jaselle's shoulder.

"Why do I have to ask something? You didn't ask me about my worst Halloween, I just told you," she says.

"I don't know what to tell you."

"Hopes? Dreams? Fears? Regrets?"

My mind naturally lingers on regrets. I think for a half second on playing Michael's song for her.

Jaselle's phone buzzes to life with the lyrics of Nirvana's "Dumb." She looks at me, then finally grabs it as the ring tone is about to repeat.

"Hey," she answers it. I hear a female voice coming through the speaker loudly but I can't distinguish the words.

"It's in two weeks," Jaselle says.

"I am."

"I know."

I listen to Jaselle's half of the conversation.

"Sins had nothing to do with it, Mom. Please just stop."

I sit up a little with interest. Her tan shoulders are tensed. I instinctively want to massage them, but catch myself before I move.

"No, I'm not," she says.

"No, I'm not!" She raises her voice a little. I wonder what this scene would look like if I wasn't here. Is she holding back for me? I've seen plenty of family drama; she certainly doesn't have to.

"Look, come if you want to, don't if you don't." She clicks the phone shut without waiting for an answer.

I sit quietly, waiting, watching. Jaselle reaches for her glass, which is nearly empty. I take it and mix a new one for her. Things keep popping in my head to say, but none of them seem right. So I sit, probably the dumbest thing of all. I zone out on the floor for a minute, searching, and when I look back, Jaselle's cheek has a shimmer to it.

"Hey," I say, finally in the soft voice I've been searching for. I gather her up in my arms instantly, effortlessly. Other people's tears usually freak me out, but hers don't bother me. I wrap one arm securely around her, holding her to me. The other is caressing her, touching her face, wiping away the tears, smoothing her wild dreads.

I can feel her trembling, shaking under the sobs she's trying to control.

"Parents are great, huh?" I say.

She laughs despite herself, then straightens up out of my embrace. It ends too soon. "My last art show didn't go very well."

"Because of your sins?" I put it together easily.

She looks a little surprised that I do. "Yeah." I wait for her to elaborate, but she doesn't. She just stares, blankly. My eyes keep wandering to her lips. I feel guilty. She's sad, eyes are the appropriate thing to focus on when someone's sad.

"Real Jesus freak, huh?" I finally say.

"Definitely. Every bad thing that ever happens to me is because of my lifestyle. It's all my own fault."

"You mean because you're gay?" That's where my mind automatically goes with the word "lifestyle."

"Well, yeah, definitely that. And because I get high, and drink. That's what she kept saying. 'You're high again, Jaselle.'" She mimics her mom's nasally voice.

"But you *are* high," I timidly point out, sneaking a sly smile in there.

She beams back brightly. I breathe in relief. "Of course, I am," she says. "And I'm about to get higher now that I talked to her." She reaches for the pipe with a grin. She takes a huge rip and passes it my way. I take another too and physically feel myself getting higher, my blood vessels expanding in my skull as I take in the burning smoke. The rawness in my chest reminds me of something. Too far away to know.

"And anyway," Jaselle continues, "she thinks I'm not painting because I get high. I painted tonight, motherfucker."

With that taken care of, we both down the rest of our drinks. My head is swimming.

Time is changing. It's usually sequential, maddeningly precise, unforgiving, inflexible. It ticks past you one second at a time. There goes your life. Tick. Tock. Imagine if life were counting down to your death, instead of up. No one would wear a watch. We're all just walking time bombs. Tick. Tock. Here comes your death.

But when you're high, stoned, drunk, rolling, tripping, take your pick, time is different. You can move through it, forward and backward, not confined to the rules anymore. Three days can go by, five years can come back. His face can come back. And I can reach out and touch him again. But it's not real, Rainn. Why not? It's real to me.

His face is real again. Not quite the way it was, fractured by my memory. A picture of a picture of a picture. Him, but just slightly warped, something slightly wrong, a reflection in a rippling pool.

"Michael!" Jayden rolls over on his skateboard. When did he get here? His face is right. But his Mohawk is shorter, and it's blue. "Hurry, man!"

Michael jumps on his board and propels himself forward. He looks over his shoulder. "Let's go, Rainn!" I'm here? I look down. I'm on a skateboard too, my ripped jeans fluttering in the chilled midnight air.

We're behind a skate ramp. The beams that hold it up offer some false sense of invisibility. Shiloh puts a can of black spray paint in Michael's hand. Jayden puts a can of red in Michael's other hand. He goes to work, making long strokes over the wood. The hiss of the can is constant. I look over my shoulder, paranoid we're being watched.

"Come on, dude. We should bail," Jayden says, slapping Michael's shoulder, but Michael won't stop, or even acknowledge him. The concrete is slick. It's been raining.

Michael is lost in the paint, spraying and spraying, flinging his arms across the ramp, his focus impenetrable. I look past him, past the mist that separates me from what he's painting. It clears. It's mostly black, some more concentrated than the rest, all sweeping diagonally. And there's a man in the center, a red man collapsed on his knees, reaching for something. But he's being swept backward, dissipating into the wind, disintegrating.

A light blares on us. "Hey!" It's a cop. Michael drops the cans of spray paint. Jayden reaches down and sweeps up the red. I reach for the black, but kick it away with my foot. "Shit!"

I take another swipe and retrieve it. We grab our skateboards and run. You know you have an ineffective method of transportation when it's faster to just pick it up.

"Freeze!" Yeah, they actually say that. We all get to the fence at the same time, fling our boards over, and climb. The cop is at the fence already. How's a fat ass like that move so fast?

"I said freeze!"

He reaches for my leg just as I'm trying to swing over the top, attempting to pull me back down. Michael is on the other side now, the only one on the ground already. He kicks the cop in the gut through the chain-link as hard as he can. The force knocks Shiloh, Jayden, and me to the ground next to Michael. We jump up and run.

My heart is pounding through my chest. I can hear the guys' labored breathing and the thud of their feet beside me. A layer of slick sweat covers me. We run and run long after we can't hear the cop's fury anymore. It's Shiloh who finally reaches out for me.

"Rainn, stop." He has to put some muscle into slowing me down. "Stop." He's panting so hard he can barely get it out. I stop, turn, and see Jayden and Michael leaning over on their knees trying to catch their breath. We're in the woods now, a small little clump of trees on the hill by our house. It's cold.

Jayden starts laughing first, then we all do. I keep staring at Michael, his colorful hoodie, his gray eyes, slim figure. We look so alike. Everyone says that, but not a thing like our mother. Neither of us have ever been convinced we're related to the woman, but we are certainly related to one another.

I notice a giant black stain on my hand from the can of spray paint I put in my pocket. I look down; it's bleeding through the fabric. "Ah, man." And this is my favorite hoodie.

"Is that one dead?" Jayden asks. I nod. "That's okay," he says. "This one has some life." He pulls out the red can and the paper bag it came in he's been storing in his pocket. He sprays the paint in the bag and passes it to Michael. Michael looks so young next to Jayden, tiny.

I watch silently as Michael puts the bag over his nose and mouth and inhales deeply. I see the euphoria ripple through his limbs. His posture slumps. His hands droop to the wet grass like a monkey.

Jayden takes the bag next, freshening up the paint even though that's completely unnecessary. The bag comes to me then. Michael's face is drooping. I half expect the skin to melt right off.

I put the bag to my face and breathe in. Choking. Bleeding lungs. Paint them red. Can't breathe. Drowning. Gasping.

"Rainn!"

Gasping.

"Rainn!" Cold fingers on my burning skin. "Wake up, sweetie." I'm covered in sweat still from running. Soft comforters. Not running. My chest still hurts from the paint. Sun rays. I still see Michael. He's gone.

"Open your eyes."

Voice of an angel, pulling me from the ground. I open my eyes. Jaselle. Dreaming. When did I fall asleep? My brain hurts, resisting my attempt to recall going to sleep, or anything for that matter.

"You okay, honey? You need to puke or something?" she asks.

"No." I groan and try to sit up. As I straighten up, whatever's in my stomach sloshes around and I rethink the throwing up offer. She's rubbing my back. It feels so good. I'm sore everywhere, tender to the touch.

"Are you okay?" Jaselle asks. I can finally see the room clearly. I'm still a little drunk, I think, dizzy. The sun is bright. It's late.

"You feel really hot, babe."

"I'm okay," I finally answer her. Some fraction of me tingles from her calling me babe, but the sensation can't overcome the lingering dread of Michael's face.

"Bad dreams?"

"I'm fine. I should go." I nod like it's the best idea I've ever had even though just the thought of standing up makes me sick. I start trying to get to my feet and Jaselle bounds up.

"You don't have to go. Take a shower, have some breakfast. You don't always have to run away."

I look at her and catch her eyes. They're full of something I can't quite identify. Then it's covered with embarrassment. She didn't mean for me to see that much.

"I could use a shower," I confess. I can use Benny's any time I want, but he's definitely your classic man. I bet Jaselle's shower is clean and has conditioner. She smiles.

"Good. It's in there. Take your time."

I resist the urge to rummage through her things. I look in the shower and smile. No conditioner after all. Of course, dreadlocks, she doesn't need it. The tub is free of the standard layer of slime in Benny's, though.

The steam is suffocating. There's black fuzz closing in my vision. I wobble light-headedly, rushing through before I collapse. I turn the water off and wretch in the toilet, my wet bare knees sliding on the tile.

I wash out my mouth and then just sit there breathing, taking in the pain, feeling it flow through my skin. There's a gentle tap on the door. "You okay?" It's Jaselle. I stagger to my feet and open the door. I stand feebly in front of her, naked. Her eyebrows weaken and she reaches out and touches my face.

And then something happens. My knees buckle. Jaselle helps lower me to the floor, softening the fall as best she can. She grabs my head with both hands, weaving her fingers through my wet hair, and she kisses the top of my head.

There's shattered glass in my lungs. Waves of burning fumes. "I should have never let him hang out with us," I choke out. Jaselle squeezes me tighter. "I killed him."

"Shh." She rubs my back. She doesn't say a word, no questions, just holds me. I wipe away the tears and look up at her. It comes back to me that I'm naked. She seems to remember at the same time. She looks at me. I watch her eyes wander. I can see her desire, almost painful. I stare at her, waiting for her to kiss me, lunge at me, take me. I'm certain she will.

But then she sighs and pulls down a towel from the counter. She drapes it around my shoulders, closing it in front, then touches my face and smiles unconvincingly.

"I should go," I say.

Jaselle nods. "Always going."

She watches me get dressed from the doorframe of the bathroom. It looks like she wants to say something, and I'm moving at a crawl to let her, but the silence just drags through the space between us.

All dressed, I walk over to her again. "Well, see you."

She nods. "All right."

I shift my weight awkwardly. I don't know what I'm expecting, but it doesn't seem time to leave yet. The silence is unbearable, the distance unconquerable.

"Jaselle," Noah calls from the other room. I close my eyes and nod irritably. Jaselle just watches me, not answering him yet. She's right there, within my grasp, waiting for me as much as I am for her, yet I can't move. Friends. You've made it this far. Turn around and leave.

I reach out stupidly and hug her, my arm sliding around her neck. She hugs me back around the waist, and we linger there for a second. When I drop my arms, it feels totally inadequate.

"Jaselle," Noah yells louder. We emerge from her room together. I stride past Noah, determined not to so much as look at him.

"See ya, Savage."

I shut the door hard, only pulling back from the full slam at the last instant.

CHAPTER SIX

The longer I stay away from the alley the harder it is to go back. That's why I rarely take the guys up on offers to spend the night. It only makes it harder. But tonight is the worst night I've had in a long time back here. It's freezing. And when I say freezing I mean it in the Denver, Colorado, literal way. Freezing.

It's starting to snow. I look to my flip down storage unit. It's just big enough to fit in if it gets too intense out here, but I have to take all my stuff out to get inside, which I really don't want to do. Plus, it's cramped. I can't lie flat in there, and it's pitch-black, obviously. Claustrophobia kicks in pretty fast.

It seems darker than usual tonight. Maybe it's the cloud cover. Maybe it's the memory of Jaselle's warm bed, the feel of her skin. Or maybe it's the memory of something darker. Benny's bedroom light flicks on, and I see his silhouette. His window is on the second floor and has a perfect view of me. I roll my eyes and flash a peace sign at him.

I hear people talking, their voices echoing off the walls, bouncing down the alley. I clench up involuntarily, a shiver of uneasiness. No one actually walks past me. The voices just fade away. I take a breath of relief, then hate myself for it. I hate that it only takes a night or two away and this place is as scary as ever. The chance that someone will come within a fifty-foot radius of me sends my heart pounding to a heart attack worthy rate, but usually even when someone does come by they don't mean any harm.

Usually, it's just gray, homeless men digging in trashcans and mumbling to themselves, stinking like a dead dog. Sure, you kind of wonder if they'll snap one day and murder someone for no reason; sure, they like to talk to you even though you can't really understand them, and sure, they're a little quirky and often times have a mental disability. But the homeless never hurt me.

Gang members in the alley are the ones you have to be afraid of. They come through, pants falling off, surrendering to boxers, shiny chains, and sports hats. Most of them deal their drugs and move along, but rarely do they go without comment.

I've found just the right tone to ward them off, strong, stern, but not insulting and definitely not inviting. Acknowledge but don't encourage. You're not afraid. You're not lonely. You are definitely not vulnerable.

But some of them just can't pass by a young woman alone in an alley.

So, I've been raped. Once.

Ever since then Benny has developed an obsessive and involuntary tic that keeps him peering out the window at all hours of the night, making sure I'm okay. And when he does stop looking out the window, he leaves it open so he'll hear if anything is amiss, even when it's freezing. He stopped locking the back door too thinking that if only I hadn't had to look for my key I would have gotten inside before anything happened.

Poor Benny, stuck in a state of perpetual worry. He can't stop seeing me the way he found me that day, bloody and broken into a collapsed ball of mush on his back step, shaking in the pouring rain, watching a river of my own blood navigate its way through the alley. It was like I relished the pain in some sick way, the same way I relish it now, reflecting in the heat of my dream about Michael, soaking in the agony, fulfilling some unspoken debt by reliving what they did, by suffering.

I picture their faces, the way they came sauntering through my alley, a backpack full of drugs freshly emptied.

Most people assume I'm a hooker, a drug addict, or a drug dealer when they see me out back; can't say I'd think different. They almost didn't even see me they were so elated, fanning out handfuls of crisp Benjamins. But the last one saw me, a short, loud little shit.

"Hold up, hold up, hold *up*." He drags the last "up" out forever and stops his buddies with an outstretched arm.

"What, motherfucker? Get your hands off me." He dusts himself off. The third one says something, but I can't understand it through his grill.

"Oh shit! Look at this little piece of white pussy." All three of them head my way. I stand up and back away, trying my best not to look afraid.

"How much, baby?"

"Not for sale."

"Come on, baby, you seen the paper. You know we're good."

"That's great, take it 'round the corner then. There're some nice girls on 15th. I'm sure they'd love it."

"Maaaan, youz a grmmm shaw crra mmmm bras shaw," the inaudible one with the grill says.

"I didn't hear a word you just said, man."

The short little thing gets in my face. "He said take your mother fuckin' clothes off, bitch." He gives me a strong shove to let me know he's not playing around anymore.

The other one, the one that isn't grill guy or short shit rushes up on me and slams me against the wall and presses his forearm against my throat, hard.

My arms are acting instinctively, swatting at his face, scratching, flailing, trying to relieve the pressure that's threatening to crush my windpipe.

He grabs my jeans and his hand slithers inside.

He's rough, pressing too hard. He forces his fingers inside me. A surge of power pushes me off the wall, but he slams his forearm into my throat to control me.

"That's my pussy." Flakes of spit fly out of his mouth as he says it.

Short Shit and Metal Mouth are laughing and slapping hands next to me.

"What you gon' do to her, Ice?"

He doesn't answer Short Shit. Instead he looks at me. "Should have taken the money, bitch. We woulda paid. Now don't be a cunt about it and it won't hurt."

He pulls my pants down as far as he can, which is only halfway between where they started and my knees, but that's plenty. I slap him as hard as I can, only slightly satisfied that it connects.

Both of his hands close around my shirt. He pulls me toward him then slams me back on the wall. My head snaps back from the momentum and smacks on the brick. I'm dizzy and certain I'm bleeding. I'm shocked at how completely ineffective my struggle is. I always considered myself so much stronger than this.

"I said quit fightin' it, bitch."

"Fuck you!"

He punches me. He punches again and again. He pulls my neck down and knees me in the gut. I absorb the pain of each blow knowing it's an extra second he isn't inside me. Maybe something will save me if I can just keep him busy hitting me long enough. Then the blow that knocks me out cold, an elbow to my face.

I'm only out for a second, but when I come to his jeans are unzipped and he's already on his way in. I flail around trying to stop him but it's too late. He uses his entire body to pin me to the wall and shoves himself inside me. Pain erupts, a pain I've never felt before, and it's not just where he forces himself in. No, it's everywhere, like an electric shock, spreading to every inch of my body.

I'm crying, not sure when I started. And for the first time, I scream. I beg them to stop, and I mean beg. I hear the sound of a gun cock by my ear. Short Shit has a 9mm pointed at my temple.

"Shut the fuck up, bitch, or I'll put one in you. No screaming."

I silently endure it, trying to focus more on the cold tip of the gun against my burning skin than the shooting jolts of pain that come with every thrust "Ice" makes. I can feel him getting close and I feel like there has to be a way to stop him. I *have* to stop him.

And like Short Shit reads my mind he presses the gun against my head harder. Ice starts moaning a little and pulls me against him by my waist, going deeper yet, and then he comes. He comes inside me, no condom, nothing, disgusting little piece of shit Ice semen inside of me.

He kisses me and pulls out, finally, and then just for fun grabs the gun from Short Shit and pistol-whips me.

"Your turn," he says to Short Shit and now Ice is holding the gun. I cry harder as I take in the fact that all three of them will be inside me, passing me around like a damn joint.

To be completely blunt, at least his cock is smaller, but he's got this triumphant look on his face and keeps making comments about how at least I'm not so dry anymore (because I'm bleeding) and how I'm his slut.

He grabs a handful of my hair and kinks my neck in a strange and aggressive way the whole time he's fucking me. He comes a little faster. I guess watching Ice got him halfway there.

And last, Metal Mouth. He's a little gentler, but by now I'm so destroyed it doesn't really matter. He comes quickly and gets out.

Ice and Short Shit still aren't done. They pistol whip me again, which sends me to the ground. They each kick me several times, and I'm convinced they're going to kill me now, beat me to death, and the funny thing is the only thing I think about it is, I should have just taken the bullet.

They spit on me before they go, and Short Shit leans all the way down to the pavement to meet my eyes.

"Thanks, baby." He sticks a one-dollar bill to my bloody face.

The aftermath is simple. It starts raining. I lay there in some sort of trance of misery, watching a river of my own blood navigate down the alley, allowing myself to feel the pain, not try to conquer it. Eventually, I lose consciousness.

Benny finds me at six the next morning and thinks I'm dead. In an hysterical frenzy, he borrows his cook's truck and picks me up and puts me inside. He's headed to the hospital.

I open my eyes a little, and he sees I'm alive. He starts talking, but he sounds far away. The only thing I understand is, "I'm sorry, Rainn, I'm so sorry."

I wasn't sorry. I was destroyed, but I was glad I was destroyed. It felt appropriate. It felt like punishment, punishment I desperately need.

They didn't bother counting the stitches. Some were on my face, a lot weren't. Benny was a basket case.

"You are moving in. I am going to sleep on the couch. You are taking the bedroom, and I don't want to hear a thing about it."

For weeks, that's exactly what had to happen until I healed up a little.

After that though I went back to the alley, because when something kicks your ass, the thing to do is go back out and look it in the eye again. I would not live in fear. I would not leech on to people who would have no moral choice but to let me.

I won't pretend it came easily. I won't pretend I didn't sneak back up to Benny's some nights when the quiet was too quiet or laughter was too close. I won't tell you I wasn't scared or even that I don't still get scared sometimes. What I *will* tell you is that I refused to let fear dictate my life.

Benny however, poor Benny, he's very afraid. I think he'd honestly prefer I just move in so he could stop looking out that window. But I won't.

Benny's bedroom light flicks back off. I know he's still standing there, peering through the blinds. My fingers are too stiff to bend. I hear the crunching of tires on loose rocks. A car? My stomach clenches, and I shrink back into the corner.

I bite my lip angrily. Too scared. Take a deep breath and overcome it. I see the headlights painting the asphalt, highlighting the falling snow. The car stops in front of me, and a ripple of anticipation overcomes me. The car door opens.

"Get in the friggin' car." It takes me a minute to process her voice. It's Jaselle. I didn't even recognize her Celica under the layer of snow and darkness. Her face is angelic. She's dusted in snowflakes. I warm from the core, somewhere deep inside. And then I feel myself fight it, try to resist.

She makes a quick "come the hell on" gesture, I'm sure trying to fathom my hesitation. I'm doing the same. She feels so good. So why my constant resistance? Am I punishing myself still like Benny says? Or am I just afraid she'll destroy me? I made a choice a long time ago not to live in fear, and that applies beyond the alley.

I stand up and go to her, around the car and into her arms. I meet her lips hard, taking her kiss. She yields to me, going soft in my embrace, holding me close. She grabs me, pulling my hips to her.

I feel like we're standing there forever, melting into each other, tasting each other. I could have stood there for another forever, but she finally pulls away. A smile spreads across her face.

"Hi."

I smile back and kiss her again. "Hey."

"You know it's like, negative ten degrees right now?"

"I knew it was cold as hell," I say.

"I couldn't sleep knowing you were out here."

It wouldn't matter if it were negative seven hundred; I could stand here looking at her longer, but I can feel her shivering, so I get in the car. The ride is quiet while we sneak glances across the car. Flashes of what I want to do to her are running wild. It feels so good to let them go, leave them be, and see how they develop.

But when we finally get to her house she has her own plans. She slams me into the wall with no hesitation. She presses against me, pinning my hands while she kisses me. Her strength is overwhelming, surprising. I can't move, even if I wanted to, and that positively thrills me.

She slides to her knees, kissing her way down, breathing over my skin. She pulls my belt, undoing it with expert finesse. Her mouth is burning, a searing tease playing by my hips. I force my wilting legs to hold me. She pushes me back against the wall. I hadn't realized I was falling off it, begging to collapse into her.

She breathes on me, pausing for a moment, sending a tingle through my spine, then moving on. I sigh audibly and see her smile at my pain. I let her go on like that for a while until I can't take any more. I grab a handful of her hair and pull her to me.

I fleetingly wonder if she's okay with it, but she meets my surge of lust with one of her own. Her tongue is soft but demanding, blazing perfection.

I hear myself moan her name, and she increases the pressure with the plea. I dig my nails into her shoulders and drag. She pulls me to the floor with her and slips her fingers inside me. My back arches off the floor. With her fingers still inside, she kisses her way back up, gently biting my neck, breathing in my ear, and finally resting in my eyes while she goes deeper.

"You want to come?" she whispers.

"Yes."

"You want to come?"

"God yes."

"Ask me."

"Please, baby. Make me come."

She presses harder and grinds her hips into me in a rhythm that makes me weak, pulling me to her, delivering the moment she decides to. And then I dissolve into her. She holds me tight, kissing my head. I squeeze as hard as I can. Don't let me go.

CHAPTER SEVEN

L et's do some meth," Jaselle says, casual as can be. "I know where we can get some."

I can't explain why my stomach knots. I've never exactly been timid about drugs before. There's just something about that one that seems a little too dark. She reads my face.

"We don't have to if you aren't into it. I just thought it'd be fun."

"Sure," I finally say. "Why not?" The nerves twist one more time at the commitment, and I consciously tell myself to take a breath. You don't want to go into it like that. It's only a few hours.

It doesn't take her long at all to find some. She makes one phone call, and whoever is on the other side does the rest. An hour later, we're standing on a street corner looking out for a blue Honda with a duct-taped right brake light. I wonder absently why any drug dealer would want such a distinction on his vehicle, seems like an easy thing for cops to latch on to.

The guy is an hour late. When he finally rolls up to the stop light, Jaselle goes to the back seat window. I can't see even an outline of the person through the black tint. Again, I wonder what kind of dealer would invite random pullovers with illegal tinting. Completely doubting this guy's capability, I look over my shoulder, wishing Jaselle would drop this apparently intriguing conversation already and come back. The light turns green and he zips away, bass rattling everyone's windows.

"Subtle," I say and roll my eyes when Jaselle is back.

She smiles. "I know, right? Come on." She slips her hand into mine and squeezes. "I'm so glad we're doing this together. I really think you're going to like it."

I do like it. The second that cloud glides up the foil to fill my lungs with a silky rush, I like it a lot. The smell isn't so great. It's chemical, harsh, invoking the instinct that it was made from products decorated with hazards and warnings, the kinds of things that tell you to immediately contact a doctor should you accidentally ingest it, or to flush eyes vigorously for forty-five minutes in the event of contact.

The taste is metallic, but it goes down like a dream, none of that coughing, burning, gasping you get with cigarettes or weed. It just wraps you up in a smooth, warm hug and whispers everything is all right, or maybe that it just doesn't matter if it isn't.

Yeah, I think it's safe to say it scares me immediately, the sheer power of it. Nothing should feel so good, certainly not a drug. I don't have the finances to fall in love.

But for now, I'm floating in a dream, energized and fearless. Yes, fearless, that adjective I've been chasing, it's here, in the fold of the foil. Nothing can hurt me. I'm fucking amazing. I'm too smart to be tricked, too strong to be raped, too resilient to be broken. You know that feeling you get after you've accomplished something that took everything you had? It feels a little like that, only way better. For once you're not so ashamed of yourself.

"It's much better with someone," Jaselle says. I have nothing to compare it with, but being high with Jaselle is pretty incredible. She is the blazing flame in my chest, and I can't get enough. We fuck. And then we fuck some more. We smoke a little more, and then we fuck a lot more. I never knew meth to be a sex drug, but let me tell you, it is.

Velvet copper, silken smoke, bring me a lover. Sweet shadows, fill my soul. The room no longer extends beyond the glow of her lighter. "Though your sins be as scarlet, they shall be as white as snow." Bible verses ring randomly in my head with no origin. My mother must be climbing out of my subconscious. I know so much more than she. Gather the lonely, bring them to me. I have the answers. I'll live forever.

Smoking lies. That's meth.

"Kiss me." Yes, again and always again.

Just as I'm agreeing with this whole idea and the genius of it, my heart is beating too fast.

"There's someone coming, someone to the window."

"What?" Jaselle looks. "No, there isn't."

I keep staring.

"Rainn." She puts her hand on my face, so calm. "No one is coming. It's okay."

"No, there is. There is, they saw us."

"You're just high, baby."

Her hipbones grind into my thighs. Her breath is warm on my neck. They're coming. Have to leave this place before they get here.

"Shh." Shh like deep waters of tomorrow, forever beyond reach. Envelop me, sweet satin smoke, veil this world from my eyes, ripping away the curtain, baring my naked mind.

Something buzzes next to me. Phone call. Jaselle's phone, singing Nirvana. Say hello. She ignores it. Thicker smoke. Three huge bangs on the door. "Jaselle!" Way too loud. "Open the door, Jaselle!"

She lies across me on her back, raising her hand to my face. More pounding. She pulls me into her kiss.

"Open the door!"

"Go away, Noah." Her lips never leave mine as she yells back. The pounding gets louder. Splintering wood. She licks my lips, moving her hand down over my breasts. Pounding, crunching, breaking. She presses into me. The doorframe finally gives and Noah surges through.

"What the fuck do you think you're doing?" he screams. Jaselle laughs through his rage. He reaches down and grabs her arms, jerks her from my lap, and screams in her face. "I said—"

I lunge off the end of the bed and shove him as hard as I can. "Get your hands off her!" He stumbles back and falls against the wall. He springs back up in a fury. Jaselle steps between us, holding a soft hand to my chest and a pleading one to Noah.

"She's high, Noah. Leave her alone."

He points a finger in my face over Jaselle's protective arm. "No shit. You're high, both of you! I swear to God I could fucking kill you right now!" His eyes burn into me and I completely believe him.

"Get out, Noah!" Jaselle screams.

"Not this again, Jaselle! I'm not dealing with this bullshit again! Where's the rest of it?"

"It's gone. We smoked it."

"Bullshit. Where's the rest?"

"It's seriously gone, dude," I chime in, unsure if it really is or not.

"You shut the fuck up! I'm not talking to you right now." The finger he has in my face comes back to life. I swat it away, unsure where my nerve is coming from.

"If you think you're taking her to the gutter with you, you're wrong. I'm not letting it happen, not in my house!"

"*I* got *her* high, Noah. Leave her alone," Jaselle says.

He keeps yelling at me, his eyes bulging from their sockets. "You're a piece of trash, trash from the alley."

"Noah!" Jaselle tries to push him backward.

"You think you're the first?"

"Get out!"

"You think you're her first stray?" He's laughing at me, finally allowing Jaselle to push him backward. "Hey, you enjoy that bed tonight, Savage. I know how hard you worked to get there. You enjoy my roof, but get the fuck out in the morning!"

Jaselle gives him one more shove and slams the door, holding it in place while the silence settles since it won't latch anymore.

Her face is full of emotion, but I don't know what to make of it. Truthfully, my head hurts just thinking about trying to figure out what just happened. All I know is I don't like Noah. His rough grip on Jaselle's slight wrists keeps replaying in my brain. The rest of it is already fading. Do I think I'm her first stray? That's what he said, right? I don't know, Noah, do you think you're the first to call me trash?

Jaselle pulls her dresser over a few feet so it blocks the door. I hear the furious slams again and the helpless wood. I have no doubt Noah could get through if he wanted. But for now, at least it keeps the door closed, some weak attempt at security.

"Does he hit you?" I ask.

"Oh no," she says sincerely. "Never. He'd never hurt me. He's a good guy, underneath it all."

I roll my eyes at the cliché. "You know he totally wants to fuck you, right?" I surprise myself with that one, but it's already out, no sense backing off it now. Jaselle smiles, comes to the bed, and straddles me.

"Is that a little jealousy I hear?" She weaves her fingers through my hair and pulls, exposing my neck.

"No, definitely not."

Her kisses trail down.

"Not jealousy," I repeat.

"Play for me."

"What?"

"Play the song. I want to hear it." She pointedly breathes across my collarbone.

"You're seducing me into playing it?"

"If that's what it takes."

"I don't think now is the best time," I say.

She shrugs. "The door has a lock on it."

"Yeah, 'cause that made a difference."

"You scared?" She winks at me, so fast and nonchalant I'm not positive I saw it. It sends a ripple of warmth through me. I can't say no to her, to that face. But he's listening. They're coming.

She pulls me to my feet and together we push the dresser aside again. Noah's gone to his room, which means he can't see down the hall, but the TV is off, so I'm terrified our steps are sounding through the entire place. She shuts the door to the piano room, locking us safely inside, semi-safely.

"I don't know, Jaselle. Are you sure? It won't get him going again?"

"Play. I want to hear. Fuck him. I don't care."

I wish I was so bold. I care a lot. The thought of him breaking through another door makes me want to hyperventilate.

"Rainn, he's not going to do a goddamn thing. He's all bark, promise." She sits me down and rubs my shoulders. "Play. Please."

I hold my shaking hands over the keys. I press the A, then jump back at the giant sound. "This isn't a good idea."

"I want your secrets," she whispers in my ear. "Play like he isn't here."

I take a deep breath, remembering the notes before I begin. It's been so long since I've played this, even in private. How can I be sharing it with her? It almost feels wrong, like it was never meant to be for anyone but Michael and me. But that's all delusions. It had nothing to do with us. It was his, and I cling to it. That's the end of it. He didn't give it to me. And who am I to deny such beauty to the world?

I begin. At first, I'm timid, terrified of Noah, but gradually the song takes over. I'm lost in it, or death, or meth, something numb and quiet. It rolls through me, paralleling the waves of my high. It's something searing hot, melting, slicing through me effortlessly.

It's conquering me. I want to collapse under the memories. I'm outside myself, not playing anymore, but watching, watching like a ghost. I can see the steam coming off my back, my knuckles, my legs. Jaselle. Hear me, from somewhere outside of this. Hear me, from the black well that holds me under the earth. See me, even though these notes aren't mine, could never be mine. Feel me, giving you everything. Not one secret, the only secret.

"You weren't lying. That's the most gorgeous thing I've ever heard," Jaselle says from under the piano. When did she go there?

I look under. She's lying beneath the strings, stretched out on her back.

"What are you doing down there?" I can't help but smile. She comes out and sits beside me on the bench.

"The sound is stronger down there. It grabs you, and there's nothing else."

I pull her to my mouth. It's becoming so natural so fast to do that.

"Hey," she says, waiting for me to stop.

I finally do. "Yeah?"

"I want you to have it," she says.

"Have what?"

"The piano."

My chest tightens. I can't pinpoint which emotion does it exactly. "Absolutely not," I say.

"Shut up. I mean it. I want you to have it."

"Do you have any clue—"

"How much it's worth? A lot more to you than to me. I won't sell it. It was my grandma's, so it's not about money to me. I can't play it. It's just sitting here, alone in a room collecting dust. You play so beautifully. I think it was made for you. I've seen the way you dote on it."

"But don't you want it? If it was your grandma's don't you want to keep it? Even if all you ever do is look at it?"

"It should be played. You know that. You two are soul mates. Please." She lowers her head on the please, revealing some underlying pain. "Please, accept it. I want you to have it."

"Jaselle—"

"Please."

"I can't take something so valuable for free," I say.

She leans against me. "Can you take me for free?"

I chuckle. "That's not the same."

"Isn't it?" She kisses me. "Take the damn piano."

"I don't have anywhere to take it anyway."

"For now. You can keep it here until you do."

She says it like it's already done, like I will have a place. I'm not sure what to do with that kind of confidence. The assumption is a little intimidating.

"I have a question," she says.

I exaggerate a sigh. "I played you the song already, you trying to kill me tonight?"

"Just one little question."

"You better make it a good one, 'cause that's seriously all you get tonight."

"That's all I ever get, what are you talking about? I'm lucky if I get one."

"Okay, okay. What?"

"Do you love me?"

It catches me off guard, but I don't miss a beat. "You have no idea."

Chapter Eight

Something burning through the new sun. Jaselle, one foot propped on the box of a heater that protrudes from the wall, smoking the last of the meth, or crystal, as she prefers to call it. She lazily points her exhale to the open window above her.

"Looks like there's one more. You want it?" She holds out the foil and lighter. I go over to her, not sure if I do want it, but she's high, and I'm not one to be left behind. I pull the smoke to me, waiting for the rush of a fresh hit, but it pales next to the first one. I watch the last of it burn out, dissatisfied.

I find myself on the carpet, not sleepy by a long shot, but feeling the sun press me into the floor. We've been up all night, I realize. The quiet in the living room is starting to irritate me.

"Is he even here?" I ask.

"I don't know. I haven't gone out there."

Neither have I. I wouldn't dare. It made me uncomfortable just creeping from the piano room back to Jaselle's. No wonder it always seems like she's sneaking around. I would too. What a crap way to live.

"How do you want to die?" Jaselle asks suddenly.

I crack my knuckles. "Alone."

She nods and appears to think about it before she speaks. "Isn't that what most people don't want?"

"Probably."

"Why do you want to die alone?"

"Having someone there makes you feel better but the other person feel like shit. I'd just rather quietly slip off. I'm not dragging anyone with me."

"I guess most people are afraid to die, and if someone they love is there it's a little easier," she says.

"I guess."

"But you're not afraid?"

"Sure, I am," I say. "But I don't need anyone to drown in it with me."

"Who says it's a bad thing to be there? I was with my grandma when she died. It was sad, and it sucked, but I was glad I was there."

Paramedics and flashing lights pop into my head. Slick grass and "Clear!"

"But your grandma lived a full life, and probably died in her sleep in a bed, right?"

"Yeah…" She waits for me to continue, but I'm not sure what to say, so she goes on. "So, you're planning to die prematurely?"

I feel the corners of my mouth draw down as I think that over. "Apparently, I expect to."

She leaves her perch by the window and comes over. "I'd love to be there when you die," she says. I smile slowly and we both start laughing. "That sounded twisted," she says. "But you know what I mean."

"What about you?" I ask. "How do you want to die?"

"High."

"Really?" I'm genuinely surprised. "You don't want to feel your last few minutes? Know what's happening?"

"Not really. I want to die laughing, looking the darkness in the face and not being afraid of it."

We just sit quietly for a few minutes. Once I feel like the right amount of time has passed I sigh. "I guess I should get going before Noah gets back."

She kisses me. "Absolutely not. I don't want you crashing in the alley. You're going to be out so hard nothing will wake you up. God knows what will happen to you."

"God knows what Noah will do to me if I'm still here when he gets home. He flat out said to be gone." I try to stand up, but she pulls me down.

"He didn't mean that. He was just having an episode. He's mad at me, not you."

I smile. "No, he was definitely mad at me, and I don't have much choice if it's his place."

"Rainn, stop. I'm serious, it's not safe. Crash here, then you can go, okay?"

I see a ripple of insecurity in the "then you can go," like I want to go. I reach out and touch her face, giving in to her as my body begins to feel weighted with exhaustion.

"I don't want to cause problems for you," I say. When she doesn't answer I keep going, wishing I'd shut up with every passing word, but unable to stop. "I don't want you to feel obligated to take care of me. Just because we're friends doesn't mean you have to bring me in every time it snows, or let me stay because I'm crashing..." My mouth keeps moving but my brain is stuck on the word friend. It doesn't feel appropriate anymore.

"Really? I thought that was exactly what it meant," she says. I wince at how easily she accepts the word. Friend. It didn't even seem to bother her. Maybe we still are just that. I told her I loved her, didn't I? Does it count when you're high?

She touches my face. "I want you here."

I smile. "Okay then."

I wouldn't call Noah's threat empty, or even a threat so much as a demand, but when he gets home it turns out Jaselle is right. He doesn't say a word to either of us about it.

I wake up. Again, I don't remember falling asleep. That pisses me off. I want to hold Jaselle while we drift off together, but I always just feel like I went through a time warp instead.

Jaselle isn't next to me. No, wait, she isn't even in the room. I sit up abruptly, alarmed at the realization. My atrophied muscles complain at the jolt. The sun is way too bright. Why won't she get some stupid blinds?

Did we really smoke meth? How long have I been sleeping? Where's Jaselle? Where's Noah? Did I really push him? My stomach wrenches harder the longer I think about it.

The door opens and Jaselle comes to the bed. All my nerves calm as she slips under the covers next to me.

"Morning, you," she says. I scoot across the bed and wrap my arms around her, resting my head on her chest. She squeezes me.

"How long did I sleep?" I ask.

"A long time, babe, it's two."

I shrug. "That's not bad, ten hours or something?" She just looks at me until I'm forced to ask, "What?"

"More like thirty-four hours, honey."

I feel like I'm in the twilight zone. I clench up in horror. I've overstayed my welcome by a lot. Benny must be really worried by now. I'm completely humiliated. How long has she been up? I missed band practice.

"I have to go." I've already flown to my feet. Jaselle watches the whole thing. Her calm suddenly irritates me, too big of a contrast. She follows me to the door. I have my hand on the knob when she finally speaks.

"Will I see you again?"

I'm so startled by the question I completely forget I'm in a hurry. "What? Of course, you will." She just keeps staring, so I grab her head and kiss it. "Of course, you will."

"I never know."

That's depressing. I guess Benny was right as usual. I'm lucky as hell she's persistent. My adoration hasn't come across at all. "Baby, you're going to see me all the time." The words sound foreign, which only confirms that my instant, ridiculous, intoxicating love for this woman has failed to assert itself. "If you want," I feel like I have to add.

"You kidding? I can't seem to get enough of you."

"Good." I kiss her. She reaches in her pocket and pulls out a pen. She grabs my hand and writes her number on it.

"I'll see you then," she says.

I force myself to leave calm and slow, but once I'm on the sidewalk I jog to the nearest bus stop. My need to tell the boys I'm okay is ridiculously pressing. Like the ten minutes I shave off from power walking are really going to change anything when I've been gone for three days. But despite all the time I spend telling myself that, when I finally see the Blue Moon sign I can't stop myself from trotting the rest of the way.

Benny says he wasn't worried, that he knew I was staying with Jaselle, but he hugs me tight and I know he's full of it. "You need to give me her number so I can check on you when you do that," he says. His eyes move to the ink on my hand. I pull it away like I'm afraid he'll memorize it without my consent.

"I don't know, Benny. I'm not sure I should be giving it out," I say.

"Who's giving it out? What do you think I'm going to call her up for a date? Strictly for emergencies, I promise."

"I just don't think it's a good idea. I'll call and let you know next time, okay?"

"No, you won't, just like you didn't call this time." He makes a playful grab for my hand.

"I was too fucked up," I confess self-consciously.

"Exactly. Look, I'm not trying to babysit you. It's just not like you to miss band practice."

"I know, I know. I feel guilty enough already," I say.

"I'm not trying to make you feel guilty. I just want to know you're okay is all." Benny looks at me for a while waiting for me to say something, but I don't. He picks up the phone. "She's here," he says. "Yeah, she's fine." He hangs up. "They're on the way."

The boys show up in record time. Jayden's Mohawk isn't even spiked today. He trimmed it down too. I feel like I've been gone six months, not three days.

"Are you all right?" Shiloh asks. He's the first to make it across the room. I tell him I am. Alex gives me a fist bump and a wink. As long as someone got laid he's happy.

"Well, look who's at band practice," Jayden says. It should be no surprise by now he's the difficult one.

"I'm really sorry, guys," I say. "I—"

"No, no, it's okay." Shiloh and Alex can't forgive fast enough, but Jayden...

"She's human, good. Now she can stop busting our balls over every little thing," he says.

I don't like where this is going. Diffuse. "Look, it was a one-time thing, and I'm really sorry. Let's get back on track, okay?"

"Fucking her was a one-time thing? Was it that bad?" Jayden says.

I want to knock his smug ass out. "Missing practice was a one-time thing, jerk. Strap up." I point at his guitar.

"I know how it goes," he says with a slight weave to his posture that briefly makes me think he's drunk, only I know he isn't. "It's a one-time thing until you need some pussy again." I stare at him, willing him to put his stupid guitar on already before it's too late. "She got a good pussy, Rainn?"

I shove his shoulders with both hands as hard as I can, knocking him back a few steps. "What is your problem already, you hormonal brat?" I try to remove Alex's arm from around me. He's holding me back.

"I'm not the one who missed practice," Jayden says.

"You either miss practice completely or are late every other day. Are you really going to hold this over me?"

"I'm not the one who's a Nazi about it though!" he yells. "Jayden, you're late. Jayden, you're not playing the song right. Jayden, you're not in tune. Jayden—"

I cut off his mockery. "You don't think those things are important?"

"Jayden, that girl is a slut." His impression of my voice is starting to make me shake with anger.

"You can—"

"You're no better than anyone else, Rainn! You found some ass you had to have and you blew off the band. And that's fine, okay? But quit acting like you're something else now. You're just like us, so I don't want any more guilt trips about how *I* bring us down."

"I swear to God if you don't stop calling her a piece of ass I'm going to rip your Mohawk out," I yell.

"What do you think she is? A soul mate?"

"Stop it. Not everything is always about sex. I'm not like you."

"Oh yes, you are," he says.

"No, you want me to be so you can feel better about yourself, but we both know it's not the same."

"Hey, I feel great about myself. You're the one who has a problem with me."

"I don't even know what you're talking about anymore," I say. "I messed up and I apologized. I'm not going to grovel. I've never done this before, ever, and if you think me missing one practice is your golden ticket to do whatever you want, you're out of your mind."

"When did this become your band?"

"When I became the only person working on the music!" I'm surprised how easily I claim the band. It doesn't even bother me the way he intended.

"This isn't Rainn and the Suicidal Angels; it's just the Suicidal Angels."

"I begged you to help me with the songs, Jayden, *begged*. You won't. You want the power to do whatever you want with the songs, but you won't do the work to make it sound good? Screw that."

"Guess what, I *can* do whatever I want."

"Oh, trust me, we know, Jayden. You're so cool. You fuck whoever you want to fuck, you show up whenever you want to show up. Maybe the problem is that you don't want to be in the band, you just want the girls that come with it."

"Fuck you!" he yells and moves forward. Shiloh puts a hand out like he's afraid Jayden will actually hit me. He never would. Jayden just screams. "I made this band!"

"But you don't love it anymore!"

"Hang on, guys," Alex intervenes. "Let's just cool off here."

"No, fuck you all. You think I'm bringing us down? Fine, find a better guitar player. I dare you." He grabs his guitar and storms for the door.

"Jayden, come on, man," Shiloh yells, but Jayden won't stop. We all just stand in the quiet for a second after the door slams. I can feel Alex's and Shiloh's anxiety. Me? Well, I'm somewhere in the middle. Jayden is the best guitarist I've ever met, and he has creativity bursting from every pore on his body, but he lacks the discipline to make use of it. Maybe we're just wasting our time anyway. Watching him walk away hurts more as a friend than as a bandmate.

I look at Benny. His mouth is crooked, exactly like one of those smiley faces you type in the computer with the colon and the slash. He sees me looking at him. "Hey, guys," he says. "He'll be back."

Shiloh and Alex grunt. "He left us here, huh?" Alex says.

"Yeah." Shiloh nods.

"I guess we should start walking then."

They both give me a hug, but it feels strange. I might be imagining it, paranoid that they blame me, but they feel stiff. When they go, Benny and I just stare at each other for another minute before he waves me over. "What do you say I let José run the bar tonight, and you and I go upstairs and watch the game? We can order pizza, have a couple beers, just chill." I nod.

We flop down on his extremely worn couch. It's perfect, beaten to hell but comfortable as can be. We're in the third quarter and fourth beer apiece when he finally takes that deep sigh that means he's about to get to the point.

"He's just jealous, Rainn."

"What are you talking about? What does he have to be jealous about?" Benny stares at me like I'm a moron, but I don't bend. I just keep waiting for an answer.

"He's never seen you with anyone. You've always been all about the band. They've always had all your attention. Now they have to share."

"So I'm not supposed to date anyone?"

"Hey, you know I'm happy for you. I'm just telling you what his problem is, the real problem. He'll be back." He keeps looking at me like he's waiting for some kind of emotional reaction.

I just shrug. "I don't even know if I want him back. He's exhausting."

"Of course, you do. You guys are amazing, Rainn. It's going to happen, but you have to do it together. He may be exhausting, but we both know he's part of your sound."

"If he wants to be."

"Hey." Benny pats my shoulder. "He does. He just needs a little love."

"Loving Jayden is dangerous."

Benny's look changes. His eyebrows raise the smallest degree. I feel my cheeks get warm and wish I had phrased that differently.

He stares at me until he can't take it. "Have you…"

"No," I say sharply.

He lets a second go by before he asks more. "Did you think about it?"

"I'm gay, remember?"

"That wasn't the question."

"Wouldn't it have to be for me to think about it?" I say.

"Hell, I don't pretend to know how that stuff works."

"Have you ever thought about screwing a guy?"

"No," he says with a big grin. "Never crossed my mind."

"Then you understand how that stuff works. I want to screw a guy exactly as much as you do."

"That's not true though," he says, and he gets up to get a couple more beers. He points his finger with enthusiasm, like this is the most interesting thing he's ever talked about. "You've been with guys, right?"

"That doesn't mean I enjoyed it. You have to make room for some experimenting time."

"I never experimented with guys, though. So, we're not the same." He's got a pretty cute smile when he thinks he's won a debate.

"But you weren't supposed to like guys. I was. When you just flow with the current you don't have to experiment. It's when you have to figure out how to turn around and go against the grain."

"Wait, are we going with current or grain? Can we stick to one metaphor, please?"

"Shut up." I punch his arm.

"Seriously though, come on. You were never attracted to any guys?"

"I thought I was a couple times, I guess. I tried to be, before I knew there was another option. Before I knew what it was *supposed* to feel like."

"What about Isaiah?"

"Isaiah was a mistake, a gigantic mistake."

"But you were attracted to him." He won't let up. Suddenly, I'm irritated by this conversation.

"You know what he was like. He beat the shit out of me."

"I know. He was a piece of crap, but the only reason you dealt with him in the first place is because there had to be an attraction, right?"

"No, there was pressure to be 'normal,' nothing more."

"Okay, okay," he says.

"And what's with the interrogation? I thought you wanted me to be with Jaselle."

"I totally do. I love lesbians." His grin comes back.

"You're such a loser." I finish my beer in one swig and retreat to the alley. I don't even know why I hang out with Benny. He always leaves me drowning in some memory. This time it's Jayden peeling me off the floor of Isaiah's apartment, Jayden taking me to his place and cleaning me up, Jayden rambling about how he should kill Isaiah, asking what happened, frantic.

Now I want to hug Jayden, or slap him upside the head maybe and tell him I'll always love him. I'll always be here. He doesn't need to be jealous. But even as I think about that I don't feel the need to rush over there and beg him back into the band. I don't even feel the need to rush around looking for a new guitarist. I just feel defeated.

There's one thing I do have the motivation to do. Talk to Jaselle.

Chapter Nine

I call Jaselle from the bar, ignoring the time. She picks up right away. She asks what's wrong, and I'm shocked when I find myself choked up trying to spit it out. She doesn't press it on the phone, just tells me to come over.

The buses aren't running anymore. It's late, but I don't let that stop me. I hang up and head out. When I get there, I knock on the door. Noah answers.

"She ran out for a minute. She'll be right back."

"Okay." I nod, feeling completely awkward, waiting for some verbal jab.

He sighs. "Don't just stand there. Come in."

"Really?"

"You'd better hurry or I'll close the door."

I step inside, shoving my hands in my pockets. I follow him into the living room. He flops down on the couch, kicks his legs up, and reaches for the remote. I take the chair across from him. It seems more appropriate than retreating to Jaselle's room alone, even though that's exactly what I'd like to do.

"So, Jaselle told me to be nice to you tonight," he says. I laugh a little. "She says you're dealing with some personal shit or something."

"It's not that big of a deal. You can be mean if you want," I say.

"What is it?" he asks. I'm a little taken aback he's bold enough to ask, given our intense dislike of one another. Honestly, I can't deal with him being nice. I just feel like I'm waiting for the mean Noah to resurface, but he just keeps looking at me like he's truly trying or something. I figure I can either tell him it's none of his damn business and set this rivalry in stone, or I can loosen up and maybe not feel like I'm about to get kicked out at any given moment.

"It's just my band. My guitarist flipped out on me and quit."

Noah nods and grabs a pipe off the coffee table. He takes a deep hit. "So you need a new guitarist then?"

"I don't know. He was pretty much the best I've ever seen. And he has huge stage presence. I'm not sure he can be replaced. I can't even imagine us with someone else."

"So you need him back then." He hands me the pipe. I accept it, trying to cover my elation from the gesture.

"I'm kind of thinking about just throwing in the towel, actually."

"What?" He jolts up on the couch.

"Well, yeah. It's just—"

"Your music is the coolest fucking thing about you! What do you mean you're thinking about throwing in the towel? You've got to be kidding me!"

"I, uh…" He's throwing me off caring like this, and was that a compliment? Sort of?

"And what the hell are you going to do with yourself once you quit the band? Huh?"

"I don't know. Get a job, I guess. An apartment." I smirk. "Conform."

"You don't mean that. An apartment, maybe, so you can stop bothering me, but you're not going to quit playing music. The only time I don't want to smack your face off is when you're playing the piano. And now you want to quit? You really are in bad shape, aren't you?"

"I guess. It was already going downhill." I can't believe I'm making a solid effort at opening up to Noah. I'll probably regret giving him this much information later. "This guy, Brad, who was supposed to be a break for us, flaked for the millionth time, and even before Jayden walked out he was all over the place."

"So maybe Brad isn't the guy that's going to be your break. Cut him loose. Look for something else. And either your guitarist is worth the trouble or he's not. Decide which it is and either get him back or replace him."

"You always want things to be simple, don't you?" I say.

"It is simple. If you want it, make it happen. These problems you think you have with your band, they're pathetic, really. So the music industry is hard to break into; what, are you shocked?"

"Of course, I'm not."

"Then dry your eyes and be a bitch. Let some of that savage out where you actually need it. Kick life in the balls."

I start laughing and take another hit of the weed. I can't help but repeat him. "Kick life in the balls." I'm shocked I actually feel a little better.

"I got a question for you, and for once I'm not trying to offend you."

"Okay," I say. I figure he's earned a slightly offensive question. "Go ahead."

"How does a skinny, dirty, homeless girl from a back alley know how to play a piano like that? Chopin for God's sake. How's a homeless girl even know who Chopin is?"

"How does a mangy, stoner drug dealer know who Chopin is? And by ear?"

"Well, that's no exciting story. I just like classical music. There's more to life than reggae," he says. I hear the front door open.

"Hellooo?" Jaselle calls. She turns the corner and sees Noah and me sitting together. Concern fills her face. I wonder where she had to go in the middle of the night, urgent enough to leave me here alone with him with a plea to behave. I get up and give her a hug. She kisses my cheek.

"Everything okay?" she asks, looking from me to Noah and back.

"Yeah," I say.

"Okay, well, come on." She grabs my hand and pulls me toward her room.

"Savage?" Noah says and exposes his palms. I know it means where's my answer?

"I wasn't always a dirty, skinny, homeless girl from a back alley," I say. Jaselle studies me when I say it, trying to take in the vibe I guess, probably confused as hell.

We sit down on her bed, and she comes over and kisses me, her hair falling in my face. I grab her neck and pull her down on top of me. She backs away gently. "Are you okay?"

I nod and I pull her back down. I can't get enough of the taste of her. No matter how close she is, it's never close enough. We're wrapped in each other for hours.

It's not until the sun is rising that we get around to what happened with Jayden, and by then I feel stupid for being upset about it to begin with. Of course, he'll be back. And of course, the band will go on. Jaselle picks her pants up off the floor and digs in the pocket, emerging with a tiny plastic bag. Inside, it looks like a small piece of glass. Meth. I guess that's exactly why they call it glass.

"More?" I ask.

"Yeah, I just need to crank out some work. The show is coming up and I'm behind. I'm telling you, it doesn't just keep you awake, it broadens your mind."

"Yeah?"

"I get some of my best stuff done on this. You want some? You can go try to write some music on it. I bet you'll love it." She pulls an old piece of foil out of the drawer by her bed, already covered in little black spots where she's smoked off of it before. Where we've smoked off of it before? Yes, we.

I smoke it gently, timid about getting too high, but after the first one my conviction fades. Before I know it I'm hitting it again. Jaselle looks so beautiful through the smoke. What a bizarre thought.

She goes to work setting up her paints. I'm wired again, for sure, but not feeling particularly compelled to create much of anything. Jaselle reads my thoughts. "Try it at least. Play piano, and I'll paint what you play."

That idea fascinates me enough to get up and go to the other room. I wish she'd come in here with me, but she's already set up in her bedroom and says she can hear me easily.

I start with something low, a pulsing, deep rhythm. The sound is amazing. I get stuck on it, with no desire to complicate it. Finally, I force myself to add a layer, some high notes sprinkled in with the somber bass. Next thing I know I'm so wrapped up in every little note that they're just running away with me.

I feel like I'm floating on the surface of the ocean, rolling with the waves, smooth. But then, a jolt, a sudden fear there's no way I'll remember any of this tomorrow after I've come down. I try to pay better attention, burn it into my memory. It's exhausting. Isn't the point of being high to get lost? Not to focus.

I don't hear Jaselle come in. I just feel her arms on my shoulders, then her hands slide down my chest until her breath is in my ear. "Come to bed, baby." How long has it been? A long time already.

I let her guide me under the covers. Everything feels incredible. She tells me I'm peaking. My hand runs up her thigh, the warmth so inviting. I kiss her neck, tasting her skin while I slip my fingers inside her. She moans as my fingers go deeper and grabs a handful of my hair. I obey her pull. She grinds into me while I push into her and she drives me crazy. Every little movement she makes, every sound that comes from those lips, I can barely stand it.

Her orgasm is the most beautiful thing I've ever witnessed. Her hips thrust against me as she wraps her arms around me so tight I can't escape, like she'll never let me go. Her face is smooth and arresting. I kiss her exposed neck while she's still breathing hard, sinking back into the sheets.

I pull her closer to me. She's almost asleep already by the time I get her all gathered up. I put my arm around her waist and squeeze. She's so small I feel like I could wrap my arm around her twice. I breathe her in, making a conscious effort to memorize this moment.

I finally notice the canvas in the corner of the room, her painting of my music. There's long sweeps of deep blues and purples, with small but brilliant specks of red. The longer I look at it the more I see. I feel like it's sucking me inside this other world. I want to stay down here with her.

Chapter Ten

S o, are you going to call him?" Jaselle asks. My eyelids feel heavy still. I haven't gotten my fill of sleep. I force myself to sit up before I pass out again.

"Yeah, I should," I say.

"Just do it. Don't overthink it. You'll feel better when it's done."

How does she know I'm having so much anxiety about this? Am I that easy to read? "Okay, okay. I'm getting up." I reach for my shirt.

"You have to get dressed to call him?" she asks.

"I was going to go to that gas station, call him from the pay phone."

"You're kidding." Her eyebrows crinkle. "You're not just going to use my phone?" She extends it out to me. I take it from her, deliberately brushing her fingers as I do.

"I didn't want to be presumptuous," I say.

She scoffs. "Give me a break. You need to stop with that crap already. Are you my girlfriend, or aren't you?"

My anxiety over Jayden vanishes in favor of happiness I can't contain. "Am I?"

"You better be."

"Then I am."

"Then you should feel comfortable using my phone."

I give her a kiss and dial Jayden's number. It rings a couple times. I'm surprised how relieved I am at the notion it'll go to voice mail. But then he picks up.

"Yo."

"Hey, Jay. It's me." The silence that overtakes the line is brutal. For a second I think he hung up. "Hello?"

"Yeah."

"Uh, how are you?" I feel like a jackass. It's not helping that Jaselle is watching.

"Fine, I guess."

"Look, Jay, you know why I'm calling. I don't want it to end like this."

"How do you want it to end, Rainn?"

"I don't want it to end. I'm sorry, okay? I should have been there. I shouldn't have said some of what I said. And you're right, you made the band. It wouldn't have started without you, and it can't go on without you, okay? We need you."

"Wow," he says. "How'd that feel?"

"What?"

"Apologizing. Saying you need me."

"It felt fine." It stung a little. "It's the truth." It stung a lot. "I've never taken your talent for granted, you know that. We *do* need you." We do need him.

"I'm sorry too, I guess," he says. Was that supposed to be satisfying? I just sit there waiting for him to go on, forcing him to go on with my lack of response. Finally, he does. "I shouldn't have talked about your girl like that. That was a jerk thing to do."

"Thank you."

"And I'll try to stop being late all the time."

"What I really want is for you to write again. You know that," I say.

"I know. It's just…"

"You're so good when you want to be."

"I'll think about it."

The line goes quiet for a while. Finally, I decide that's about as successful as it's going to get. "So, I'll see you tomorrow then?" I say.

"Yeah."

"All right."
"Hey, Rainn?"
"Yeah?"
"I do still love the band, okay?"
I smile. "Okay."

Sometimes things sneak up on you. Sometimes they sneak away from you. I don't notice the alley fading out of my life. Funny how fast we adjust. I thought television would be a glamorous luxury forever, now I need some mindless chatter in the background to fall asleep. I thought her bed would swallow me in ecstasy every night.

Don't get me wrong, I still think about these things, but the bruises on my spine from sleeping on concrete are healed. Already it's becoming the past. I guess the meth does its part in that effect, but it's mostly Jaselle. She's my home now.

I don't notice I essentially live with her until she goes to her art show and leaves me in the house alone. I want to go, but she says it's pointless. I've already seen all the art, and she'll just be busy all night anyway. I can't help but assume it's because I'd damage her image. It burns a little, but this is her night, so I swallow it, kiss her good-bye, and wish her luck.

Now I'm biting my fingernails, watching *South Park*, waiting. I picture her in some classy loft with a martini in her hand, discussing abstract art with some dude with slicked back hair and a red tie. I'm sure she's raking in all kinds of money. It was hard to see her cart off the one she painted of me. I know that was always its purpose, but I'm a little attached to it.

Who needs the painting when you've got the model? That's what she said to quell the hurt I was failing to hide. That was cute enough to make me feel better at the time. Keepsakes are for people who expect it to end.

I look around the room at what's left, the ones that didn't make the cut for the show. A lot of the ones she's done recently are still here. She's been amped up on meth for the past few weeks. We both have, pushing out all the creativity we can find. And yet, all of it is still here, in the bedroom, apparently not impressive enough for her taste. I guiltily confirm to myself that they aren't as good as the ones she did take, almost all of which were done before I met her.

And my music? Can I remember any of it? Is it worth remembering? I'm questioning the artistic value of the drug we love breathing together. The truth is, I've tired of it. I'm relieved we've come to her show. This means the last-minute rushing and painting and scurrying around has come to a close. Her "need" for it is over.

The door slams. I jump to my feet as fast as I can and still she bursts in the bedroom door before I reach it. How she crossed the entire apartment before I crossed the room I can't tell you. "Hey," I say, but she goes for the nearest painting. She picks it up and hurls it into the dresser, putting the wooden corner right through the fragile canvas. I jump back involuntarily.

She goes for another. I watch her smash it into the wall again and again until it snaps in half. "Jaselle," I say it soft, afraid to intervene. She rakes the walls with both arms spread wide, knocking all the hung ones to the ground. She stomps them, kicks, picks them up and throws them. She reaches for one I particularly like, and I have to stop her.

I grab her arms by the elbows from behind. "Jaselle!"

"Get off!" She pulls away, much harder than I expected. I reach for a better grip, but she just keeps fighting. "Fucking piece of shit!" she screams at the painting in her grasp. She launches it across the room. It breaks her lamp. Glass shatters into the air. I finally have a good grip, and I pull her back.

"Stop, baby, stop!"

"Why? It's all shit, every last one of them! Might as well throw them out now!"

"What happened?" It feels like a ridiculous question at a ridiculous time. The art show went bad. Just like the last one. How does this happen? They're so beautiful. I know it's not just that I love her. They are incredible.

She tries to lunge away from me again. She gets her hands on a painting she hasn't even finished yet. Her strength surprises me. I'm holding back a little in an effort not to hurt her, but I'm trying hard, and though hindered, she's still doing exactly what she wants to do.

She tries to smash it into the wall. I tighten my arms around her more. She can't get the leverage she needs so she just throws it. I pull her to me as hard as I can, crushing her with love. She fights it, rigid and furious in my embrace. "Let me go!"

But then, finally, she breaks. She goes limp and shakes with tears and holds me. She squeezes me and I squeeze back, wanting to somehow absorb this pain for her, pull it right out of her skin and feel it for her. She cries like that for a long time. I catch my breath with relief.

I want to ask what happened again, but I fight it. She keeps muttering little clues I'm trying to piece together. "*Someone* might like it," imitating someone. "Just give it up now." "Trash." I finally recognize the nasally impersonation. Her mom.

I hold her while she relives it. "Hey," I call for her attention, soft in her ear. "You're amazing. It's going to be okay. They'll see."

She pulls her face away from my chest. "I'm sorry. I'm okay." She exhales like she's forgotten to breathe all this time. "I'll be fine. I just need a drink." I reluctantly let her pull out of my hold. She gets a drink, but she heads for the drawer too. She takes out the foil and some crystal. I want to suggest we only drink tonight, but I figure now isn't the best time to try that.

"I'm being dramatic," she says. I look around the destroyed room. "This'll fix me up," she adds. I watch her take a long hit, closing her eyes while she holds it in. She offers it to me, but I pass.

Her face goes blank as she slumps on the bed, too high to stand. I let her go comatose and start picking up the paintings that survived. I hang a few of them back up.

"What are you doing here?" she asks abruptly. I glance over at her passingly but have to shoot back for a double take. Something in her eyes makes me stand up straight, pulse throbbing in my ear. She's sitting facing me. She looks evil. My angel looks demonic, her pupils blacker than black and expanding to the rims.

"I love you," I say cautiously. "That's why I'm here."

"Put that fucking painting back on the ground." She's never spoken to me like this before. I try to ignore it.

"Your art is beautiful. Just because—"

"Put it on the ground."

"You can't do this to yourself," I say.

"And what makes you think you know anything about art?"

"I know it takes me somewhere. I know I could escape in it forever. And I know there are other people out there who will see it too. You'll come out of this, and when you do you'll want these."

"You're just a girl from an alley!"

"Jaselle." I put a steel wall between me and what she said, hoping I can build it before she continues. "Don't," I plead.

"Who the fuck cares about your opinion? You aren't a critic. You aren't educated. You aren't an artist. You don't know anything. You're ignorant. No one cares what you think."

"Art is for everyone. It doesn't matter who you are. That's the beauty of art. How can you not know that?"

"No, you're wrong again, Rainn. There are rules. There are politics just like any other business. There's a proper way!"

"And what you do isn't proper?"

"No one wants what I do. They don't understand it."

"Then do it the proper way, I guess."

"That's what you think?" she raises her voice in a fury.

"I don't know what you want from me! I tell you it's beautiful and I'm an ignorant piece of shit. I tell you to change it and I'm an asshole."

"I've painted things people can't even comprehend yet! I've shown the truth of this cold world, and they don't want to see it because it shows them their ugly faces! I am the greatest artist alive. They're afraid of me."

"Afraid?"

"Yes, because I'll expose them. It's not my paintings they don't like, it's themselves. My art is a reflection. You can't blame the mirror for the world! I am the jester."

I feel like I should say something, but I don't want to get her started on bashing me again, so I figure I'll just let this jester thing keep going. And it does.

"They think I'm the joke, but I'm the only one that sees them. I see right through you all. I see through you, Rainn."

"You're not acting like yourself," I say, afraid of where this is going, just wanting it to stop. I'm afraid of the way she's looking at me. I can't withstand her hate-filled eyes.

"You want me to tell you what your soul looks like?"

"Jaselle, stop it. You're freaking me out."

"Get out."

I tense up, shocked, confused. There has to be a way to turn this momentum around. "Look, I'm sorry you had a bad night. You know you're an amazing painter. I know you're amazing. You'll make it. You just have to keep trying. You know how many times I've heard my band sucks? Sometimes you just have to keep going anyway."

"And where has that gotten you, Rainn? Where are you now?"

"Stop."

"Maybe you do suck. Ever think of that?"

"Jaselle."

"Have you?"

"I think about it every day!"

"And?"

"And I keep going," I say.

"Is that so?"

"Yes."

"Then where is your band?"

"What?" I stop, puzzled.

"When was the last show you did with them?" she asks. I stutter, surprised to find it far away, not at my fingertips where I thought it was. She starts laughing. Her eyes are cold. What's happening? What's happening?

"Oh, Rainn. You have no idea who you are, do you? Or who you aren't. I can see you."

"Don't talk to me like that."

"Like what?" She shoots to her feet and comes close to my face like she wants to fight or something.

"Jaselle, just stop it. Just stop! I know you're upset, but—"

"Fuck you! Don't act like you know. I told you to get out, didn't I? Get out!"

"You don't mean that."

"What, I don't look like I'm serious?" She looks completely serious. She shoves me, in a methodical motion I don't see coming. It jolts me. A ripple of shock runs through each of my muscles. She raises her arms to do it again. I catch each of her wrists and hold her back. She tries to pull away, yanking me off balance. I stomp down on broken glass from her lamp. I feel the shards dig into my bare feet as we wrestle for position.

I hear her bedroom door open. I look over for just an instant, and she pushes me hard. I fall backward and smack my head on her closet door.

"Hey, hey, what's going on in here?" Noah yells. I leap back to my feet and grab my jacket. Fuck the shoes. I push past Noah without even looking at Jaselle. I hear Noah asking what happened again as I cross the living room. I slam their front door as hard as I can.

CHAPTER ELEVEN

I walk into the street, ignoring the bloody footprints I'm leaving behind me. I'm indifferent to the fact that I'm shoeless and how monumentally detrimental that is now that it's back to the alley.

No, stop. She was upset, that's all. She didn't mean it. You'll be lying beside her again in no time. Is it crazy for that to be my first thought? To even want that? I choose a wall and slide down.

Worthless street girl, why do you cry? You should have known. You should have known such love was not for you.

Stop it. I can't manage to call Jaselle a bitch, even in my brain. I want to. I want to so bad. Hate her. It's so much easier to hate her. But I can't. I pull my left foot over my right leg and go to work prying out a sizeable shard of glass. I'm bleeding everywhere, more than I thought.

I get the major pieces out and stand up, carefully testing my weight on the wounds. The concrete tugs the cuts apart. There are still a lot of little pieces in there, but I can't find the determination to pull them all out.

I don't notice where I'm walking. I just walk. I end up at the guys' apartment. I knock lightly, half hoping everyone's asleep so I can drag my lonely, pathetic ass back to the alley, justified in feeling useless to the world. That doesn't happen. I hear someone messing with the chain.

The door cracks open, Jayden's face filling the space. He swings it open in a hurry. "Hey," he says in an excited whisper.

"Hey." Why am I here? He gestures for me to come in. He guides me to the living room. Shiloh and Alex are sleeping in the bedroom. Jayden sleeps in the living room because he's always awake, so he's close to the instruments where he can pass the extra hours. And he'd prefer to take the living room and be alone than share a room with the guys, better for banging chicks.

Actually, now that I've come to my senses I can't believe there's not a girl here right now. "You're alone?"

He laughs. "Yeah, I'm alone sometimes." He finally takes in my appearance. "Are you okay?" I nod. "Dude, you're bleeding all over the carpet. What the fuck?"

"Sorry." I sit on the couch and pick my feet up.

"I didn't mean what the fuck, you're messing up the floor. I meant what the fuck, are you okay? What happened?"

"I'm fine." I choke up and have to stop. His eyes are deep and warm, brown and soft. He puts my foot in his lap and looks.

"Oh my God, do you have any clue how screwed up you are?"

"Uh, no."

"Come on." Before I can stop him, he picks me up and carries me into the bathroom. He turns on the light and flips the lid to the toilet down with his foot, then sets me on it. He sits on the edge of the bathtub, rolls his pants up, and turns the water on.

"Oh no," I say. "No, no, no. You don't have to do this."

"Quit it." He holds his hand under the faucet until he likes the temperature. Then he pulls my foot under the running water. A flaming flash of pain overwhelms me, and I jerk my foot back.

"You okay?" he asks.

"Yeah. Yeah, just surprised me. I'm fine."

"Yeah, you're messed up. Okay, come on now." He pulls my foot back. I don't even realize I'm resisting until he starts laughing. "Come on, you turning into a baby on me?"

That does the trick. I let him pull my foot. After the first couple of seconds it isn't as bad. It still hurts, but I ignore it. I watch the red water disappear down the drain. Once the caked blood is washed away, he pulls my foot into his lap again and starts working on the remaining pieces of glass.

"So," he says. "Are you going to tell me what happened?"

I take a deep sigh. "We got in a fight."

"And she took a razor blade to your foot?"

"No." I laugh. "No. She, uh, well, she was upset, and we were arguing. I guess I said some things that—"

"Rainn," Jayden interrupts. "You don't have to protect her from me. If you decide to forgive her, I'm not going to judge you. Just tell me the way it is."

My eyes water. I try to push it away, but I can't. They spill over. He stops working on my foot for a second and hugs me. I tell him what happened, every detail. I take him on his word and stop sugar coating. I hadn't realized that's what I was doing until he said so, but he's right. I don't want him to hate her. I don't want him to have ammo against her. But I believe him, and I tell him how it happened.

"I knew you guys were doing something," he says.

"What?"

"Meth? Seriously, Rainn? What are you doing?"

I'm surprised that's what he chooses to focus on, but then again, I shouldn't be. Meth. What *am* I thinking? "I know. I'm stopping."

"And what about her? You're going to stop and she's going to keep doing it? You know how hard that's going to be?"

"I can stop. I don't even like it that much. I know that sounds like a lie, but really."

"So, you'll be sober and she'll be high? And you think that's going to work?"

"She'll stop too. She was only using it to get ready for her art show." I ignore the look he gives me.

"Look—" His phone cuts him off, blaring his ring tone way too loud for the silent house. He looks down at the caller ID. "That was fast."

"One of your girls?"

"No, yours." He shows me the front screen that reads "Jaselle." I'm impressed it doesn't say something derogatory. Where'd he get her number anyway? "Are you here?" he asks me. Oh, right, I called him from her phone.

"Uh, yeah," I say. He flips the phone open. "Wait, no," I hiss. He nods cooperatively.

"Hello?" I can hear the sound of her voice through the speaker but can't make out any words. "No, I haven't seen her. I thought she was with you." He pushes the speakerphone button.

"You're a terrible liar," she says.

Jayden doesn't miss a beat continuing the charade for me. I think he sounds pretty convincing, actually. "Why would I tell you she isn't here if she was? I'd love nothing more than to rub it in your face that she doesn't want to talk to you."

"I know you hate me, Jayden. I don't know why, other than you're in love with Rainn, but she's with me, and I'm not letting her go anytime soon."

"Apparently she's *not* with you," Jayden sneers. This is escalating in a direction that's making me nervous. Even though Jayden knows I'm listening, and I think Jaselle is pretty confident I am as well, I feel like I'm hearing something I'm not supposed to. She thinks Jayden is in love with me?

"I love her, Jayden. I really do," she says. "I'm not trying to take her from you guys. I just want to take care of her."

"Sounds like you're doing a stellar job." I wave my hands at him, telling him to take it easy.

"She wants us to get along," Jaselle says.

"Rainn is my best friend," Jayden says. I can't help but smile. "If you want to be with her I come with that."

"That's exactly what I'm saying. Some day you have to acknowledge that goes both ways. If you want to be in her life, *I* come with that too."

"I'm surprised you're so confident considering you don't know where she is right now," Jayden says.

"I know where she is."

"Whatever."

"Look, just tell her I called, okay? Tell her I'm sorry and I love her, and whenever she wants to come back, I want her back." Jayden stiffens while I weaken.

"I told you she isn't here."

"Tell her I called at least. Please." He flips the phone shut. We just sit there for a second. I can't imagine what he's thinking.

"You're going back," he finally says.

I don't bother wasting both our time acting like I'm thinking about it. I want to be thinking about it. I force myself to acknowledge this is a giant red flag, that this wasn't acceptable. I make myself picture life without her, but it all feels like a formality. I know I'm going back. I can't stand for this to end. "Yes."

"Can I say something?"

"Anything," I say, but I brace myself.

"I know you won't listen, but I feel like I have to tell you. This has bad news written all over it. You've changed. I'm sure you think you haven't, but you have. And I know she's sorry now, and she probably means it, but once they get physical they don't stop. It just gets worse. You know that."

He's referring to Isaiah. I hate it when he does that, but I guess he of all people has a right to. Comparing Jaselle to Isaiah is something I just can't do though.

"She didn't hit me or anything." I feel absurd and pathetic making the argument, but it's true. She didn't hit me. And had there not been glass on the floor I wouldn't even be hurt right now. It's different. It's complicated. There's nothing I can say that doesn't sound like every girl who's ever tried to justify this, but it *is* different.

"Yeah, yeah, bounced right off your skull like I thought it would."

"I love her." Is that a case? I want to leave.

He just nods. "I know."

"I'm going back."

"Tonight?" He doesn't sound surprised, just, I don't know, sad? I nod and take my feet out of his tub. I pull my pant legs back down and carefully stand up. The pain is more than I remembered. The numbness of depression is wearing off. I straighten up and look at Jayden. I can't stand his disappointment. I reach out and rustle his hair.

"Don't worry," I say.

"I'll drive you."

"No, you don't have to do that. I walk all the time."

"Shut up, Rainn. I'm driving you. You aren't walking your bloody ass bare feet all the way back to her." I smile and follow him to his truck. When we pull up to Jaselle's, he turns the truck off. I figure that means we're going to have a little chat before he leaves me here. I just sit and wait.

"You know you can always call me," he says.

"I know."

"I'm glad you came to me tonight, but you didn't have to murder your feet first. I would have come and got you." I just look at him, not sure how to respond. "I'll always come get you." I smile and squeeze his arm.

"Thanks, Jay."

"All right, go on."

I jump out and thank him for the ride.

Jaselle and I just stare at each other in the doorframe for a minute. I can see the emotions rolling over her so clear she doesn't have to say a word. She's surprised I came back tonight. The relief is making its way through her tight muscles. Her stomach dropped when she realized what she'd done. She abruptly reaches out for me, wrapping her arms around my neck.

Her sudden movement makes me jump at first. I ignore that I just flinched. I hold her, letting her squeeze me to the point of discomfort. I can barely breathe. Who needs oxygen? "I'm so sorry," she says.

I put my hand on her cheek, trying to meet her eyes, and I feel the tears on her face. I wipe them away and try to pull her chin up. She resists a little, but eventually gives in. "I love you."

She starts crying harder. "I love you. I'm so sorry." She keeps saying that. "I'm so sorry." She pulls me inside. In her bedroom we're a little awkward, not sure how to move forward. I think my silence makes her think I'm waiting for more apologies. I'm not trying to make her grovel; I just don't know what to say.

"I didn't sell anything. A few people made offers, but they were so low they wouldn't pay for a blank canvas. The thing is worth more before I paint on it than after."

I just shake my head. I want to comfort her. I want to say all the things I've already said, but I'm afraid to.

"Mom was there, and she was just telling me everything that was wrong with me. I told her about you. Like an idiot, I thought she'd be happy for me. She wasn't."

I nod.

"Anyway, I was upset about all that, and then I got high and it just exploded. I thought it would calm me down, but it just made everything feel darker. And I just wanted to hurt something." Her eyes flick to mine. "Someone."

"I'm sorry about your show." I feel far away. I want to have the closeness with her again, but I find myself wondering what her mother said about me and if that's why she attacked me. Maybe for a second, she agreed.

"Forget the show. I just want us to be okay."

"We're okay," I say. She wraps her arms around me again. Next thing I know she's crying more. I put my hand on her head. "Hey, I said we're okay."

"I can't believe I did that to you." She just keeps crying harder the more she talks. "I don't ever want to hurt you."

Jayden's comparison to Isaiah holds no value to me anymore, if it ever did. Isaiah never apologized. In fact, I was usually lucky I hadn't gotten worse. I squeeze her tighter, resisting the phrase "It's okay," yet forgiving just the same.

"I don't want to do it anymore," I say. I feel her body tighten with panic.

"Do what?"

I realize she thinks I mean be with her. "Crystal. I don't want to do it anymore."

Her eyes soften. "Don't do it anymore then, baby."

We stare at each other for a while. I don't know how to say what I want to say. I'm terrified of what her reaction might be. I'm not prepared to react myself. Eventually, she speaks for me.

"You don't want *me* to do it anymore."

I shake my head and wait for a response. She seems to be thinking it over carefully.

"I'll never hurt you again. If you need me to stop to believe that, I'll stop."

"Really?"

She leans forward and kisses me. "Of course. I love you."

Chapter Twelve

I watch Jaselle get depressed as she comes off the drugs. I hold her while she shakes. I pretend I believe her insistence it's easy even while she gets sick. I barely leave her side.

And then one day she's walking around again. She's okay again. But there's a darkness that doesn't leave. There's a layer of despair, not tangible but constant. It starts to make me doubt what I've done to her. She's so unhappy. And our conversations are growing darker. I pretend they don't scare me.

She's usually so lost in her head that by the time she talks she's so far down a chain of thoughts it seems random to me. She snaps out of a daydream and says, "When I was in eighth grade a guy that lived three houses down from me hung himself in his parents' closet."

"Were you friends with him?" I ask.

"Not really. Barely knew him."

"Why his parents' closet?"

"I imagine he must have wanted to hurt them. He wanted them to see."

"He was blaming them?" I feel like a therapist, cooperating through a conversation while trying to discover the deeper meaning.

"That's how I'd take it," she says.

"How's that for a skeleton in the closet?" I feel a little guilty when she laughs.

"I thought about doing the same to my parents," she says. I just stare at her, waiting for more. "Well, not exactly the same. I wouldn't hang myself. But I thought of making them find me."

"Why?"

"Because they were always trying to change me, what I wore, how I spoke, what I did, who I loved. They still do. I wanted to just say, 'Fine, you hate me. I get it. I'll put you out of your misery. I'll let you get back to your American dream, but first I'm going to bleed all over your white picket fence.'"

I nod, understanding completely the feeling of being rejected for who you are. But why kill yourself? Why punish yourself? Leave. That snarky voice in my head taunts me for always thinking running away is the answer, but then, isn't killing yourself the ultimate running away?

She seems to interpret my silence. "Death is so easy. It's ridiculous how we fear it. All the pain stops. What's so scary about that?"

"You don't have to die to escape the pain."

She chuckles, thinking I mean drugs, scoffing at me for mentioning the one relief I took from her. "You can detach from it," I say. "Don't let people make you feel like shit. They don't like who you are? Cut them loose."

"By that logic shouldn't I have told you to go fuck yourself when you asked me to stop doing crystal?"

That stops me in my tracks like a kick in the face. I roll around in space trying to recover for a second. "I asked you to stop because I do love who you are, not because I don't. I wanted you back."

"We did drugs together from the beginning. When did it start hurting you?"

"When it took priority. When it made you angry."

"You're my priority, and the drug wasn't what made me angry. It was the failure. It was feeling like a loser, again. It was my mother having more ammo to shoot at me when she already has way too much."

"I'm your priority?" I should be focusing on the fact that what really made her mad was the evidence that the drug wasn't good for her, but I don't.

"Haven't I proven that?" she asks. "I'd do anything for you. I stopped for you. I wouldn't do that for anyone else, not because I couldn't, because I didn't need to. But that didn't matter because you were upset, and I love you."

"I love you too."

"And you'd do anything for me too?" she asks.

"Anything."

"Then talk to me."

"Talk to you?" I ask.

"Yeah. You don't tell me anything. Who the hell are you? I don't even know where you're from, or who your parents are, or your middle name, or—"

"Okay, okay, I get it." I take a deep breath. I always knew she'd probe one day. She's so patient and gentle, but eventually everyone gets too curious. "My middle name is Marie. Rainey Marie Shimmer."

"Rainey?"

"Yes. I turned it into Rainn."

"Sounds preppy."

"That's why I changed it."

"Rainey. Sounds like a rich kid name."

"We were rich," I say.

"How rich?"

"Maids, cooks, private schools..."

"Gate around your mansion?"

"You got the idea," I say.

"You look embarrassed."

"I am."

"Why?" she asks.

"Because it's disgusting. I hate the wealthy. Pretentious, ostentatious, covetous bastards, so wrapped up in their silverware and curtains and landscaping. And everything is a trophy. God forbid your children have aspirations of their own or personalities."

"Gave you quite a vocabulary though. Throw one more *ous* word for those bastards at me, it's sexy."

I laugh and gradually lean over her as I search for another word. "Uhh, avaricious."

"Mmm." She giggles and kisses me. "You really do hate money, huh? Is that why you wanted to live in the alley?"

"I don't hate money. I hate what it does to people."

"I think people are either just assholes or they aren't. I don't think it's the money's fault."

"Maybe," I say. "But an asshole with a ton of cash has more ability to impose their asshole will."

"They become a super asshole," Jaselle says.

"A new breed of asshole." I chuckle and kiss her neck.

"I'm not done with you." She kisses the top of my head and pushes me back up. "What about your dad? I don't think you've ever said a word about him."

"He wasn't around. He shot himself," I say. Jaselle looks jarred. I feel like I can see her poring over our little suicide discussion. I put her out of her misery before she starts to feel bad. "I was a baby. I never knew him. Mom could have told me he had a heart attack and I would have never known different. She probably *should* have told me something like that."

"You think so?"

"Sure, beats the hell out of thinking your dad would rather throw in the towel than raise you."

"Yeah, I guess it does."

I can tell she's holding back what she really wants to say. She doesn't want to upset me. I say it for her. "But it's not the truth." She nods somberly. I don't let myself fall into depressed silence the way she seems to want to. "So, anything else you'd like to know?"

"Why'd you leave?"

My ears start ringing with my mother's voice. I can smell her Chanel perfume and feel my fingers ripping out her bleached hair.

"She asked me to," I say. She screamed at me to. Physically pushed me and told me I was a useless, evil piece of trash.

"Why?"

Mom's voice comes full force into my head again, washing Jaselle away, a slight indentation in the sand after the wave. "He did every damn thing you did. If you and your idiot friends had never gotten to him he would be alive right now! You killed him! You killed my baby boy! Did you have fun getting high, *Rainn*? Was it worth it?"

I struggle to come back to Jaselle. Her face is smooth. I wonder if she'll ever have wrinkles. My mom's face was smooth until Michael died. Then she got ugly. The creases went deeper. Or maybe she just stopped covering them. Maybe she just didn't care anymore.

"Things just couldn't work after Michael died," I say. Her dissatisfaction is palpable. I take another deep breath. "I guess we both blamed each other."

"Why?"

"I thought she strangled him, tried to force him to be the little businessman she was expected to raise. She didn't care about what he wanted; it was all about her."

"And what did she say about you?"

"That I led him wrong. I was supposed to protect him, guide him. I let him fall in love with all the wrong things."

"It wasn't your fault," Jaselle says. Everyone says that. But she says it so soon, with so little information. She doesn't even know what happened. How can she know it wasn't my fault? Maybe it was.

CHAPTER THIRTEEN

South Park is on TV. Cartman is rattling off about Jews, and I'm watching the ice cubes in my glass melt under the rum. When I look over, Jaselle is digging in a small plastic bag. In between her fingers is a rock of meth. My stomach clenches, and I watch her go through the routine of putting it in her pipe and digging for a lighter.

She doesn't make eye contact with me until the pipe is to her lips and her hand is raised to light up. She looks over the glass, waiting for me to do something, I guess. Am I supposed to offer my consent? It's not going to happen. Finally, she drops the pipe back down to her lap.

"What?" she says.

"How long have you been doing this?" I ask.

"I haven't. You think I've been hiding it from you?"

"I didn't know you even bought it, so yeah."

"No. I haven't done any since I told you I'd stop."

I look at the plastic bag, wanting to ignore its worn appearance and believe her. "So why now?"

"I enjoy it. Haven't I proven I can handle it yet? I completely stopped when you asked." She snaps her fingers to demonstrate the speed. I just look at her, wanting to argue, but anxious. She continues. "You like to drink sometimes, right? Does that mean you're an alcoholic?"

She enjoys drinking more than I do as well, but I get the point. I understand the situation all too well. She wants to do this. If I tell her no, she'll put it away, but for how long? Will she just start doing it when I'm not around? Do I want her to feel like she has to lie? She did stop when I asked. Maybe I'm being paranoid.

I don't know if she reads all of this on my face or if my silence somehow conveys defeat, but she leans over and kisses my cheek, then puts the lighter to the pipe, rolling the pipe from side to side as she heats up the bowl. Back and forth, back and forth, not letting the flame stay in any spot too long so as not to burn the meth.

It doesn't bother me once she's smoked and puts it away. She makes me laugh until my sides hurt. I guess as long as it's not in my face it doesn't worry me so much. And my last memory of her being high and angry seems further away now that she's high and happy.

I force myself to relax. I force myself not to be controlling. I force myself to realize the harder I squeeze, the faster I'll lose her. I can't stand the thought of losing her. Trust her. She says she's fine. She quit. She's fine.

That night I hold her as close to me as I can. Even when I'm hot and want to roll over, I refuse. I just hold on. I smell her hair, rub her arms, kiss the back of her shoulder. A tear rolls down my cheek. I'm not exactly sure why.

Chapter Fourteen

Michael bursts through the front door. My brain immediately goes to the dent in the white paint he just made, how Mom will use that as a constant reminder of how reckless we are, how little value we hold for our nice things.

Mom and I look up. I lift my fingers off the piano keys. The pressure of Mom's fingers on my shoulders releases though her hands stay in place. We're frozen, waiting for Michael to explain the abrupt entry.

"I'm not playing violin anymore," he says.

"Yes, you are." Mom doesn't even pause to think.

"No, I'm not. I don't like it. I don't want to do it anymore."

"I've already invested thousands of dollars in your violin, your lessons, your recitals, your—"

"I never asked you to do that. It's a miserable, boring instrument and I won't play another note on it. You can't make me."

"You're already signed up for auditions. You're going to the academy in the fall. It's already done."

"I'm not going."

"Michael, yes, you are."

"No, I'm not! And I'm not going to law school either!" he screams.

"Oh really?" Mom starts to laugh. "And what is it you're going to do then? Be a janitor?"

Michael looks at me. I burn my eyes through as many layers of skin as I can penetrate, willing him to shut up. Don't say it.

"Well?" Mom asks again.

"I'm going to be a drummer. Rainey and I are going to LA, and our band is—"

Mom holds up her hands brusquely to stop him. It's a small gesture, but the fury is enough to make Michael pause. I shake my head at him, trying to ask him why he would do this. Mom drops her hands from my shoulders finally and walks to the side of the bench so she can make eye contact with both of us.

"Your what?" she growls.

"It's just something we do messing around," I say.

"No, it's not!" Michael yells. "We're good, Mom. If you would just listen you might even be proud."

She starts laughing again, that evil hyena laugh. "What? You're going to be rock stars now? Is that it? I send you to the finest schools and tutors, have world famous musicians come to our house to teach you real music, and you want to bang on drums and scream?"

"It's not all trash just because you don't like it. It takes all the same skill."

Mom spins on me so fast I don't see her lash out, a snake striking and recoiling back into herself before I know what happened. I just feel my neck turn too far, a shocking sting spreading through my face, the warmth of my cheek flushing. The sound of it echoes in our hollow stone mansion.

"You did this to him," she snaps. "It's one thing that you run around with your drug addict friends, but now you're bringing him down with you?" She keeps ranting on about how my music is dark and corrupt, how I refuse to behave, how I've ruined my life and now am trying to ruin Michael's too because I can't stand to burn alone. Her words start to blur together, faded and far away next to the ache in my face where my hand still clings to my wet skin.

"Leave her alone!" Michael's voice is thunderous and pulls me back into the moment. He storms to the corner where his violin is propped. He opens the case and pulls it out, grabbing it by the neck and flinging it with everything he has so that it flies into the wall and bursts into splinters, the neck and body only held together now by the sad strings.

Mom's jaw sags, and she stammers for words. Michael points the bow at her. "I hate you! You think just because people aren't who you think they should be that they're trash. Not everyone wants to be you, okay? I'd rather die than be you!"

"Settle down!" She desperately tries to take back control, but he won't have it.

"Who are you to laugh at people's dreams? You make people feel like shit, Mom. No wonder Dad killed himself. You make me want to kill *my*self."

I can feel her go rigid beside me. I'm not sure I can breathe either while I wait for something to happen. Michael's face is hard, showing no sign of remorse or guilt. His pupils are dilated, I finally realize.

Michael turns and goes out the front door that's still gaping open behind him. Mom and I are afraid to look at each other, or maybe I'm the only one afraid.

I get off the piano bench and raise my hand for her shoulder. She pulls away hard. "Don't." And I hear her heels click out of the room.

I stand alone for a minute, not sure what I'm going to do next. Then my muscles take over. I switch to autopilot. I grab my jacket, throw it over my shoulders, and start walking to Jayden's. When I get there, Michael is already there with Jayden and Shiloh.

They all sit up straight when they see me, their chatter dying. They look afraid of me. I'm not sure what they're expecting. I walk past the couch they're lounging on, not saying a word to any of them. I step in front of the mic we have permanently set up, flip it on, and take a few deep breaths.

"*You're such a pretty girl, but you just can't let go,*" I start to sing. The guys scramble to their instruments. Jayden starts strumming on guitar, Shiloh comes in with bass, and Michael eases in with a soft rhythm.

"Yes, I know I've lied, but you just didn't want the truth."

We play all night. I begin to appreciate Michael's drumming in a way I never have before. I've always known he was talented, but when you compare violin with drums, well, drums just don't have the same magic. Appreciating perfect timing requires a deliberate focus on something that's not supposed to draw attention to itself. It can certainly wow, especially when he breaks into a solo, but the violin, my heart will never stop breaking that I can't hear him play anymore.

We go for hours. My voice is getting raspy. Michael has blisters from his drumsticks. Jayden and Shiloh's fingertips are raw.

I look at Michael. Part of me is still a little mad at him for what he said to Mom, for crushing her, for taking me out with him, but I realize I need Mom's approval in a way he never has. He doesn't care. He wants Dad's approval. He'll never have a chance. Maybe all he did was say what I didn't have the guts to. Maybe he forced the confrontation I would have avoided. Maybe he freed us. And should he feel guilty for doing what he wants to do? Was it selfish? Or was it just taking control of his life?

Our band isn't something we do just screwing around. It's our heart and soul. How dare I say anything short of that? No, I can't be mad. I'm a coward. And he did what we both needed. Overkill bringing Dad's suicide into it? Definitely. But if that's what's in his heart, maybe not. Maybe I try to shelter people too much. Maybe I should just let things be what they are. Don't sugarcoat every little thing. Hurt people, if you have to. I don't know anymore.

"So, can we stay here until we go to LA?" I ask Jayden. His smile spreads wide across his face, and I realize my approval was all they were waiting for.

Michael comes and gives me a tight hug and whispers in my ear. "I'm sorry. I couldn't take it anymore." I just squeeze him back. Jayden breaks out celebratory beer. We clink bottles and take healthy sips. Michael raises his lighter to his lips, not striking the flame awake, simply inhaling the butane.

Jayden whoops his approval and Michael inhales longer. I want to smack the shit out of Jayden. Is Michael taking the extra pull to impress him? He always was enamored with Jayden. It was Jayden who handed him his first joint, Jayden who handed him the spray paint that first night, Jayden who handed him drumsticks before he even had drums to play, Jayden who showed him the magic of banging on pots and railings and cardboard.

Maybe it's Jayden's fault. Jayden handed him everything. But I handed him Jayden. I watched it all happen. That's why Mom slapped me. I watch Michael's eyes dilate a little farther. I watch his muscles relax lazily. I watch him char his lungs for a petty high, a trick of the mind, oxygen deprivation and brain cell death. I watch and I try to focus on something else, leaving town, the band, desires I gave him, things I desperately want to be good.

And then my mind wanders back to Mom, crying in her empty mansion, bereft of her husband and her children, crying out to God or anything that will listen that she did everything right, demanding an answer, why has this happened to her?

Chapter Fifteen

Jaselle's shoulders are tan. She's wearing a tank top that shows them off, and I can't stop staring. They're feminine, slight and lean, but I know how strong they are. They beg for a kiss. The rest of her says don't touch me as she goes through the contact list in her phone irascibly.

"How does everyone in the city run out at once?" she asks. She means meth, and she doesn't want an answer. I shrug and put my hand on her thigh. I don't know what else to do. She keeps clicking away.

"Let's just smoke some weed, babe. What's the big deal?"

Someone answers their phone and I get ignored while she talks to them. When she gets off, she has a new number to call. She doesn't close the phone, just presses end and dials again. When I hear her half of the new conversation, I know she's found some. She clicks it shut and confirms it.

"You ready?"

"What? I don't want to go." Her face changes. She looks hurt and a little panicked. I don't understand why. I don't smoke it with her anymore, so I usually don't buy it with her either.

"Come on, I don't know these guys."

I roll my eyes. "Where'd you get them?"

"A friend of a friend. It'll be fine, but just come with me, okay?"

I go through the visual of her in some weird guy's car buying drugs and things going wrong. I conclude I'd rather be there if it does than sit here and worry. I sit up with a groan. She leans over and kisses my neck. "Thanks, sweetie."

I try to resist her. I still pout every time she wants to do meth even though it doesn't change anything. She keeps kissing, working up to my ear and breathing warmth into it, then whispers, "I love you." I smile without enthusiasm and kiss her cheek. That's not good enough for her. She keeps going, running her hand between my legs, telling me how sexy I am, until I submit and really kiss her back. Once she's worked me out of my crappy mood she gets off the bed and slips into flip-flops and puts her shades on. Tease.

It's one of those sunny winter days that like to spring up in Colorado, and Jaselle's car has been gathering and trapping the rays long enough it feels like a sauna inside. I close the door and let it suffocate me. She rolls the windows down and we jerk away. She's bobbing her head to Nine Inch Nails, chewing on a toothpick, so at ease.

My mind is on road rash and rotting flesh. Heat makes me think of that kind of stuff, death and the like, maggoty wounds and unnoticed bodies in the alleys. Some would say dark nights and bad weather lend themselves more to those sorts of thoughts, but for whatever reason this kind of day just makes me think of how fast a body would decompose under the merciless sunrays. Weird? Yeah, okay, I'll stop.

Jaselle stops in front of a house that doesn't look nearly ragged enough, the kind of house that's not supposed to know what crank is. I shoot her a glance and she looks unsure too, but she double-checks the address that was texted to her and nods.

"This is it." She opens her car door.

I reach out and grab her arm. "We're going inside?"

"Yeah, they said ring the doorbell."

My stomach knots again. I hate this, but I get out and follow her up the path between the way-too-green grass. She reaches up and rings the doorbell twice, once long and one tap. I wonder if that was some kind of code given to her or if she just rings that way. She looks over at me and reaches out to touch my face, concerned again, it seems.

I hold my breath when I hear the doorknob twist. It swings open and I feel the blood drain from me, head to toe. I have no more blood, or breath, or bones to hold me, or equanimity to pretend. I dig deep down for strength as a beam of light reflects off the grilled teeth that disappear as quickly as my pulse.

I stare into the black eyes that once were the kindest of three sets, and I see his terror. I harden my gaze and nod, hoping he interprets what I intend, that I want him to shut up and act like he's never seen me before. Shut up, and don't make this seem weird. Shut up, and don't give the slightest indication that you've been inside me. And I'll act like I don't remember you. I'll act like I don't still feel the cold metal of the gun on my temple.

He steps out of the way so we can come in. I know I can't be satisfied with my small victory just yet.

Metal Mouth. He says some fucking shit I can't understand just like old times and heads down a hallway out of view, leaving Jaselle and me alone in the room. With him gone, I take in our surroundings. All the trashiness this place lacks on the outside it more than makes up for on the inside. There's garbage covering every inch of carpet. I try to pay closer attention to the details, and not see it just as clutter.

There are propane tanks in the corner, spray painted with bent valves coming out. There's plastic tubing, empty pill bottles everywhere, paint thinner, rock salt, funnels, those camp stove fuel things, mason jars, everything you can imagine. A scuba tank? And all the bottles seem empty, empty toluene cans, empty hydrogen peroxide bottles, empty starter fluid. Ingredients, no doubt. I'm creative enough to imagine how all these things come in useful, but it all just looks scattered, discarded.

I'm wondering where the working version of all this is. Which room contains what surely looks like a sixth grader's science project?

I hear talking down the hall, voices starting to rise. Jaselle's hand slips around my arm like she's afraid. I squeeze back. Three guys come back in the room. Three way too familiar faces. Ice bounds down the hall, jubilant, and comes all the way up to my face, too close. Jaselle pulls my arms a little when she backs away from him. I won't move. I stare him down, knowing shutting him up will be a hundred times more difficult than Metal Mouth.

We stare and stare. I can't feel my limbs. I'm not in the alley. I'm not alone. But really, what's the difference? There are three of them. I'm sure they still have guns. And we're in their house. They could all rape Jaselle and me right now. Maybe I should have grabbed her and run the second Metal Mouth opened the door. Why didn't I think of that? I was so preoccupied with Jaselle not finding out who these men were to me. But now, who will they become to her?

"Leave her alone, man." Metal Mouth has never been more audible. Part of me wants to thank him, the other part just says yes, you owe me this. Ice looks from me to Jaselle, catching up with what Metal Mouth has already interpreted: Jaselle is in the dark.

"I hear you're a good friend of Shane's," Ice says to Jaselle. I hate that he's speaking to her. I want to step in between them. I don't want his eyes roaming over her.

"Yeah, we go way back," Jaselle says.

"Shane's our boy. We'll hook you up," Short Shit says. I look at him for the first time. He was the loudest. I probably should be the most worried about him, but Ice is the boss. Short Shit looks me up and down exaggeratedly. "We'll *definitely* help you." He reaches out like he's going to touch me. I swat him away, hard. Ice shoots him a look that says back off. Jaselle squeezes my arm again.

"What can I get you ladies?" Ice says.

Jaselle flashes a wad of cash that would be impressive were it not made of ones. "Teenager?" I don't even know what that means, but Ice nods. He sits down on the couch and leans over his pile of crap that I suddenly realize is hiding a coffee table. He pulls out what looks like a cell phone but is actually a scale and goes to work.

Short Shit gets closer to me again. I can smell his bad breath. "So, how you been?"

"Fine."

"You know I was on 15th the other night, looking for some fine bitches, wasn't shit out there."

I look at Jaselle to see if she's finding this unusual, but she clearly thinks it's just small talk. I look back to Short Shit. I'm a little surprised he remembers me telling him he could find hookers there, my feeble attempt to save myself.

"There're always girls on 15th," I say.

"Sure, there were girls, but once you taste something sweet it's hard not to come back for more. Makes that crap on 15th not even worth it."

I wonder if Jaselle can feel me shaking.

"You'll fuck anything," Ice blurts from the couch. "Your standards of sweet are pretty low."

"You fall in love?" Jaselle uncomfortably asks.

Short Shit's smile spreads across his face like wildfire. "With her pussy, maybe."

Ice gets up and walks over with the bag of meth. He hands it to Jaselle, brushing her finger with his while he gives me a look. "Y'all can stick around if you want, have a drink, shoot up." My skin feels like it has a million ants crawling under it.

"I don't shoot it," Jaselle says. My eyes fly to hers, wanting to shake her. That's her only response? Not, we have to go? Not, no thanks, we're fine?

"You need some rigs?" Ice asks. I'm a little proud of myself for knowing that means needles. I want to shake him now. She didn't say we don't have needles, she said we don't shoot. Jaselle lingers longer than I'd like. She seems fascinated.

"We have to go," I blurt. I was trying not to do that, but enough is enough.

Metal Mouth crosses the room. "All right grmm, y'all shha have a nice high." Weird, I'm starting to understand him easier. I think my eyes say thank you.

I tug Jaselle toward the door with the arm she still won't let go of. Finally, I hear the deadbolt behind us. I don't feel any better yet. I want to be in the car. I want to be going eighty miles per hour. I want to forget their faces, their snotty little laughs.

The car door closes. I can't feel anything. Jaselle gets in the driver's side. She's waiting to turn the ignition, looking at me, wanting to ask what's wrong.

"Go," I say.

"Are you—"

"Jaselle, just go."

I can tell she still doesn't want to. She's considering trying to get it out of me some more before we leave, but she doesn't. She puts the car in drive and we go. When we pull up in front of her house, she tries to do the sitting in the car thing, but I just get out and leave her there, so she's forced to follow along. She catches up to me on the stair in front of her building. She gave me a key to her apartment, but I still don't have one for the building, so I have to wait for her. She stops in front of me.

"I wasn't going to do it," she says.

"Huh?"

"I wasn't." I realize she means shoot up. That's what she thinks is wrong with me. I'm not thrilled about that little inner struggle either, and after what she just blurted, I obviously should be concerned.

"Good." I can't think of anything else.

"You don't believe me?" Her eyes water up. I don't say anything. "Don't be mad at me. I didn't do anything."

"Don't ever go back there again."

"Excuse me?"

"You heard me."

Her posture changes completely, the gloss over her eyes disappears. "Don't talk to me like that. Who do you think you are? I'll go wherever the fuck I want."

"Not there."

"What is your problem? You act like you've never seen a drug deal before. You live in a fuckin' alley and you can't handle a sixteenth of glass?"

"I don't give a shit about the glass. I told you not to go back to that house."

"I don't know what makes you think you can *tell* me anything."

I stop and take a deep breath. I should have known this was the wrong approach, my rebellious angel. I try to smooth out my voice. "Okay, you're right. But—"

"I'm not going to be anybody's dog. I've done that. You—"

"For God's sake, Jaselle, shut up for a second!"

"Fu—"

"They raped me, okay?" I have to scream it, partially to make her be quiet, partially because I don't think I could have gotten it out any other way. Her face goes blank. I've never seen someone so without words in my life. "All three of them," I say. "In the alley…" A tear spills over. "Held me down…" My knees buckle. "Gun…" She's holding me immediately. I'm gasping in air, trying to compose myself, but it all just keeps coming out whether I like it or not.

She squeezes harder, plastering me to her chest, not letting me move an inch. The tighter she holds me the harder I cry. The sympathy is too much for me. It gives the fumes I'm choking on a flame and I burn from the inside. It's like I've never allowed myself to cry over this before. It's like it was never worth crying over until I had her to comfort me.

"Don't go back. Promise," I say. She promises. "Promise," I demand again. She promises again. And I keep asking like that, over and over again in some mindless babble. I can't stop saying it, "Promise and again always."

Somewhere along the way she realizes I'm out of my mind and she just rocks me back and forth, promising her heart out. "I promise, baby. I promise."

Her arms are so strong. They were powerful when they pushed me, but they're stronger now, holding the pieces of me I'm certain would scatter to the ground were she not keeping me together. I bury my wet face in her neck and dive into her scent. There's nothing but her, nothing but her smell and her arms, her chin on my head, her hand rubbing my back and her soft voice. "Breathe, baby, breathe."

A couple of kids with their dog walk by us on the sidewalk. They pull me out of my little episode. I come back to the present and realize I'm falling apart on Jaselle's front steps, in front of the world. Seeing them see me is enough to make me take a deep breath and wipe my face off.

Jaselle helps me up. "You okay, sweetie?"

"Yeah," I say. "I think I'm going to go to the Chapel. I haven't practiced with the guys in a while." She looks concerned but just gives me a kiss. I finish pulling myself together on the walk. I do want to see the guys and practice, but I think I mostly just don't want to watch her smoke.

Chapter Sixteen

Jayden gives me an extra-long hug. "You okay?" I haven't seen him since the night I came over with bloody feet, so I guess it's reasonable for him to ask, but I don't like it. He thinks of Jaselle as dangerous now. I wish I hadn't gone to him that night. I can tell he hasn't told the guys. They're completely normal, so I try to focus on them, playing up my happiness on purpose.

"We miss you, girl," Shiloh says. "We never see you anymore."

"I know, I know. I'm sorry."

"Don't you still love us too?" Alex says.

"Of course, I do." I give him another hug like that'll make everything go away. I breathe in the familiar Chapel smell: beer and mildew. Benny hands me a Corona and touches my cheek with his chubby hand. That's a little strange. Usually, I just get a smack on the back or a rustle of the hair. I'm not used to tender gestures. Maybe Jayden chose Benny to talk to about his fears of abuse. That makes me grit my teeth. No, Jayden, you didn't convert Benny. I need Benny. He pushed me into this; I need him to stay on board.

I try to fall back into my rhythm, to feel as natural as I always have, messing around in the empty bar while the sunlight exposes all the dust in the air and slime on the chairs. I try to take comfort in peeling my shoes off the sticky floor step by step, but my mind isn't here. My mind is in Jaselle's bedroom, watching the smoke swirl past her lips, satin dreams.

"So, are we going to play or what?" Jayden asks. I nod emphatically and grab the mic stand from the corner, putting it back in my spot, center. Jayden starts us off, strumming into one of our oldest songs. It doesn't sound the same to me for some reason. The words come easy as ever though, strange how lyrics never leave you.

"*I want you to watch me, someone should watch me burn. I love your psychosis. Criminal activity to damage what damaged you. And I'm just a phantom. I'm not really here. Now you can't see me. I'm just a breath in your ear.*"

I can't focus. I see Jaselle stretched out on the bed, naked and high, in a stupor. Do you feel good now, my love? Is the pain gone?

"Rainn?"

I shake my head like I can rattle the image out of my ears. The guys are staring at me. I clear my throat. "Sorry, let's go." Shiloh cautiously starts in on bass again. I can't believe this feeling. "*Frozen chest and bleeding lungs, surrender now to what you've done.*"

It takes everything I have to finish the song, to make it through a couple more, to stay for another half hour after that, to try to act like I'm having fun, to stifle the painfully uncomfortable urge to leave and go back to Jaselle.

When I finally feel like I've stayed long enough not to qualify myself as a complete ass, I excuse myself. The guys groan but don't know what to say, so they hug me good-bye. On my way home, I immediately feel bad. I know they saw me watching the time. I know I wasn't fully present even for the short duration I spent with them. I know I'm rude. I know they think they're losing me. I know they are.

And still that doesn't change the fact that I'm walking the now-familiar, long journey back to Jaselle's. When I'm outside I buzz the apartment so she can let me in. The line is connected to her cell phone, so when it goes to voice mail I leave a message that I'm outside. I wait fifteen minutes and try again. Still nothing. I wait another half an hour, trying my hardest not to get frustrated.

Eventually, someone is leaving and opens the door. I slip inside, ignoring the glare I get.

I head down the stairs into the basement and let myself in. Noah gives a lazy nod when he sees me. I wave by slightly raising my fingertips and turn into Jaselle's bedroom. She's not here. I stand awkwardly in the room alone for a second, turning like I'll find some clue as to her whereabouts. Now her not answering her phone is bothering me a lot more. I fully expected her to just be sleeping, or watching a movie and not paying attention, but she's not here.

My stomach knots. I swallow it. I internally yell at myself that I can't be like this. I can't torture myself. It's not worth it. I'll drive myself crazy, and for God's sake, I can't very well forbid her to be in public, even though I'd be lying if I said I wouldn't like it better that way. Just because she's out doesn't mean she's cheating, nor does it mean she's in mortal danger, so just take a deep breath, psycho, and relax. You went out. Now she's out.

Eventually, I can't stand being alone with myself, so I go to talk to Noah. I sit down next to him on the couch. He doesn't say anything for a while, just passes me his bong. I milk it hard, filling it to a thick white smoke.

Noah whistles when he sees it. "Take her gentle," he says. I look at the wisps that are escaping from the top for a second. "It's going to get stale," Noah says. I remove the slide and inhale, slow and gentle just like he said, determined to clear it completely.

I'm successful, but on my next breath in I go into a coughing fit that makes my eyes water and cheeks feel hot. When I finally can repress the coughs, I fall back into the couch. My skin is full of static. "So, where's Jaselle?" I ask.

Noah shrugs. "What makes you think I know?"

"She didn't say anything when she left?"

"Sure, she did. 'Bye.'"

We pass the weed back and forth for hours. I nervously keep pulling on it, smoking just to smoke, taking small hits, just enough to keep me numb. I don't want to feel this anxiety. I don't want to worry about her. Every time I look at the clock and get a jolt of panic I just take the weed from Noah and try to drown it out. I'm desperate not to cry, not to fall apart. I figure keeping Noah next to me will force me not to.

I reach for the house phone to try calling her again, but Noah just gently touches my hand. We stay like that for a second, his hand on my hand on the receiver, and he shakes his head almost imperceptibly. I take a deep breath and nod.

"Thanks." I look at the clock again. It's almost one in the morning. The tears well up, and I'm not even exactly sure why. I don't know where I think she is. I don't know what exactly I'm afraid of. I just know my insides hurt. I feel like I'm huffing paint again. She must know I'm home by now. I went to band practice, and she probably thought I'd be there longer than I was, but at this point she must know I'm wondering where she is. Doesn't she know I'll call? Wouldn't she check her phone for that reason alone if nothing else? Where could she be that she can't talk to me for five seconds?

"You talk to your parents ever?" Noah asks.

"Huh?" I know my expression is pure bewilderment.

"Your parents."

"No. My dad is dead and my mom and I don't get along," I say.

He nods and goes quiet for a while before he speaks again, too loud. "She doesn't like that you're gay?" he guesses.

"Among other things."

"Jaselle's mom hates that she's gay too. She's a real piece of work. I'm sure you'll meet her someday."

"I hope not," I say.

"So, you never talk to your mom? Not even on Christmas or whatever?"

"Especially on Christmas."

He takes another rip of weed. "So, where you from?"

I repress a sigh of frustration and look at the clock again. It's almost two now. I realize Noah is just trying to take my mind off

Jaselle. I turn soft for a second. He knows exactly how much I'm suffering, despite my attempts to hide it.

"Where the fuck is she?" I blurt. I figure I might as well since he obviously sees through me anyway. He just looks at me sympathetically. "Would it kill her to just call and tell me she's okay? I know she's seen my calls by now, how could she not?"

"She's fine. Don't waste your energy worrying."

"But this isn't like her. She's never done this. What if she's not fine? What if she went back to that house or something?" What if she's shooting up?

"Rainn, she's fine."

"How do you know?"

"Because, I hate to break it to you, but this *is* like her. This is exactly like her. You've just been too glued to her to see it yet. She likes her freedom, and if you don't give it to her, she'll take it. Now relax, hit the bong, and she'll be home when she's home."

I let that settle for a minute. I know he's known her longer, but I still feel like I know her better. He sees me fighting his advice and pointedly holds out the bong.

"You have no way to find her. You have no choice but to wait. Why spend that time going crazy when you don't have to?" He jabs it at me again. I cave and take it from him, taking a huge hit.

It's three in the morning. The TV is a blur of colors and sounds, white noise in my ears. And I can see you there, somewhere, falling to your knees, and the things you locked away are ripping through your seams. There's a part of you, apart from me, and when I breathe it eats through me.

"She'll be home tonight, right?" Sandpaper eyes. "Noah?"

"What will it mean to you if she's not?"

It's four in the morning. The streets call to me. They're swallowing my love into a gutter where the mud that isn't mud carries disease, and the flies love your skin. They love your gray eyes, glass and glossy liberation. Who broke your fall?

It's four thirty in the morning. Greasy-haired sympathy, passed out on the couch next to me, and he sees what you'll never see. Hazy smoke and broken scales, profit off another's inhale. Let them die if they so choose and wait until it comes to you.

A key, pulling me, scratching in the lock.

"Rainn," Noah says, "keep your cool." He gets up to leave, retreating to his room. I hear them say something as they pass in the hall. I can't pick my head off the couch, my neck won't stand for it.

She turns the corner. Her eyelids are dark and heavy. She stands by me, quiet. I'm not here right now. I can't see you. She squeezes my arm. I'm too far away for that. She descends to her knees, gently maneuvering her way between my legs. Her lips brush over my neck. Her fingers trail down and she corrupts my silence, pressing against me, smothering my misery. She tries to pull me back to life. She wants my surrender. If I don't stop her soon, she'll take it whether I like it or not.

I make her earn it, resisting every step of the way. She weaves her fingers into my hair and pulls so I have to look at her, forcing me to reconnect with those damn eyes. She's too warm. She's too good. I love her too much. I'm too afraid this is the last time. I pull her against me as hard as I can, hoping it hurts. You've broken me. I'll break you too.

"Come to bed, sweetie," she says when I release her. I lie on the bed next to her. I can feel she won't sleep. Her body is too alert, too wired. I breathe her in and close my eyes, knowing she'll watch me fade away.

"Jaselle." All I have strength for is a whisper. "Where were you?"

"You know where I was," she says. The truth is I don't. I feel like I should, but I don't. Smoking, obviously. Partying, somewhere. Maybe that's what she means. I know she was getting fucked up. Does it matter where?

"Not there though?" Not at the house. You promised.

"Of course not, love."

She's painting when I wake up. I sit up slowly and let the night come back to me. I can't believe I let her touch me, no questions asked. The rage I was too worried to feel last night creeps into my chest and squeezes. For some reason, I hear Noah again, telling me to keep my cool. Keep my cool? Like she doesn't deserve an interrogation? No, Noah, I will not.

"Where were you last night?"

She spins around. She hadn't even realized I was awake. "Good morning," she says.

I keep staring at her. "Jaselle, you scared me to death."

"I was out."

"Where?"

"Why does it matter? You went out. I went out," she says.

"You knew where I was. And I wasn't out all night."

"You could have been if you wanted. I wouldn't grill you about it."

"Because you don't give a shit what I do?" I snap.

"Uh, no, because unlike you, I trust you."

"This isn't about trust, Jaselle. I haven't accused you of anything. I was just worried about you. Why don't you get that? All you had to do was call me and say you were going to be late. I wouldn't have said anything."

"That's horse shit and you know it. You would have wanted to know exactly when I was coming home, where I was, what I was doing, who I was with…"

"What's wrong with that? If you wanted to know those things it wouldn't bother me to tell you. There's a reason you don't want to tell me. What are you hiding? Why don't you want me to know?"

"Because I'm not thirteen years old. I don't need a mother. I don't need a parole officer."

"You can do whatever you want, Jaselle. All I want is to know you're safe."

"Why wouldn't I be?"

"Really? Because I know you're out getting high and then you don't answer the phone for twelve hours. Don't act stupid."

"You're the one acting stupid. I didn't answer the phone because I knew you'd be like this."

"I'm acting like this because you didn't answer the phone."

"No, you would have been like this anyway, or at least wanted to come with."

I fight tears with all my soul. I expected her to at least make up some crap lie about her phone dying or something, not just blatant admission she didn't want to deal with me.

"God forbid I come with you."

"Yeah, 'cause you get all weird and freaked out about me smoking and you just fuck up my high," she says.

"You're an asshole."

"You wanted to know, Rainn. You had to push. You should have just left it alone. I need to be able to go out if I feel like it without you having a meltdown. I'm not dealing with rules. I didn't cheat on you. I didn't lie to you. I just went and saw some friends. Deal with it."

"Don't you see yourself?" I scream. And as I pore over all the features I want to expose to her I find I'm exposing them to myself. Her face is gaunt, hollow cheeks. Her bones jut out. I want to scream. I want to slam into her frail skull what's happening, but when I open my mouth all that comes out is a pathetic squeak worthy of her dying lungs. I sink to the ground. If she can't see it in the mirror, at least can't she see it in my face?

But her expression is stone. "Don't be dramatic."

"I can't do this, Jaselle. I can't watch you die."

That seems to touch her, but the depth it's gaining comes to a halt with the ring of her cell phone.

She looks at the screen and smirks. "It's your boyfriend."

"What?"

She turns her phone around so I can see Jayden's name. "You can't be serious."

"*You* can't be serious. What do you think I'm a fucking moron? I've seen you two together. He calls constantly. He tells you what a piece of shit I am all the time. I'm sure that's why I can't go out without you being suspicious in the first place. He put shit in your head, didn't he?"

"This is stupid. There's nothing between Jayden and me."

"Tell me I'm wrong," she yells.

"You're wrong."

"He doesn't tell you I'm no good for you?"

I put my hands in my pockets.

She steps closer. "He doesn't give you the pathetic puppy eyes and tell you that you deserve better while he shoves his cock against his girl jeans hoping you'll notice?"

"God, what is wrong with you?"

"Tell me you honestly don't think he jerks off to you."

"Wh—"

"And I bet you think of him too, don't you?" She lowers her voice to a whisper in my ear, pressing close in a cloud of her smell.

"Who *are* you?" This is not Jaselle. Her eyes are so cold. Her movements are inhuman. Slimy. She's a demon. A demon takes over her body when she's high.

"You want to fuck him, don't you, Rainn?"

"No."

"You want to be with him? Is that why you started this fight? You want to go be with him, but you can't stand being the one to blame, can you?"

"I want to be with you if you'd fucking let me!" I yell. I can't let go of this demon concept now that I've pinpointed it. This is not Jaselle. This thing has raised straight up out of hell. Its every gesture is evil. Heartless.

"Tell me he doesn't tell you I'm a piece of trash!" she screams.

"It doesn't matter what he says."

"Tell me he doesn't tell you to leave me!"

"What do you expect!" I scream. She winces a little, but I pretend I didn't see it. "You hurt me, Jaselle. You pushed me and screamed at me and you do this fucking shit all the time." I slam my hand over the bag of meth and hold it in her face. "You're a drug addict. Of course he tells me to leave you!"

"Then fucking leave!"

I fling open her bedroom door and do just that.

"Go fuck your boyfriend!"

Chapter Seventeen

I choose to lock myself inside my storage unit for the night. The weather isn't as severe as it normally has to be for me to pull this move, but for some reason I crawl in there anyway. Maybe because as pathetic and uncomfortable as it is, this little space is the only thing in the goddamn world that is mine. If I want to close a door to the world, this is the only way I can do it, and I need to slam that door. The only thing I can afford to focus on is not going back. Any break in my concentration and I'll fold. I know it.

Benny doesn't even know I'm back until he catches me crossing the bar to use the bathroom a few days later. He appears on the back step with a soggy sandwich and coffee a few minutes later.

"You want to talk about it?" he asks.

"Nope." I pull out my keyboard and start setting it up. Maybe that'll be a strong enough hint to get him to leave me alone. I notice my middle A key is missing. "Shit."

"Are you okay?"

"Sure," I say. I know I'm being a super bitch to Benny, who totally doesn't deserve it, but the realization isn't enough to make me stop.

"I probably shouldn't mention this but…"

"Then don't," I snap.

"Rainn, Jayden says you two have been doing some pretty nasty drugs over there."

"Benny, I said don't."

"If you need help, Rainn, getting off…you know, whatever. I'll help you. I'm here for you."

"I'm not on anything."

"Jayden said—"

"Jayden needs to shut the fuck up. He doesn't know what he's talking about."

"He just loves you." Benny's face is sagging. He looks older. What is he, a parent? My misbehavior isn't supposed to make his face droop. That's reserved for moms.

"Yeah, well, he just loved me out of a relationship." I notice the loose key in the corner of my storage unit and start trying to put it back in place.

"What?"

"He kept calling her. She thinks there's something going on the way he's acting," I say.

"Jesus, Rainn, give the guy a break. You were best friends, couldn't separate you. He doesn't know who you are anymore. None of us do. Then you tell him you're doing meth, of course he's freaking out."

"I'm glad to see whose side you're on."

"There shouldn't be sides. We want you to be happy. Don't treat us like the enemy."

"But you didn't even ask, Benny. You just listened to precious Jayden. Do I look like a tweaker to you?"

He looks me over. I stop trying to jam the loose key into my keyboard for a second in case the frantic effort does, in fact, make me look like a tweaker.

"Well?" I ask aggressively.

"No, I guess you don't look any different."

"That's because I'm not."

"And Jaselle? Does she look the same, Rainn?" Images of Jaselle's hollow cheeks seize my rebellious brain.

"Mind your own business, Benny!"

He recoils from me in shock. I stare at him, hurt that I've hurt him but not backing down. He gets up and goes inside. I know I've given away the truth. I throw the loose key back into my storage space and try to play without it, angrily pounding the empty space when I need the note, which, of course, is constantly.

It takes me a while to realize I'm waiting for Jaselle. Every crunch of gravel or flash of light has my head snapping up looking for her Celica. I wait and wait. Days are passing and she must be thinking of me. She must want me to come home. Soon, weeks are passing. Why hasn't she called? I jump every time I hear the bar phone ring. It's never her. Why doesn't she come to me? Can she feel time at all anymore?

I'm not breaking. You have to come to me. You have to change. I'm not running back, damn you. I can't run back. This can't go on.

Libido hasn't moved, obviously. His smirk hasn't changed either, mocking me. Always mocking. "Fuck you!" I pick up the nearest empty beer bottle and hurl it at him. "You think you could have done any better?" The small splash of beer that was left in the bottle makes his blue paint a little darker.

Some guy interrupts my episode by sticking his head out the back door and puking, barely missing me. I catch a glimpse of Benny behind the bar before the door swings closed again. I sigh and go inside to get the hose. I can't sleep next to puke.

Benny looks flustered. He's overrun. I try to ignore him but can't. I groan and pass through the "employees only" gate. I start pouring shots for the violently angry half of the bar Benny hasn't gotten to in half an hour.

After ten minutes, I'm caught up and the tips start rolling in. I wonder why I don't do this more often.

"Rainn!" I recognize that too-happy-to-see-me chirp. I look up. It's Shelby.

"Hey," I respond as monotone as possible like that'll balance her out or something.

"Where have you been?" Her energy level doesn't change at all, but she sounds a little mad now.

"Uh, around." I figure she means because we haven't played a show here in way too long. Fucking groupies, making me feel better than I am, missing me, jerks.

"I saw Jaselle yesterday," she says.

Stab of jealousy. Grit your teeth and absorb.

"She looks like shit, Rainn. Why aren't you with her? She needs you somethin' bad."

Confusion scatters, reaching every corner of the brain. "Did she say that?"

"She said you left her. She keeps saying that. 'Rainn left me.' For some guy? What the fuck, Rainn? I thought you were gay?"

"Oh my fucking God. I *am* gay."

"Well, she says you left her for a guy."

What a sick interpretation. "*I* left *her*?"

"That's what she said. And that's messed up, Rainn, you guys are perfect together. I was kind of mad at first 'cause you were supposed to marry me and all." Shelby turns into a bad movie and looks into the distance. "*Sing me to sleep…*"

"Shelby."

"Yeah, anyway, I don't know what she did to you, but get over it and get back over there. She's a damn mess."

"She told me to go."

"And you took her seriously? Rainn, no penis is worth messing up what you guys have."

"Enough with the penis crap," I say.

"I got a penis for you, sweetie." Some jackass slobbers his way over Shelby's shoulder. I ignore him.

"I'm *not* fucking Jayden."

"You can fuck me." I ignore the drunk asshole again. Shelby keeps pulling away from his lean so we're side-stepping gradually down the bar.

"She really thinks that?" I ask.

"She seems to, yeah."

"Hey! Bitch! If you're not going to do something with my dick at least get me a fucking beer."

Benny appears at my side like magic and slams his hand on the bar so hard Shelby and I jump. "Listen, fuck face." He points a finger in fuck face's face. "If I ever hear you talk to her like that again I'm going to cut your dick off, all right?"

Fuck face turns into an ashen statue and retreats from the bar altogether. Benny grabs my arm and pulls me in the back where José is clanging away cleaning dishes.

"Don't let them talk to you like that. Not anyone," he says. I just nod, stiff and still a little shocked.

"I know you're going over there," he says. "I know that face." I nod.

"Be careful." His eyes tear up.

"Oh God, please don't," I say.

"Just say you'll be careful. Don't drown in it. Come back sometimes, Rainn. Come up for air. Don't let her consume you."

"I have to go. I have to make sure she's okay." I hate that I'm still being cold, but I know I can't promise what he's asking. I give him a long, firm hug and tuck the tips I've made into his shirt pocket. I don't feel right keeping them. "I love you, Benny. Don't worry."

Shelby gives me a ride, dropping me off outside Jaselle's. Part of me can't believe I'm here after I swore I wouldn't come crawling back. I swore she'd have to come get me if she wanted me. She'd have to prove herself. It would have to be different. But if she needs me, she needs me.

I wait until I can sneak in behind someone rather than buzz her. I let myself into the apartment. It's the same as the day I left, but it feels foreign now. Why does that happen so fast? I hate the immediacy with which I live my life. Wherever I am, that's all there is. Noah gestures for me to come into his room when he sees me. He closes his door behind me. I don't think I've ever seen his door closed before.

"What are you doing here?" he asks.

"Am I not welcome?"

"Shut up, of course you are. But why would you want to be here? I thought you got out. I was a little proud of you."

"Got out?"

"Of this." He gestures at the walls of his room, but I know he means the entire apartment, this hellhole of a situation. "You don't want to be here, with the drugs and the late nights, with her driving you crazy and me calling you an ignorant savage. Why are you here?"

"Because I love her."

"Yeah, they all love her. She's so mysterious, so dangerous, so…"

"Real."

"But it's not real, that's exactly the problem. Nothing's real. It's all illusion, images in smoke."

"You're acting stranger than I remember," I say.

"I don't know if you want to see her like this, Rainn. It's gotten worse since you left."

A stab of guilt. I left her when she needed me. She was drowning in the drug, and I was her last tie to the surface. And I left. She's been picturing me with Jayden and the silence was too much. Don't I know the feeling? Don't I know waiting? Don't I know silence? And don't I know breathing in chemicals for the burn of melting flesh and organs disintegrating?

"She needs me."

"Yeah, she does. But is this what you want for yourself?"

"She needs me." I separate the words for emphasis. Can't he see that's all that matters? I hear glass shatter on the other side of the apartment. I give Noah a slight scowl and go to her.

She doesn't notice me at first, but when she does her knees buckle and she bursts into tears. I kneel down beside her and gather her up. I cringe, almost pulling away from the feel of her protruding bones bending in my embrace. She's dirty. I don't imagine she's showered in a while. There are cigarette burns all over her arms, self-inflicted. She's so skinny. I feel her feeble rib cage threatening to break from the mere expansion of her lungs, and I know I could squeeze her to death without even trying. She's so weak I cry.

She cries and I cry, and I just want to hold her forever. Just let me take care of you. Let me help you back to life. Don't you see you're dying? My rebellious angel, just let me love you. I think this is the first time I've seen it, not the problem, not the use, not the pain, but the threat of death. It's so real now, with her wheezing breaths, her pattering heart. What have you done?

CHAPTER EIGHTEEN

I can't undo the damage. She rages, breathing spider venom into my veins, and she's the demon more and more. Her eyes are glass more and more, dark orbs without color, black expanding too far, all black, the demon exhales smoke. She hates me. She hates everything. Life has killed her.

I'm the only one who dares stay in her reckless path, bound to her forever, addicted to her kiss and the way it destroys me, those glimpses of Jaselle still inside, bound and gagged, scared and crying while the meth eats her. And I stay for the moments she remembers she loves me. I breathe her in and pull so deep, and my cheeks are wet and she begs me don't leave, don't leave me alone with it. It's alive. It whispers to her and the voices don't stop, not even as I hold her, as I plead for her life, it feeds on her death. That's what it wants, but not until it's taken everything.

I hold on to her, grabbing her golden gaze, her laugh and memories of times when love mattered, and I fight the battle she can't. I carry her weight, even as the flame burns through and she screams for me to just stop. Just stop. Don't leave me. Go away. I'm afraid. I want to just die. I need you. I'm so afraid.

But death is quiet. Death is submersion into the water, finally beneath the waves that bash into you again and again, setback after setback, mouths full of salt and burning eyes. It's so fun at first, but then frustrating, enraging, exhausting, unconquerable. Finally, submit. It's so much easier to submit.

It's Jaselle speaking. It's not the demon this time, but it's winning. She's closing her eyes, and her fight is gone. Life will happen until death does, and she wants the quiet. I'm the pleading that won't stop. I'm the last siren going off. Her muted instincts don't care anymore. I have replaced them, that useless voice telling her to live just because. Why? Because. You have to. Live.

And the demon screams, just shut up! And it strikes me, swift shock and Jaselle cries. And another inhale, hot foil and black spots, spots like her eyes, burned out, windows no more.

Guilt owns me. It never ends, never fades, never easy, not to forget that she became this when I left. Because I left? Warm in the self-value? The proof of love? Or dead in the guilt? "You left," the demon whispers. You left her; now she's mine. She smoked and smoked, and she breathes it so easy, silk death. This is your doing. You left when she needed you, and she burned every rock in sight and pictured you on top of him, and she felt his hips digging bruises into your thighs while you wept in an alley.

Yes, the demon hates you. No, the demon is pure indifference. It's Jaselle who hates you, Jaselle who loves you, Jaselle who cares that you left her, Jaselle who was alone without you, Jaselle gasping for breath ever since you let her go under.

Jayden calls, and he calls again, and it looks like what she thought. He seems the broken lover, and it's not your phone to silence. And he's not your enemy to kill. He's just confusion the demon is using. And now you've lost a friend because she can't watch you call him; she won't understand. And you must undo what you've done. You will remind her what it's like to trust and to love. You will wait.

He calls again, and you watch yourself lose ground. And she's distant again. She's impossible again, forever licensed to hurt you at will because you hurt her. "How did his dick taste?"

"We're just friends. We've never done anything." Nothing matters. Nothing sinks in. And she's using again. She's dying again. She's crying again. She's screaming again. She's sick again. She's shaking again. You're on the curb again, buying the drug you desperately want her off of, selling your soul for a bag the size of a quarter because she's dying without it. She'll fall asleep in your arms and the shallow breaths will just stop. You pick change out of the gutter. You rip off the kids selling lemonade who can't count change. You wish you kept the tips from bartending instead of turning them in to Benny. You let the creepy guy outside Walgreens touch your hair. And you go back to her. She's in the same spot because she's too weak to move.

Her thumb is shaking on the lighter. Ah, that feels so much better. She's on top of the world again. Nothing has changed, but nothing matters. And she wraps her arms around you and pulls you closer, kisses your cheek. "I love you, Rainn. Never leave me? I love you so much." And nothing has changed, but nothing matters.

Chapter Nineteen

I hear the door to the apartment close, but Jaselle doesn't appear. I get up and go down the hallway to find her. Her back is to the door. She's breathing hard. It doesn't take much to exhaust her anymore, but this looks different.

"Baby?" I ask. "Are you okay?"

Her eyes flash to mine like she hadn't realized I was here. Her gaze jumps around. She can't settle on any one thing. She looks scared, I realize. I go to her and touch her cheek.

Paranoia is a common symptom of methamphetamine addiction, or so Google tells me, along with irresponsibility, loss of appetite, child neglect, criminal activity, intense rages that often lead to violence, and suicidal tendencies. Thank you, Google.

I've never been much of a researcher. I guess worrying has turned me into one. Only a fucking moron could really think they'll find all the answers on the internet, but I tried.

"Sweetie?"

She wraps her arms around my neck and squeezes. She stays there, clinging on like a child. I hold her and wait for whatever is going on to pass. Is she just paranoid? Are the cops really coming after her? Or maybe someone else? Is she hearing voices? It's impossible to know.

What Google doesn't tell you is what *your* symptoms will be once you've fallen in love with a methamphetamine addict:

paranoia, irresponsibility, loss of appetite, intense rages that often lead to violence, insomnia, uncontrollable urges to stalk said methamphetamine addict.

"Baby, what's wrong?" I pull her face away from my shoulder and wipe away tears. There's a deep shadow below her eye. I touch it. She winces. "What happened to you?"

She pulls away. "I'm okay."

"Jaselle." I reach out for her again. I'm shocked she lets me. "Who did this to you?"

There's a knock on the door. She jumps and presses against me, hard. It's the most strength I've seen her exhibit since I've been back. I try to lean forward to look out the peephole. My heart is pounding. I wonder if she can feel it the way I can feel hers.

She pushes against me, preventing me from reaching the peephole. "No."

"Baby, what's going on? Who is it? Tell me."

She bursts into tears.

"Jaselle." I grab her face and force her to look at me. "Jaselle, breathe."

"Don't." She clings to me.

"I'm here, okay? I'm here. Just tell me what's going on."

She doesn't answer. I let her stay glued to me, but muscle past her attempts to stop me. I look through the peephole, then back at her.

"It's Jayden," I say.

Her tears dry. Her back straightens, and I'm not sure if I ever saw the fear at all. "What the hell is he doing here? Did you invite him here?"

"No."

"I can hear you guys talking," Jayden says through the door. "Morons."

Jaselle and I are stuck staring at one another. I don't want this to turn into a fight, but he's here, on the doorstep. I do the only thing I know to do. I open the door. Jaselle scowls and walks away.

Jayden's Mohawk isn't spiked. I can't read his expression. I don't know if he's perfected his iron stare or if I've just forgotten the subtleties of his face that give him away.

"What are you doing here?" It seems cold, like I've evolved into a heartless shell, but that's a pretty standard question when someone shows up unexpectedly, isn't it?

"What day is it?"

"Uhh, Saturday, I think."

"The date, Rainn. What's the date?"

"I don't know." Is that the point he's trying to make? I'm so deep in this cave I can't keep track of the date anymore? Well, I could never do that.

"It's the sixteenth," he says. I stare blankly. "Of January." I stare some more. "Which means…"

I know I'm failing a crucial test. "It's National Drop in on a Friend Day?"

"Is that what we are?"

"Jayden—"

"Shut up, Rainn, for two seconds. I don't know who you are. You used to be there whenever any of us needed you, especially when I needed you. You used to be the most badass musician in Denver. You used to be the leader of a band that was going all the way." He pauses. "The old Rainn would have never done this to us."

"I'm not trying to *do* anything to you guys. I just have to be here with her right now. Jaselle needs me. I know you don't like her, and I know she's made mistakes, but—"

"Shut the fuck up about Jaselle for two seconds!" I feel the doorframe vibrate under my hand from his voice. I'm ready to slam the door in his face, but I can't fast enough. "Brad was at the Chapel last night, Rainn. He came to see us. You blew it for us. You weren't there. You blew it."

My heart drops into my stomach. I'm about to ask why he didn't call me, but he did. I've been ignoring his calls. For Jaselle.

"I am so sorry." I choke up. I've never had to apologize about anything like this before. I've never hurt him like this. I've never been the sole jerkoff in a situation before. "Oh my God, Jayden, I'm so sorry." I put my hand on my forehead. I can't meet his eyes. "Where are Shiloh and Alex?"

"They don't want to see you."

I find that hard to believe, even given the circumstances. "They don't want to see me or you don't want them to want to see me?"

"You are so fucking self-deluded. You're really going to try to make it seem like I want you to be the dick? No, Rainn, I wanted you to be the hero. You can't treat people like they don't matter and expect them to keep loving you."

I let that sink in for a minute. I can't decide what I think of it. It hurts. It's just, I suppose, but haven't I been treated like I don't matter more times than I can count? Don't I keep loving anyway? Why doesn't it work that way when I'm the one who needs the mercy?

"I'm sorry, Jayden. Really. I screwed up bad."

"We're finding a new singer, Rainn."

My ears start ringing, and I'm groping for the meaning to what he just said. "What?"

"You were amazing, Rainn, but a good singer who shows up is better than a great one who doesn't. We can't wait for you to get your shit together any more. We're moving on."

He turns and walks away, leaving me speechless in the doorframe. Part of me wants to scream at him that they aren't the Suicidal Angels without me. What a joke to kick me out. I am their voice. I am their face. Well, Jayden might be their face, but I am their music. I want to tell him he better not even think about using any of the songs I wrote. *I* wrote. Alone. Without their help. Before I was the weak link, when I was the only link holding together a bunch of monkeys on a jungle gym. How many times did they goof off? Show up late? Leave early? Forget the song mid-performance? Did I ever try to kick them out?

But I watch him turn the corner without saying any of that. I know I deserve this. I know showing up late and not showing up at all are different. I know I let them down on the wrong night. It wasn't just a mistake to miss Brad Schafer; it was a betrayal. My entire being aches knowing how good they all are, knowing they'll still be amazing musicians without me. Will they find another singer? Will it be as easy as he made it sound?

When I turn around, Jaselle is standing there. I look her up and down, taking in her black eye all over again, and I'm grateful I didn't make any desperate pleas to Jayden not to kick me out. I can't be there for them the way they deserve right now, and I can't keep lying and pretending I will.

"Are you okay?" she asks. She heard everything Jayden said. I'm impressed she didn't intervene. I'm even more impressed she's setting aside her hatred of Jayden and suspicion long enough to realize I need her.

She comes over and holds me. I cling to her the way she clung to me, and it feels so good. It feels so incredible to be the weak one.

"Let's get out of here," I say.

She perks up. "Really?"

"Yeah. I have to get out of this house."

We hardly ever go out anymore. I try my best to keep her here, where for whatever reason, I feel like she's safe. Safe from the world, sure, but that won't keep her heart from telling her to go fuck herself.

She does seem better, though. I've been forcing her to eat. She hates it, but at least she has enough strength to walk around without passing out. She even seems a little happier, but when was the last time we laughed together? I can't even remember it. I remember plenty of crying, fighting, lovemaking, but when was the last time we had fun? We're both dying in this apartment.

"I'm going to get dressed." She springs off. I know she'll also be smoking before we leave, but we don't need to talk about that. If she doesn't smoke, she'll get sick. If I ask her not to smoke, we'll fight. If I convince her not to, she'll be in bed feeling like she's going to die, and I'll be taking care of her. Maybe I'll hate myself for this later, but tonight I'm taking the easy road. Tonight I'll let her have her way without a screaming match. We'll go out, and maybe for just one night I'll remember what it's like to just hang out with Jaselle. Maybe the world won't revolve around crank for just one night.

Are we even in a relationship if we don't try to have fun together every once in a while? Who knows, maybe if I stop being her opponent for once, she'll remember I'm her lover and her best friend, and she'll tell me what happened to her eye.

CHAPTER TWENTY

Jaselle wears all the clothes she knows turn me on, revealing enough to drive me crazy but not so much she looks trampy. Our sex life is one of the only things that hasn't suffered from the drug use, but it's still refreshing to see her dress up for me.

I want to go to a gay bar, but we don't have much money. Jaselle convinces me a straight bar will be better because guys will buy our drinks. I don't relish the idea of dealing with a bunch of drunk straight dudes all night, but Jaselle says leave it to her, so I do.

We buy our first round ourselves and settle in at a table in the corner. She looks beautiful, except for the black eye that won't stop demanding my attention. I don't want to jump straight into that though, so I waste time on Jayden for a while.

"I really let them down."

Jaselle holds my hand. "They'll forgive you."

"Why should they? I haven't really been in the band for a while now. They just made it official."

"You know what?" She brightens up.

"What?"

"You're better off without them. You're so much more talented than they are anyway. Just focus on your own stuff for a while. The songs you've been playing on the piano are so beautiful. Maybe you should be a composer. Do you even like the band anymore?"

"A composer?" What does she think we're in 1750 Vienna? "There's no audience for classical music anymore, babe."

"Of course, there is. What, no one listens to anything except Beethoven and Bach and Mozart?"

"And Chopin. And yes, the list pretty much ends there, give or take a dead guy."

"I think you're wrong," she says. "And anyway, if that's what you love..."

"I loved the Suicidal Angels. And that's not even the point anyway. The point is that they're my friends, and I completely failed them."

She frowns, and I know she's thinking all kinds of Jayden thoughts again. I wish I could figure out how to stop that. I live like I cheated on her, constantly tiptoeing around his name and not hanging out with someone I have no reason not to hang out with, just because she's under the unfounded misapprehension that I slept with him. Suddenly, I'm angry. I take a swig of beer. This is not what was supposed to happen tonight. I force myself to relax and smile.

"I started a new painting," she says.

"That's good. What is it of?"

"Death."

"Oh? And how exactly do you paint death?" I ask. I hate it when she says intriguing things like that, and I have no choice but to get sucked in.

"I'll show you when I'm done. It just hit me. Even if it's just a feeling, I know how to put it on the canvas. That's why paint is so amazing. You can capture anything."

I lean across the table and kiss her.

"Well, you know the feeling," she says. I raise my eyebrow a little. She looks at me like I'm missing something super obvious. "You do it with your music all the time. Hell, you probably do it better than I do. I know you've played death on the piano. I've heard you."

"Oh?"

"You didn't feel it while you were doing it?"

Remarkably, I know exactly what she's talking about. I did play death, though I might not have called it that in the moment. I wrote it for her.

"I used to say Jayden on guitar was the sound of heartache." I say it without thinking. I hover on the edge of guilt for a second, but I pull myself away from it.

"Yeah, he did sound like that." She looks sad. "Rainn, I want you to be happy. I love you."

"I love you too."

"If you want your friends back, go get them back."

"I'm not sure it's that simple anymore," I say.

"They'll forgive you. You know they will. I don't want you losing them on my account. You'll only resent me for it anyway."

I'm pretty sure I already do, but I don't say that.

"Go see them more often. I'll be okay without you for a day here and there. Don't think about the band right now; just get your friends back."

She looks so sincere. I realize as easy as it is to blame her, it was never her fault. They're my friends. It's my responsibility to make time for them, not hers to shove me out the door. She didn't keep me from them, I kept myself from them, perhaps with the exception of this Jayden thing recently. Still, I shouldn't have let her do it.

"Are you sure it's not going to bother you?" I mean me hanging out with Jayden, but I don't want to be that direct. She answers as if I was anyway.

"You are not allowed to fuck him," she says.

My mouth opens wide, and I raise my voice without meaning to. "I never did! How many times—"

She puts her hand over my mouth and kisses my cheek. "Okay. But you're still not allowed to. Right?"

"Of course not. What kind of idiot do you think I am that you have to tell me that? Why can't you see you're the only one I want?" She kisses me again. It's so warm I melt into it. She wraps her arms around me and squeezes.

"Can I get you girls some drinks?" A guy with too-big shoulders interrupts us. I pull away, irritated, but Jaselle speaks before I can tell him no.

"Sure, you can, handsome. What's your name?" I forgot we're relying on guys buying our drinks tonight. I hate relying on the male species for anything. Now I have to listen to this jockstrap try to talk his way into a threesome for the next two hours.

"Trey," he says. Jaselle introduces herself and, unfortunately, me too. As predicted, when Trey returns with drinks he makes himself comfortable at our table.

"So," he says, "I'm trying to hook up with this girl over here. I've been in love with her since like third grade. I figured a couple lesbians might be able to give me a few pointers, huh?"

I smile against my best efforts. Well, that's more interesting than being hit on. "You've strictly been friends the whole time?"

"Yep."

"Does she know you want more?"

He shrugs.

"Make it clear you're interested," Jaselle says. "You have to be confident but not creepy or aggressive. If it's been that long, she either has no clue you like her or she thinks you're a total chicken. You have to use your balls."

"Use my balls?"

"Yes," we say together.

"That's not what I'd figure two ball-less lovers would advise," he says.

Trey keeps buying us drinks, and we keep giving advice. He turns out to be excellent company and even fairly easy to get rid of. When we've had enough of him, we send him off on his mission to get his girl.

Jaselle nods at me when he's gone, as if to say she told me she'd handle it. We're both plenty drunk now. Jaselle disappears to the bathroom. I don't think anything of it, but when she returns I know she's high. I can't imagine wanting to get high on top of how drunk we already are, but she does it all the time. She comes straight over to my chair rather than her own and kisses me. I expect a peck, but she makes it clear she wants more, pushing against me and waiting for me to invite her tongue.

I wrap my arms around her and give a deeper kiss. I'm conscious of the room around us and the fact that this is getting pretty showy for a straight bar, but I chance it. There are other couples making out too, and it's so nice to just have a normal night for once. We're us again, finally, if only for tonight.

"Dykes."

Jaselle spins around to spot the culprit. He looks like a frat boy, of course. "You got something to say, cock breath?"

I grab Jaselle's arm as a precaution. She looks like she might spring at him. I see it coming way before Jaselle does. The collection of girls accompanying the douchebag head our way, one charging forward in a rage, the others fulfilling the obligatory friend backup.

"Cock breath?" the girl says. I have to stifle a laugh at the phrase coming from this choir girl looking thing. "Just because you have no problem throwing yourself into the fires of hell doesn't mean everyone in this building is a fag like you."

"Hah, I nailed that one," I say to Jaselle. "I knew she was a Christian."

"Oh, that's hilarious, making fun of the love of our Lord and Savior. That'll go over well when you're trying to explain yourself to Him."

"Is she trying to fight me?" Jaselle turns to me and asks. I force myself not to laugh and address the offended Christian.

"How about if you stay on your side of the bar, and we'll stay on ours?" That's peaceful, right? I insulted her religion, she insulted my basic composition; I think we're even.

"How about if you stay at home, and *we'll* stay in the bar. No one wants you here."

"She's definitely trying to fight me." Jaselle takes a step closer to the choir girl. I can't believe the little thing has the guts to hold her ground. She's so small and fragile looking, and I'm pretty confident she's never been in a fight before. Meanwhile, Jaselle looks like she got in a fight two hours ago with her black eye. I try to wedge myself in between them.

"Back off," I say sternly to the choir girl.

"Sin is an infection. If we turn a blind eye to you then—"

"You'll catch homosexuality? Yeah, it's really been going around lately," I say. Jaselle laughs and puts her arms around my waist. Before I know what she's doing, she licks my ear just to agitate the girl.

Choir girl's face contorts and she raises her hand. I think she only intends to point at us and deliver another misguided interpretation of the Bible, but the second Jaselle sees movement she assumes it's an attack and pushes choir girl away with all her strength. Choir girl stumbles backward. She probably would have fallen down were it not for her wall of friends.

I throw myself in between Jaselle and the recovering choir girl. I hold a hand to Jaselle's chest, pushing her back, and a hand in front of the five girls springing toward us.

"We'll leave!" I yell. My mind is going crazy. Jaselle is high. What if the cops are called and she's caught with meth? "We'll leave!" I repeat.

"Fuck you!" one of choir girl's friends yells and pushes me. Her shove knocks me into Jaselle, which sends her into a fury again. I recover and hold her back before she lands a blow. I desperately hold my hand up again, but it's too late. Another of the girls pushes me, then another, and I'm in a mosh pit trying to resist throwing punches.

I see Trey trying to make his way over to help break it up, but the crowd is thick now between people wanting to get in on the action, managers trying to find the center, and people who just want a good view.

One of the girls throws her glass. Beer showers us all, but the glass connects with Jaselle's head. I hear the crack and Jaselle staggers back. Then my mind goes blank. My body takes over and my fist is swinging. I feel the glass thrower's face break, her skin splits and she falls back.

Someone tries to grab me. I throw an elbow over my shoulder. It connects too. I shove choir girl. She trips and starts to fall. She's clawing at people's clothes on the way down trying to stop herself. She gets a grip on someone's arm and starts to recover, but I kick her square in the chest, hard.

I've created a couple feet of space. I know I'll only have the window for a second, but I spin and find Jaselle. She's on the ground. There's blood dripping from a cut over her eyebrow. I scoop her up. Between her frailness and my adrenaline, she weighs nothing.

There's a scramble behind me. I realize Trey has made his way over and is trying his best to hold three girls back. Thank God his shoulders are five feet wide. The managers close in. The crowd is thick. The stairs aren't far. I head straight for the densest area of the bar, trying to get lost in the people. Attention starts to turn to the girls I injured. I hold Jaselle tight to me and weave. I will us invisible.

I can hear one of the girls trying to tell someone to stop us, but everyone is confused now and thinks the fight was between the girls I knocked down. I creep down the stairs.

"Jaselle? Can you walk, baby? This looks weird." I'm thinking mostly about getting past the doorman now with her in my arms and blood on her face.

"I'm dizzy," she says. Speed is my only option. I walk into the employees only area rather than to the front door. I speed walk past the bartender, who knows I don't belong but can't react fast enough. I go right past her and out the side door. My heart is pounding while I wait to hear a voice behind me, telling me to stop.

I turn the first corner I come to, and the first corner after that, and I just keep going like that, turning as much as possible until I feel like I've created a maze no one from the bar will follow. I find a secluded corner in an alley, lit by a sad little lamp, and gently set Jaselle down.

The amount of blood flowing from her head is terrifying, but I force myself to be calm. I know head wounds bleed a lot naturally. It's just a cut. But she's dizzy. She's dizzy half the time, though. Meth ruins your perception of everything. Infuriating.

I wipe the blood away. Doing so pulls the edges of the cut apart, and I swear I can see skull. That can't possibly be right. It can't be skull. It's some kind of white tissue, that's all. It's her forehead, Rainn, how much tissue do you think there is? It's her damn skull. But that's not the end of the world, right? Skin covering your forehead is only what, a quarter inch thick at most? I feel my own forehead like a moron, trying to judge how thick my skin is and therefore how deep Jaselle's cut is.

"Are you still dizzy?"

"I don't know. If I move my head too fast, I guess," she says. I look at her eyes. Did I hear somewhere that if the pupils are different sizes it means she has a concussion? Is that true? Her pupils are the same size: too big.

"Can you walk?"

"Yeah, I think so." She stands up and waits for a second, testing herself. Eventually, she nods. I wrap my arm around her waist just in case, and we start walking. I decide trying to go back for the car tonight is too risky, so we have several miles to go.

CHAPTER TWENTY-ONE

Noah doesn't even get off the couch when he sees us come in. It's like he doesn't notice the blood caked dry on Jaselle's cheek, only I know he does. The rage swells up for a second, but my exhaustion quickly pushes it into a corner. Noah doesn't matter.

I take Jaselle to the kitchen and pat the counter for her to sit down. I know she's ready to collapse. We split the effort of getting her up there, her half jumping, me half lifting. Her head slumps forward. Her eyes are closed. I dampen a washcloth and lift her chin. Her eyes flutter back open as I dab at the blood. She starts to doze off again as I work, resentfully coming to when her head starts sagging too much and I have to lift her chin again.

I'm still wondering if I should let her sleep. What if she does have a concussion? You aren't supposed to sleep when you have a concussion, right? Is that all the time or only in certain cases? And what happens if you do sleep with one? Do you go into a coma or something?

I work on cleaning up the actual cut. Jolts from me pressing too hard keep waking her up. Once I've woken her up at least five times, I'm pretty secure sleep isn't going to kill her. I finish cleaning her and kiss a safe spot on her forehead. I wrap my arms around her and hold her, so happy to be home and safe. I laugh a little to myself. That took care of wanting to go out. We'll see the next time I have *that* itch.

I pick her up and carry her to the bed. I set her down and cover her with the blankets, tucking her in carefully. In the bar I was irritated she was being confrontational while I was trying to pacify our antagonists, but already I'm back to adoration. The second she's in danger it's so much easier to forgive. I guess she's always in danger these days. Does forgiving instantly make you godly like Jesus? Or does it just make you an idiot?

I kiss her cheek again and head to the living room, closing her bedroom door as quietly as I can. I sit in the chair across from the couch, across from Noah. He's puffing away on a joint. I suddenly realize I've never once seen him without weed in his hand, whether it's a pipe, a bong, or a joint.

I take a deep breath and sink into the chair. My muscles are screaming from all the stress, the tension, the fighting, carrying Jaselle, walking.

"What a fucking night," I say.

"Looks like it," Noah says. "Are you proud of yourself? You're still savages."

"Oh, don't start. You know what? Shit happens, and I'm just glad we're home safe. I am a little proud of myself, actually."

"You would be." He takes a puff off his joint. "Savage."

"How does a drug dealing bum end up so judgmental? You haven't even asked what happened. You just think you know already."

"Oh, this is the part where you try to surprise me, huh? Okay, let me see." He rubs his temples like he's trying to pick it up psychically. "You went out for a few drinks. You were minding your own business and someone came and started shit with you? You had no control over it. You did nothing wrong. You defended yourselves. Sound about right?"

"Bite me." I take the joint he's offering and smoke.

"You're smarter than this, Rainn." He gets serious.

"Smarter than what? Fighting?"

"This." He gestures around the apartment. That's the second time he's done that.

"Obviously I'm not."

"That's what's sad though, you really are."

"Do you realize you're the biggest hypocrite in the world?" I ask.

"What happened tonight?"

I scowl. "Yes, it was a bar fight, and yes, they started it. We might have escalated it a little. I won't say we did nothing wrong." It's funny that admitting we did some wrong somehow ends up being my redemption just because my story isn't exactly what he said it would be.

"And by 'we escalated it' what you really mean is 'Jaselle escalated it,' huh?"

"Do you care at all that your best friend's face is smashed and we could have been arrested and we had to walk home ten miles? Does any of that even matter to you? Or is it just about you being right and feeling superior?"

"Does it matter to *you* that any of that happened?" He sits up abruptly on the couch, startling me a little. "Does it matter to you that you had to deal with all that? That you put yourself at that kind of risk?"

"Your best friend is passed out from a head injury in the other room and all you can do is try to talk me out of taking care of her?"

"Oh, fuck off. Are we going to play this game? She isn't passed out from any head injury, you donkey. She's passed out because she's crashing."

That silences me for a second. My stomach knots, rebelling. "She—"

"No. Stop. She couldn't keep her eyes open because she's crashing, just like she does every week. Just because this particular evening finds you with an excuse doesn't mean you should try to use it to shove the truth aside. You piss me the fuck off."

"You piss *me* the fuck off. If you don't care what happens to her and you're so above all of this what the hell are you doing here? You're worse than I am. You live with her. You support her. You let her do it in your house. And you have the nerve to tell me what a moron I am because I do what I do with conviction? At least I'm trying to help her. I'm trying to make it better. You don't care if she gets better or not so long as nothing uncivilized happens in your bubble."

"You're so wrong it's sickening," he says.

"But you won't tell me why, will you? You'll just insist I don't understand and continue acting superior."

"Your life has gone to shit since you've met her. Please look me in the eye and deny that if you can."

"In your opinion, maybe," I say.

"Deny it!"

"I deny it."

"You've lost your friends, you've lost your band, you don't even play your piano anymore, you've lost your home."

"Hah! My home? You must be joking."

"Yes, your home. Don't be dense. I'm not talking about the sidewalk, I'm talking about the Chapel. You might not have had a house, but you had a home, Rainn, and you've lost it. If you go back there right now will it feel the same?"

"I have a home here now. And I have the love of my life." I want to cry because I know he's just feeling more and more self-satisfied with every passing word. I'm trapped in a losing battle, and it's sending me into a rage. Why does it have to be this way? What's so wrong about standing by someone you love through their struggle? Why do I feel right but sound wrong?

"Are you happier?" he asks. I sit and brew. I want to say yes. I want to say no. Both are true, but he takes the silence as a no.

"What are you trying to prove, Noah? That you care about *me*? That you want *my* life to be better? Because that wasn't the question. I want to know why you don't care what happens to Jaselle."

"I care more than you can possibly believe. I've just accepted what you can't."

"What?"

"That I have no control over it."

"She can't get off of it alone, and you won't help her."

"She can *only* get off it alone. She can't do it for you, Rainn. She has to do it for herself. And I don't know if you've noticed, but she isn't even trying. What is it that you think you're supporting here? Because it's not her quitting, it's her using."

"She is trying!"

"You believe that?" he asks.

"Can't you see she's tortured? Can't you see she's locked in her own skin? Don't you feel her pain?"

"That's just it, I'm tired of feeling her pain. It isn't mine to feel. I won't do it to myself anymore. I'm trying to help you see that you shouldn't either. Let her go."

"Well, aren't you just a selfish son of a bitch?" I say. I want to hit him. I want to spit on him. I've never had that urge before, but I want to spit on Noah. "It's not enough that you've given up on her, you have to try to convince other people to do the same? You're just determined to leave her helpless and alone? Hopeless? Are you going out of your way to kill her?"

"You have to learn how to live your life for yourself, not for her. Your entire existence can't revolve around someone else, don't you see that? You are letting your happiness depend on Jaselle, and her happiness depends on the drug. You might as well be addicted your fucking self."

"Yes, and I can see how well not being attached is working for you. Aren't you just a model of happiness with your weed business."

"Yeah, well, I didn't get in a bar fight and almost arrested and walk home ten miles, did I?"

"Worse things have happened to me, Noah! I'd rather get in the fight and almost arrested and walk home than not be there when she needed me and she ends up dead. How will you be able to stand yourself if she dies because you're not there?"

"It's not my job to rescue her every two hours! It's not yours either," he yells.

"I like rescuing her. I like it a whole lot better than letting her die because 'it's not my job.' I like Jaselle alive."

"Fuck you." His eyes well up. Finally. I don't even feel bad. I'm just angry it took this long. "You sit there and tell me what a dick I am like you know me." His voice is shaking. He stops for a second to try to pull himself together. "You go ahead. You tell me how wrong and heartless I am. I'm a fucking human being with a life too. I was there the first time she did meth, you little shit. I watched her face light up like she just found the missing piece in her life. I watched it take her down to ninety pounds. I watched her do horrible things to get it. I watched her hurt the people closest to her. I watched her lose everything. I went to funerals with her as her party buddies died from overdoses. I took her to the hospital when *she* overdosed. I watched her melt that beautiful mind of hers. You think she's fucking smart now. God, you should have known her then. I watched her scratch her skin off because she thought there were bugs in it. I watched her talk to herself.

"I watched her finally say enough. I saw her get clean, and I felt that amazing hope that things would be okay again. And then I watched her collapse into the same bullshit. She broke my fucking heart, Rainn. Do you have any idea what it does to you to finally see the nightmare end and think you have her back and then have it smashed to pieces? I want you to try to fathom that for a second, genuinely. I want you to picture her getting clean right now, all your dreams come true. And a year from now, two years from now, she starts again. You tell me you'd have the energy to start over.

"No, Rainn, I buried Jaselle. If that means I'm weak and selfish and you're strong and loyal, then fine, you go ahead and think that."

"I'm going to be there, Noah. I can't bury her before she's dead."

"She is dead."

"It's easier for you to think that, but she's not. She comes back sometimes. She's still in there. I know you prefer not to see it. I know it's easier for you when she's fucking up, because that's what you expect, that's what you're prepared for. And as long as you don't see Jaselle you can keep her buried. It pisses you off when she comes back, doesn't it? Because you know you're wrong. And if Jaselle shows you she's still alive in there then you feel like a piece of shit for abandoning her."

"She's not in there, Rainn. Even when you think you're seeing her, you're not. You're just seeing a projection of her designed to manipulate you. She will do anything for the drug. She will be anyone."

"No. She's in there. She's in there fighting with the demon still. I can see past him. I can still see her."

"You see what you want to see." Noah offers me the joint again. I smirk and turn it down.

"The demon wants you to think she's not there. He wants you to give up on her so he can have her."

"I think you're taking this demon thing a little far," Noah says.

"Would you be more comfortable if I called it 'the drug' or 'the addiction' like a doctor?"

"Probably."

"It's alive though. You know what she becomes."

"Yes, I know exactly what she becomes, but that's your problem. You can't admit that it's her. You have to pretend it's a different entity entirely. 'Jaselle didn't hurt me, the demon did.' All you're doing is lying to yourself so that you can preserve this image you have of her where she's still a good person."

"She is a good person still. If you don't think she is you're confused. She still loves you. She still loves me. She's just trapped," I say.

"You're the one who's trapped."

I can't deny the reverberation of truth in that word. Trapped. I am, but so is she. "I can't give up on her."

CHAPTER TWENTY-TWO

Jaselle doesn't wake up for two and a half days. I'm playing piano when she finally comes to. Her call for me is quiet and weak, but my ears are trained for that. I jump off the piano bench and go to her. She reaches out for me, but she can't lift her hand high enough. I kneel down next to the bed and guide her fingers to my cheek.

"What is it, love?" Her shirt is soaking wet with sweat. She tries to squeeze my hand. I can barely feel it.

"I'm sick."

The trash can is already by the bed so she can throw up. I try to help her sit. She can't. She just manages to scoot to the edge so she can lean over the trash can below her. I pull her dreads out of her way with one hand and rub her back with the other. Her entire body seizes when she throws up. The pain of the effort makes her cry. "It hurts so bad."

"I know, baby, I know."

"Make it stop." She cries. "I can't…" She cries harder and curls into herself, leaving the sentence unfinished. I don't notice I'm crying too until a drop falls off my face to the carpet.

"I'm so sorry," I say. I wish I could feel this for her, even just with her would be better than this. I feel so useless. She pushes me away so she can throw up again. Her temperature is scaring me. I picture her brain steaming inside her head, melting.

"I think I'm gonna die, Rainn," she squeaks. I cry harder as the image enters my mind so easily, her body seizing and then going limp, her last breath pressed from her lungs.

"No, you're not." I put both my hands on her face and sternly demand, "It's going to be okay."

"The joke is on me, Rainn. I was wrong. I'm not the jester. I'm the clown. I'm going to die a fool for what I've done."

"You're not going to die." I shake off this weak person and become the one I need to be. I dampen a washcloth and put it on her forehead. I get her water and a couple crackers. She doesn't want any of it, of course, but she drinks, for me. She timidly nibbles the corner of a cracker, for me. I help her take her sweat soaked clothes off.

"It hurts so bad."

"I know."

"Make it stop." She flops onto her back again. Even sitting up on her elbows is too difficult.

"I'm trying, baby."

"I need a shot."

"You are not drinking right now. Are you crazy?"

"No, Rainn. I need to shoot."

My mind gets fuzzy. "Shoot?" I look to the inside of her elbow. Track marks are perfectly visible. How have I not seen them before now? "When did you start doing this?"

"He did it." She closes her eyes and starts to fade away.

"Who did it?" I shake her a little. "Jaselle! Who did this?"

"I'm so cold."

"How long have you been doing this?"

She starts to mumble. I try to discern it, but it's nearly impossible. Finally, I recognize it. It's a melody. She's singing one of my songs.

"*Drown me in the blood of yesterday's heartache. I am tomorrow's tragedy.*"

"Jaselle!" I shake her as hard as I dare. She throws up, still on her back. It doesn't even wake her up. I jolt into action and yank her on her side, then scrape the puke out of her mouth with my finger before she inhales it.

Shoving my finger in her mouth makes her jump awake for a second, and instantly she's fading again. She can't say more than a few words without drifting off.

"I need it," she says. "Please."

"No."

"I can't..." She gasps and winces. Her skin is burning hot. I can feel her heart beating too fast. The shadows around her eyes are getting darker, jarring contrast to her pale skin. "It hurts." She reaches weakly for her nightstand drawer where she keeps the meth. "Rainn..." She can't finish the sentence, but I know what she's asking.

"Don't make me do this," I beg.

"She's withdrawing super hard," Noah says from the doorway. I spin around. "You'd better give it to her."

I choke up. "I don't know how."

"Sure, you do."

"I can't. You do it. Please."

"You wanted to be there for her. Have fun."

"Noah!" I scream. He turns his back. I grab the closest object, which happens to be a shoe, and hurl it at him. It misses, but it's still satisfying.

"Jaselle," I whisper. "I don't know how to do this." She reaches for the drawer again, signaling me to get it more than attempting to herself. I open the drawer and take out a clear bag of crank, a lighter, a spoon, and a needle. I know the gist of this. I've seen other people do it before, but doing it myself seems so much more demanding, and doing it for someone else so much more precarious.

My heart is pounding. I put the crank in the silver spoon. There are too many emotions in my blood. I feel them flashing through me like one of those Japanese cartoons that give people seizures.

"Mix it with water," she says.

"What?" I forgot about that. The fact that I already missed a step makes me realize this is beyond me. I want to run away. I want to demand she does all of this herself, but I know her hands are shaking bad, and I don't want her stabbing around her arm fucking herself up.

"You can't just heat it up like that. You need water."

"How much?"

"You see where it says one hundred?"

I look at the markings on the syringe and find it. "Okay." I go to the bathroom for the water. I fill it up to one hundred and carry it back into the bedroom. "Is it okay to use tap water?" What a ridiculous question. I'm about to shoot drugs into her veins and I'm worried about the water. Jaselle just shrugs like she's thinking the same thing.

"You're going to need cotton," she says. I nod. I remember this part. The cotton acts as a filter. I go to the bathroom again and rip off some fluff from the end of a Q-tip. I set it down on the nightstand until I'm ready for it. I pick up the spoon, now full of crank and water. I use the end of her syringe to mix it a little.

"Don't burn it," she says. I haven't even started heating it up yet. I guess that's her way of telling me to get moving. I strike the lighter under the spoon and move the flame around in little figure eights. If you leave it in the same spot too long it will burn. It will smell really bad, and you will get in giant trouble with your drug addict.

It starts to bubble. The drug dissolves in the water, but there's some crap that floats on the surface. That's whatever the meth is cut with. I look at the who-knows-what that won't dissolve and try to focus on the positive, that this crap won't be in her system like it would if she smoked it. When it's ready, I grab the needle and stare at it for a long time.

"Is this clean, Jaselle?"

"Mm-hmm."

I can't tell if she's even listening. "No one else has used it, right?"

"Nmm-uhh."

I sigh and drop the little piece of cotton in the center of the spoon.

"Don't let the needle touch the spoon," Jaselle says.

"Why?"

She sighs like she can't believe I'm forcing her to go through the effort of explaining this. "Because the spoon is hot. It will melt the tip and make it dull. Then it'll hurt a lot when you try to inject it."

Jesus, when did she become such an expert at all this? I want to puke. I muscle past the nausea and put the tip of the needle in the cotton. I pull up the drug, careful to not to let the needle touch the spoon as instructed.

Then I tap the needle. I don't know if that matters or not, but I figure it can't hurt. Air in blood is bad. I might be stalling a little too. I turn my attention back to her arm.

"Use my belt," she says. I set the rig back down on the bed and sigh. I rip the belt out of her jeans and loop it just above her elbow. It doesn't take long for her veins to be easily visible from the pressure buildup. I touch her skin and my eyes well up fresh.

"Are you sure you want to do it here? You already have a bunch here," I say. It looks sensitive. It looks like it's trying to get infected too. I should probably clean it first.

"I'm so sorry, Rainn," she whispers. I kiss her cheek and wrap my arms around her neck. She starts sobbing. "I fucking hate myself. I want to die."

"Shh. It's going to be okay."

"Remember the boy on my street who hung himself in his parents' closet?"

My throat closes at the image of Jaselle hanging herself, and I can't even answer.

"I don't think he did it in their closet because he hated them anymore," she says. "I don't think he wanted to blame them. I think he just wanted them to see his pain. He wanted them to know how miserable he was so that they would be able to let him go."

"Jaselle, we're going to get through this. You know it's going to get better right? We're going to fix this."

"No. You're going to hate me."

"I could never hate you," I say.

"I slept with him."

I'm a thousand miles away. The world is on mute, and the only thing I can hear is a dull ringing in my ears. I see her lips moving, but I don't know what she's saying. I'm falling away, falling backward. I'm Alice. I'm falling down the rabbit hole. I'm falling infinitely into nothing. And her face at the top of the hole is getting farther away. It's just a shape now. It's just a shadow now. It's just a memory now.

"I slept with Ice." Her mouth makes the words. Her voice can't.

I'm on the brick wall again. Gravity is sideways. I'm lying on the wall. His forearm is crushing my throat. He's pressing his hips into me so hard my jeans he could only pull halfway down are cutting into my thighs. He's ripping my flesh with every thrust. He's pulling my hips. He's determined to go deeper than either of our anatomies will allow. He's excited by my pain. He crushes me into the wall even after I've surrendered. Cold metal on my temple. He pushes harder. A moan in my ear. Helpless. Weightless. He has all of me. Pressed against him far too completely. His possession.

"Rainn?"

Her lips are wrapped around his dick. He grabs her hair. He pulls her closer. He pulls me closer.

"I'm so sorry, Rainn. I hated every second of it. I hate myself. I hate myself."

"How could you?"

"I couldn't stand it. I needed more."

"You fucked him for drugs?"

She gets on top. He holds a bag of meth over his shoulder. She pushes harder trying to reach it. He goes deeper.

"It hurt so bad. I needed it. I'm so sorry." She sobs. She's hysterical. "It was the only way he'd give it to me."

"You should have bought it from someone else."

"With what, Rainn? We don't have any money. We haven't had money for weeks."

"I would have found you money!" I scream.

"Out of the gutter again?"

"I told you never to go back to that house! You promised me, Jaselle! How many fucking times did you promise me?" I get up and punch the wall as hard as I can. I punch the wall so I don't punch her. Her bones would break and her face would be mush and she couldn't fuck him with that face.

"I know. I know! I want to die! I deserve to die!"

She moves her body like a wave on his cock. She fucks him hard, the way he likes it. He tells her, "More. Harder, baby, if you want it." She pulls his head back and rides him, watching the meth. Dreaming of the smoke.

He grabs her hips. He grabs my hips.

She kisses him. She kisses me.

She rips my shirt.

She grabs his cock.

She sucks my neck.

She breathes me in.

He shoves again.

She takes it in.

He makes me bleed.

She's on her knees.

I'm begging please.

"I'm so fucking sorry." She's falling apart. "He shot me up, and I can't breathe without it. It's fucking killing me."

"Why him, Jaselle? Why did you go to him?"

"He's friends with Shane. He was the only person I could think of that might spot me some."

"But he wouldn't."

"No."

"But he made you a deal, huh?" She shrinks into herself. "How many times?"

"Rainn…"

"How many times!"

"A lot."

"Fuck you." I turn away from her. I don't want to see her face. I don't want her to see mine. I hit the wall again. Then I do it again. And again. I just keep punching the wall. I feel my knuckles split open and I scream at the top of my lungs, trying to scream some of this pain, any of this pain out.

I feel her hands on my sides. She's somehow found the energy to sit up. She wraps her arms around me and squeezes. I pry her interlocked fingers apart and push her hands away. She starts sobbing harder.

"I'm so sorry, Rainn."

"How could you do this?" I know there's nothing she can say, but I just feel like screaming. I slide down onto the floor and bury my face in my hands. "Do you even love me?"

"You're the only thing in this world I love," she says.

"Why did you do this, Jaselle? You could have done anything but this. Not this. How can I get over this? How can I look at you?"

"I didn't know what else to do."

"You should have bought it."

"I couldn't."

"Then you should have fucked someone else for it!" I scream. The space between us expands. I regret it instantly, but her face isn't full of the shock I expected, just sadness.

"I know I don't deserve you. I'm just a fuck up. You'll be so much better off without me. Will you hold me while I die? Please? And let me hold you too."

"What the fuck are you talking about? Don't be like that," I say.

"It's over for me, Rainn. What do I have? I'm stuck in this shit and I can't get out. I can't breathe. I can never breathe. I love you so much. I need you. But I'm just fucking you up too."

"Stop it."

"Will you hold me while I die? I want you to be the last thing I feel. I don't want to die high anymore. I'm not scared. I just want to hold you. I want you to know I love you. I'm just not cut out for this shit. I don't think I was ever supposed to be here."

I start crying again. The sadness is so deep. It never ends. Hers. Mine. Now it's rage tears. "I said stop it! Don't turn this shit around so that *I'm* begging *you* to stay."

"I'm not trying to turn it around, Rainn. I know I'm the one that fucked up. I'm always the one fucking up."

"Goddamn it! Why won't you just love me?"

"I do love you."

"Love me!" I crumble again, and she wraps her arms around me. I try to push her off of me again, but she won't let me. Finally. It feels fake. It feels stupid after I screamed it at her. What is it worth now?

"I love you," she says.

"No, you don't."

"I love you so much. I love you more than anything."

She loves meth more than anything.

"Rainn, don't you know I'd be dead without you? Don't you know I'm only here for you?" I can feel myself shaking in her arms. "I'm so sorry, Rainn. I wish I was better. I wish I was stronger." She rocks me back and forth. "I love you." She squeezes me harder. "I need you." She buries her face in my neck. "Please don't leave me."

"You want to be with me?" I ask.

"Of course, I do."

"I mean it, Jaselle. Do you want to be with me?"

"Yes."

I grab the rig we still haven't used off the bed, stab the wall with it, and yank so that the needle breaks off in the dry wall. The drug spills out, down the wall, in the carpet, irretrievable. The needle is useless now.

"Got it? This is it," I say, daring her to protest. She nods. "We're done with this shit." She opens her nightstand drawer again and pulls out what remains of her meth. She stares at it for a second, then presses it into my hand, deliberately closing my fingers around it.

"We're done with this shit."

I hold there, waiting for her to try to rip my hand back open, but she doesn't, so I stand up.

"Where are you going?" she asks.

"I'll be back in a while." I head for the door, but I can feel her panicking behind me. I can feel her wondering if I'll come back, where I'm going, what I'll do, who I'll fuck. I can feel it as vividly as if I were feeling it. I'm connected to her forever, whether I like it or not. I turn and look at her. She's still beautiful to me somehow. I hate her. I love her.

"I'll be back," I say again. I know she wants to hear "I love you," but I just can't right now. I leave.

Chapter Twenty-three

A crowbar makes an incredibly satisfying weapon. When Ice opens the door, I swing it at his head. I hit my mark. Blood spatters through the air. He staggers backward, and I send him to the ground with a kick in the gut before he can compose himself. I crouch down over him and punch him in the face. While he's still dizzy, I grab the gun from his jeans.

I have no intention of using it. I don't even intend to threaten him with it. I just don't want it factoring into this encounter at all. I don't dare walk away from Ice and give him time to find another weapon, so I scan the room carefully, searching for signs someone else is here, locating all places someone could come from.

There's the front door, obviously, which is behind me. There's a hallway to the right that leads into bedrooms, and there's a doorway to the left that goes into the kitchen. I listen for voices, for footsteps. Nothing. I tuck the gun in my own belt, by my back so it's not as easy to get to.

I hold the crowbar over Ice's face. "I want you to listen to me carefully," I say.

"You're going to regret this," he says. "I'll fucking kill you."

"Shut up." I put the bag of crank on his chest. "You are not to bother Jaselle again."

He starts laughing. "You think I'm the one bothering her?"

"I know you will be when you stop hearing from her."

"Look, it's not my problem your bitch likes crank. I'm just a dealer. I'm not a fucking rehab center."

"You will not sell to her again."

"I haven't *sold* to her in a while, baby, if you know what I mean," he says. I punch him again, and again. Has he forgotten I have every reason in the world to kill him?

"She's not going to talk to you again. You will not try to contact her. Do you understand?"

"What if I like her pussy? What if it's not about crank? Maybe we'll go out sometime." He smiles.

"Are you high? She doesn't like dick."

"She sure seemed to like mine." I hit him again. His face is getting pretty messed up. "Hey, baby, it's cool if you want to join. I know you two have a little thing going on." This time I use the crowbar. That takes the smile off his face. "Fuck, bitch, would you quit hitting me?"

"You want me to stop hitting you?" I do it again. "Do you even remember who I am?" I hit him again. Blood sprays from somewhere this time. I know I need to hit the brakes before I kill this guy, but the rage is too much to contain. "Do you remember me?" I yell.

"Yes. I remember you."

"Then what the fuck makes you so goddamn sure I won't blow you away right now?" He doesn't answer. "If you can't keep your dick to yourself I will shoot it off, you hear me?"

"I hear you."

The second I say it I realize I want to shoot it off anyway. I don't want to threaten it, I want to just do it. He's already lost dick privileges. It's liberating to hate someone as completely as I hate Ice. I have no guilt. "Maybe I'll shoot it off anyway," I tell him.

"No." I finally hear some fear in his voice.

"Yeah, that's a good idea. I like that. What better revenge for what you did to me?"

"I'm sorry," he says.

"And it'll certainly take away your motivation to see Jaselle. I mean what do you need her for if you can't fuck her, right?"

"I won't fuck her again. I promise! I'm sorry!"

"Threaten your life, you don't blink. Threaten your dick, you turn into a little girl. Have you ever wondered if you're a sex addict?"

"Naw, I'm just an asshole."

"Wow, a little honesty."

"I'm sorry," he says. "I'm really sorry."

"So much for that."

"No, I'm for real. I'm—"

"Shut up. I didn't come here to hear you apologize. What did I tell you, Ice?"

"Don't fuck your girl," he says. I don't allow myself to think about that too thoroughly. I don't want him to see any pain.

"And?"

"Don't sell to your girl."

"That's right. I think that's reasonable, don't you?"

"Yeah."

"Do you doubt my psychosis?" I sang something like that in a song once. Funny how lyrics I wrote a long time ago are starting to make more and more sense to me now.

"Huh?"

"Do you doubt that I am fucking crazy enough to come over here and kill you if you fuck with me again?"

"Naw, man, I got you."

I hear a key slide into the lock in the front door. I take the gun from my waist again and point it at Ice. The doorknob turns. I don't know why I'm not more afraid, but I'm really not. The door swings open. Metal Mouth walks through. He stiffens when he takes in the display before him.

"Yo, man, what a grmm mash err?"

"I was just having a chat with Ice, but I think we're done now." I look to Ice.

"Yeah," he says. "We straight."

"Your gun will be in the mailbox. You can come get it after I'm gone." They both just stare at me. What can they say? I get up and walk past Metal Mouth. I watch for any sign he might try to grab me, but he doesn't move. I reach in and close the door behind me, leaving Ice bloody on the floor and Metal Mouth stupefied in the entry.

I walk straight down the driveway and put the gun in the mailbox like I promised, like honoring that will prove I mean what I say, and therefore make Ice think twice about retaliation. My heart rate skyrockets when I think about how real that possibility is, Ice coming after me. It starts to sink in how insane what I just did is, for so many reasons. I can hardly bear to even think about Jaselle I'm so furious and disgusted, yet here I am courting death in her name.

My mission is complete, but I still can't stomach going back to her. I can't deny she broke something. It's not the same, and I'm not sure it ever can be, or should be. She tore me in two, and the discarded piece feels like a lost limb. There's no bringing it back. It's just dead. What's left is the same as ever. I still love her as much as ever, but there's less of me.

None of that adds up to regret. Ice earned his punishment, and I need him to go away if Jaselle is going to have any hope of getting clean. I guess I have to hope I was convincing enough he doesn't try to kill me, or that it's just not worth it to him to step into the ring with me again.

CHAPTER TWENTY-FOUR

The first time I met Jayden he put gum in my hair. Now he's rubbing two quarters together between his fingers, trying to remember how to talk to me. I stare at his guitar in the corner wishing I could hear that heartache sound again.

"Do I even want to know why there's blood all over your hands?" he asks.

"Probably not."

The thing about friends you've known since you were in the sticking gum in someone you like's hair phase is that they have to let you in, even when they're mad at you, even when you're covered in someone else's blood.

"What are you doing here, Rainn?"

"I, uhh…" I struggle. What am I doing here? "I guess I just don't want to be around her right now," I say. "I'm coming up for air." I wish it had been Jayden who told me to do that instead of Benny so he would feel the impact.

"What'd she do to you this time? She hit you again? That why you're covered in blood? You get in a fight?" His stare is so cold. I feel like I'm fishing around trying to find him and pull him to the surface again. It feels exactly the way I feel with Jaselle most the time. I know you're in there. Come back. Be you again.

"Jayden, I know this may be too much to ask, but can you be nice to me? I really need you to be nice right now." I fight the tremor in my voice. I don't want to cry my way out of this. I know that's not fair. "You can be mean again after this if you want, but can you just be nice for a little bit? I need you."

He stares me down for a long time. I'm determined I won't be the one to break the silence. I've asked a question. I'll wait until he answers. Finally, he takes a deep sigh, and like it's the most painful thing he's ever done he opens his arms.

I hesitate for a second. I'm not sure if I want this this way after all. But who am I kidding, yeah, I do. I get out of my chair and sit next to him on the couch, filling up the space in his arms he's offered. He wraps his arms around me, soft at first, like he'd really rather not touch me, but soon it's back to his strong Jayden hug. He takes a deep breath and holds me, and I start crying.

I wish I was crying for him. I wish I was crying because of what I've done to our friendship, about what I've done to Alex and Shiloh and Benny. I'm sure he thinks that *is* why I'm crying. I'm sure he thinks this is a plea for forgiveness, missing the band I have yet to even ask about. And in a way, it is. In a way, I'm crying for him. I'm crying that I hurt him. I'm crying that I know I won't stop. I'm crying in relief that he still loves me. I'm crying in dread that he still loves me.

But if I'm being honest, I'm also crying for me. I'm crying for Jaselle. I'm crying for what she's done to me, at the images that are on loop in my brain. I'm crying about Ice. I'm crying that life went this way, that I don't know how to break free of this net I'm tangled in.

"What did she do?" he asks again.

"I don't really want to talk about Jaselle."

"Are you guys still together?"

"Yeah."

"Whose blood is this?" he asks.

"No one important."

He scoffs. "So you don't want to talk about Jaselle, and you don't want to talk about whose blood you're covered in. What should we talk about?"

"Who says we need to talk?"

He sighs and squeezes me harder like he understands. I just want to sit here. I just want the quiet. He ends it too soon. Why can no one just shut up? For five minutes?

"Rainn?"

"Yeah?"

"I love you."

"I love you too."

His hand slides under my chin, and he pulls me up to face him. His lips land softly on mine. He just barely touches me and pulls away. His stare gets intense. I instinctively break it, but the second I do his hand moves to my cheek, much more demanding, and he kisses me again. I pull back. His mouth is hot, chasing mine, determined he'll overcome my decision, but I put my hand on his chest and push him back. It's just as easy as I always thought it would be, stopping him.

"Why do you do this to us?" he asks. "Why do you resist it? We're supposed to be together."

"Jayden, I am going to say this one time, and I want you to really listen to me. I am gay."

"I'm so much better for you than she is. You know I'd take care of you. I would never hurt you, Rainn."

"Of course you didn't listen."

"You're not gay," he says. "If you're gay why do I feel this way?"

"I said *I'm* gay, not *you're* gay."

"But I can feel that you love me too. I can feel it. We don't have a friendship, Rainn, we have a relationship minus the sex."

"I could not disagree with you more. What we have is the definition of a friendship."

"You're not understanding what I'm trying to say."

"No, I understand." I know this will hurt him, which is the last thing I want to do right now, but this conversation is overdue. "You're saying we have the chemistry of a relationship and that we have romantic feelings for each other, we just haven't acted on them."

He doesn't say anything.

"It's not true, Jay. I do love you. I love the shit out of you, and I will always care what happens to you, but we are close friends, nothing more. We used to pick up girls together, for God's sake. Does that sound like a date-type activity to you?"

"I wanted to take you home," he says.

"You looked just fine with your skanks."

"And that bothered you. You were jealous. Does that sound like a friend-type emotion to you?"

"I was jealous because I wanted your time, not your dick. I wanted to write songs with you and play music."

"Wow, that's sure changed."

I look at the ground. "I'm sorry, Jay."

"You remember Isaiah?"

I roll my eyes. Why does this name keep getting thrown in my face? I swear to God, you have sex with a guy and everyone assumes you liked it. "Of course, I remember."

"You remember that night he fucked you up and I came and got you?"

"Yes."

"What happened that night? What'd he do?"

"I told you. He beat the shit out of me," I say.

"Why?"

"He was wasted and thought I was cheating on him."

"And?" Jayden presses.

"And when we started fighting about it I wouldn't back down. I called him some names. He slapped me. I hit him back. It escalated. Jayden, you know all of this already. What is your point?"

"He didn't beat the shit out of you because he thought you cheated. He beat the shit out of you because you mouthed off. That's what you told me. You fought back, and his women weren't supposed to do that so he beat you until you couldn't fight back."

"Yeah, I was there."

He sighs. "My point is that I know guys have done some shitty things to you, Rainn. I know why you don't like guys. I know your dad wasn't there for you because he killed himself. I know you were raped. I know Isaiah treated you like his slave. But I don't want to be that guy. I've never been that guy. I'm the guy who picks you off the bathroom floor and fixes you up. I'm the guy who takes care of you. I'm the guy who's always there."

"I know you're that guy. But you're still a guy. And if you think the reason I don't like men is because they've done shitty things to me then by that logic I should just be asexual, because women have done some bullshit to me too."

"Why are you with Jaselle? I want to know." His eyes flare with anger.

"You already know. I love her."

"But she treats you like shit. I don't know what she did, but I know she did something. You don't have to tell me what it was, but please don't insult my intelligence by saying you guys are fine."

"We're not, but I still love her."

"She's killing you both!" he yells.

"You don't abandon someone because they have a problem."

"You aren't helping her by being there. You're just watching her die. And I'm watching you die watching her die."

"I'm not leaving her to deal with this alone. She won't make it."

"You can't save her!" he screams.

"I can!"

"It's too late, Rainn!"

Flashing lights seize my brain. I choke on fumes and Jayden's voice. My lungs are bleeding. "Just like Michael, right?"

"Don't you dare compare them!"

"Why not? I could have saved him, and I will save Jaselle. Don't fucking tell me I can't. Last time you said that someone died."

"Last time I said that someone was already dead. How could you have saved him?"

I'm stuck in my head. Blue. Red. Blue. Yellow. Clear!

"How could you have saved him, Rainn? You were going to raise him from the dead?"

"No. Before that."

"How?"

"Shut up, Jayden. Shut up!"

"You're acting insane. There's nothing you could have done. It was just the way the cards were dealt. There was—"

"I could have kept him away from you!"

He recoils. "What the fuck did you just say to me?"

"Jayden, I'm sorry."

"Get out."

"I shouldn't have said it. I—"

"Get out!"

"You know what? Fuck it. It's true. You were the one who taught him how to do it. You were the one who gave him the idea. 'Try it, Michael, it feels so good. You'll love it.'" I start crying. I know I'm losing Jay forever, but I've had this on my chest way too long.

"That's what you think of me?" he says.

"It's not an opinion, Jayden, it's a fact. You sprayed the paint in the bag. You put that butane in his hand. You taught him that and it killed him! And you know what? It's my fault. I saw you doing it and I knew it was wrong and dangerous and I let you do it anyway. I accept that, okay? I know it's my fault, but look in the mirror. It's yours too. My little brother is dead, Jayden! So fucking shoot me if I don't want to lose anyone else."

Chapter Twenty-five

M y tongue hurts," Michael says.
I hear the sound of his voice but not the words. I'm too focused on Jim Morrison's voice seeping through the speakers. It's like overhearing an intimate moment happening in the apartment next door.

"Rainn." Michael throws a pen at me. I look up. "I said my tongue hurts." What a strange complaint.

"You want a Popsicle?"

He shakes his head. "Forget it. Let's just go."

We grab our skateboards and go to meet Jayden and Shiloh at the bridge. We get there before they do and just sit by the water. It's a pretty small stream, but ducks float by sometimes. It's big enough for a bridge, I guess, although the bridge is old and probably isn't safe anymore. Whatever it was built for is long gone now, so we're the only ones who ever come over here. It's quiet and peaceful, and perfect for songwriting. It's also perfect for anything you don't want to be caught doing since no one will find you.

Jayden and Shiloh arrive, Jayden with his guitar slung over his shoulder, Shiloh with his bass. Michael has his drumsticks. He sets up some rocks to hit with them, testing the sounds they make and choosing a couple of his favorites. We mess around playing music for hours. Most of it is complete garbage, but it's fun.

Jayden breaks out some beer and a bottle of butane you would use to refill lighters. "Here, everyone have a whiff of this." He holds out the yellow bottle for me. I pour some out on a rag and inhale it, as is expected. I feel it burning the inside of my esophagus. Another breath in and it's pulled into my lungs. I choke, cough, but clean air doesn't ease the feeling.

"One more," Jayden recommends. I take another, and he's right. You take a little of the chemical in and it hurts. It chokes you. It makes your eyes water. Take a little more and you're too high to notice. I pass it to Shiloh and fall to my back. My muscles won't do anything. I'm outside myself. I don't think I can come back if I want to.

The thing about huffing is that it's fun for a few seconds, a few minutes, no not a few hours, not even one hour. It fades, and you end up doing it again, and again. So we ride it out, drink some beer for a while, sing for a while, then start over. It's about two in the morning when we throw our last empty beer bottles at the bridge wall and watch them shatter. Why do we destroy the things we love, littering our favorite little piece of nature with broken glass?

I wrap my arm around Michael's neck and pretend to be drunk enough to need his support. He laughs and does it right back. "Rainn?" he says.

"Yeah?"

"My tongue still hurts. Why does my tongue hurt?"

"You been licking too much pussy?" Jayden asks. I'm irritated at the interruption. Michael's question had been practically whispered to me and obviously wasn't intended to be a joke. I smack Jayden's chest and wish he would go away.

"Don't worry, Michael, big sis can give you some advice on that," he says. I flip him off and shoot him a look I hope conveys that I sincerely want him to burst into flames right now. Jayden holds up his hands innocently and goes to terrorize Shiloh.

"I don't know why your tongue hurts, man. Is it bad?" I ask.

"I don't know. It's just weird, I guess. Your tongue never hurts, does it?"

"No."

"Hey. You ever miss Dad?" he asks.

"Uh, no." The question throws me off. "Why would I? I never met the guy."

"Yeah, you did. He held you when you were a baby and stuff."

I laugh. "I'm not sure that counts."

"More than I got."

Dad killed himself while mom was still pregnant with Michael. I was two.

"What do you think is worse?" Michael asks. "Having your dad not even care about meeting you or having him meet you and still not care enough to want to know you?"

"I think it's about the same," I say and rustle his hair.

"I love you, Rainn." His words slur together just the slightest bit. I smile and figure he's pretty messed up. He holds his mutilated lighter up to his nose and sniffs. I start to tell him I love him too, but his head slips out from under my arm as his knees buckle and he hits the ground. Jayden and Shiloh think he tripped or something and are laughing, but I know something is wrong right away.

I kneel down and turn him over on his back. His eyes are closed. His breaths are labored and irregular. "Michael?" I shake him. He wheezes pitifully. I can tell his attempts to breathe are absolutely useless, like a fish trying to breathe air. "Michael!" My scream stops Jayden and Shiloh's laughing and they run over.

I put my head on his chest and listen. I can't hear his heartbeat or a lack of one over his fruitless breaths. "Call someone!" I yell. The wheezing stops, a slow exhale and silence. "Michael!" There are chemicals in my throat, burning their way through, acid chewing through my organs. I can't breathe. I hear Jayden, frantic on the phone.

"I don't know what's wrong! He just fell down and he's not breathing. I think he's fucking dying, man! Get up here!"

My pulse is pounding in my ear. I open Michael's mouth and breathe into it. I try to remember that fucking health class I took, but the only visual I get is of Sasha Walter's cleavage. All I did that entire course was flirt with her. Fuck, Rainn, think.

I try to listen to his heart again to decide if I should do chest compressions or not. Compressions? Is that right? Focus. Jayden is panicking too.

"I don't know, we're not on a road! We're by a bridge, sort of."

Five chest compressions, two breaths. Wait, is it five? Or Fifteen? Shit, I can't fucking remember.

"I don't know what it's called! We drove here on Willow Street and then walked a mile or something."

One, two, three, four, five, center of his chest? A little to the left but not far? Compressions. Compressions? Two deep breaths, hold his nose. Shouldn't it feel like my breath is actually going somewhere? Like, into him?

"Guys, what direction from the road did we walk?" Jayden screams, then into the phone. "Hold the fuck on, I'm trying!"

Where are the mountains? We walked away from the mountains, that's east, but not directly away, away and to the left. Which direction is left of east? Never Eat Soggy Wheat.

"Northeast."

"Northeast," Jayden says, and I know this is taking too long. I slow down and try to do this right instead of just in a panic. One, two, three, four, five. Yes, compressions is right. Five doesn't seem like enough though. Maybe I'll do more, but the lack of breathing seems paramount. This whole thing is way too imprecise. I have this hole in my stomach that knows this isn't working. Hold his nose, two breaths. I exhale into him slowly, sealing the gaps carefully, and I feel his chest expand a little. I do it again. And again. I'm starting to feel dizzy. Again. Where are they? Again. Are they even coming? Again. Black speckles are making it hard to see. Again. Tears are making it hard to breathe. Again. Jayden grabs my shoulders. Again. I muscle through his gentle pull.

"Rainn," he says.

Again.

"Rainn." His voice is barely audible through his tears.

Again.

"Rainn, he's gone."

Again.

"You can't save him, Rainn."

Again.

"It's too late."

It takes the ambulance an hour to find us. They yank me away from Michael and try to work on him. A guy with soft eyes and gray hair puts a blanket around me. He tries to ask me what happened, but I can't speak. The ambulance lights are overpowering in the moonless night. Blue. Red. Blue. Yellow.

"Clear!"

I figure I'll hear them do that several more times, but they don't. Just once.

I lie down in the grass. It's moist like it's rained only it hasn't. It soaks through my clothes. I don't care. Jayden comes over and lies with me. I wish he wouldn't. Shiloh comes over and lies with us. I let him wrap his arms around me.

Too quick, they're asking us to get up. The ambulance has already left with Michael, but cops are here now, asking for statements. I'm still underage by a few months, so they take me home, to my mother.

Just seeing me standing in her doorway between two police officers is enough to send her into a tirade about how all I ever do is cause problems. The cops cut her off pretty fast to tell her about Michael, using words like "asphyxiation," holding a hand in front of me like I don't deserve to be yelled at right now. My mother couldn't agree less.

She's about to boil over, but she knows she has to let the cops leave first. I slightly consider pushing her over the edge so they can see what a psycho she is. Maybe they'll reconsider leaving me in her care. But I don't. I think I want what's coming to me.

My mother, ever the class act, invites the cops in, but they refuse, saying they understand we probably need to be alone. Boy, is that an understatement. The second she closes the door she slaps me as hard as she can. She then has to hold her aching wrist, subtly behind her back like she doesn't want me to know she's hurt herself. My ear is ringing.

Her eyes are watering, and she just looks at me with the most hateful stare I've ever seen. "You were supposed to protect him," she says. I don't say anything. I can't say anything. "He was your little brother. You were supposed to help him grow, not drag him into the gutter." I'm paralyzed. It's true. "Are you listening to me?" I make eye contact to show that I am, but I still can't speak. "You killed him," she says.

"No."

"Yes, you did."

"No. I didn't mean to."

"Obviously you didn't care. You've never cared about anything but yourself."

"I loved him!"

"Then why did you do this to him?" she screams. Her eyes are bloodshot. "He did every damn thing you did. If you and your idiot friends had never gotten to him he would be alive right now! You killed him! You killed my baby boy!"

"No! I didn't mean to!"

"Did you have fun getting high, *Rainn*?" That's the first time she's called me that. "Was it worth it?"

Something snaps in me. "Maybe if you weren't such a bitch he wouldn't have wanted to get high! He was trying to drown *you* out!"

"You better watch yourself," she warns me.

"No, fuck you. All he wanted was to be himself and you acted like there was something wrong with that. You rejected who he really was. That's why he ran away from you. You think you're such a good fucking parent just because you threw money at his education? All you had to do was listen to him. I don't want to play the violin anymore. That's it! That's all he asked of you, don't make me play the violin anymore. How hard is that? Was *that* worth it, Mother?"

She winds up to slap me again. I push her so that she misses. Fury lights up her eyes, and she's so desperate to hurt me her arms start going wild. "You are a useless, evil piece of trash! You are not my daughter!"

Her sweet Chanel perfume washes over me, and I realize I will never again associate it with her tucking me in at night. It will forever be this moment now. "Yeah, I know, Mom. I know you fucking hate me. You always have. You've always loved Michael and hated me."

"You are an ungrateful, spoiled, selfish little girl." Her hand is on my face, pushing. I don't know what she's trying to do exactly, just hurt me. My fingers are weaved through her hair, and I'm pulling as hard as I can. It feels like straw from too much bleach.

"I hate you!" I scream.

Somehow we both know it's time to let go. We give each other a hard shove and detach. "Get out of my house," she says. "Now. And never come back." She pushes me again, toward the door now. "Go!"

I couch hop for a month, crashing with each of my friends for a night or two at a time. When I run out of friends I start at the beginning again. Everyone is a little extra lenient because they know about Michael, but sympathy doesn't go as far as you think it will. I know I can't keep this up. I know there's an easy answer. I don't feel ready yet, but I bend.

I take my bag and walk to the apartment that used to house all of us, Jayden, Shiloh, me, and Michael. I don't know how I'll look in his room, but I have nowhere else to go. I haven't spoken to the guys since it happened. I don't know how they're doing, but I'm surprised when I get to the door and hear music coming from inside.

When I open the door, the music pours out. Jayden's sound is unmistakable, his guitar cries. I walk down the hall. Shiloh is playing bass. I turn the corner to the living room. Some guy with a scruffy face wearing a wifebeater is playing drums. I heat up from the core. He's not just playing drums. He's playing Michael's drums. Jayden and Shiloh spot me and stop immediately. They look petrified.

"Rainn." Jayden starts to take off his guitar so he can come hug me. I'm not interested.

"Who the fuck is that?"

"He's, uh…" Jayden scratches his head.

"I'm Alex," the guy on drums says. "It's really nice to meet you. The guys say you're an amazing singer."

"Who the fuck is that?" I ask Jayden again.

"He's Alex."

"Jayden." I stare into him, daring him to tell me.

"He's our new drummer."

"The fuck he is. Get out!" I scream at Alex.

"Rainn, he's good," Shiloh says.

"I don't give a shit. Get him off my little brother's drums right now." I storm toward Alex, smacking a mic stand intended for me over on the way. Did they think I was just going to jump in and sing? Did they think this would be okay?

Jayden tries to grab my arm. "We would have asked you, but we didn't know where you were. We have to keep playing. Michael would want us to keep playing."

I pull my arm out of Jayden's grasp and smack him, then push Alex as hard as I can, square in the chest. He topples backward off the drum stool. His head hits the wall so hard he puts a hole in it. Shiloh rushes over like he thinks he might have to restrain Alex from attacking me, but Alex just holds up his hand that he's okay.

"Hey, I didn't know these were his," Alex says. "I'm sorry."

"Whose did you think they were, asshole? He was our drummer!"

"I'm sorry," he says, holding his hands up like I might attack again. "I won't touch them again. Ever, okay? I'm sorry."

I spin on Jayden. "You think you can just replace him?" I turn to look at Shiloh too. I wish they were standing on the same side of the room so I could scream at them simultaneously. "You think you can just give some other guy his drumsticks and the beats and everything will be cool?"

"You know that's not what we think," Shiloh says.

"Well, that's what this looks like. You know what? Replace me too. I'm sure it won't be hard for you."

I leave the apartment. It's snowing now. I walk until I can't feel anymore. I walk until I'm numb. I walk until I can't see their faces, until Jayden and Shiloh are gone, until Alex is gone, until my mother is gone, until the guy with gray hair is gone, until the flashing lights are gone, until Michael is gone.

I turn down a quiet little passage behind some buildings. I lay down on the wet asphalt that's just starting to collect snow. I hold my arms out to my sides. Look, Mom, I'm an angel. Look at the snow angel. A pair of shoes is strung over a telephone wire, silhouetted by the nearest glowing streetlight. The snow blurs the light to yellow. My tears blur the blob to streaks.

A door beside me opens. Music streams out. A guy walks right past me with a bag of trash in one hand and a cigarette in his mouth. When he turns to go back inside he sees me.

"Whoa, whoa. What are you doing? There's no dying allowed here." There's a smile in his voice. Does he think this is funny? Next thing I know there's a big friendly face entering my view. "You all right, there? You on something?"

I shake my head.

"Drunk?"

"No."

"Looks like you ought to be. You want to come in?"

"I'm seventeen." He only hears "seventeen," or maybe he just pretends that's all he hears. I can't be sure.

"No, it's worse than that, negative three. You're out of your mind, and in short sleeves? Come on, let's go in. I'll get you a hot chocolate." He grabs my arms and starts to pull me up. At first, I'm being difficult, but then I realize I actually can't stand up. My legs hurt too bad from the cold.

"Come on, sweetie," he says. "It'll be okay."

"No, it won't." I feel lightheaded. I'm almost completely limp in his strong supportive grasp.

"Come on now, stay with me," he says. "What's your name?"

"Rainn."

"Rainn? That's pretty. I'm Benny."

Chapter Twenty-six

The blood on my hands from Ice has dried and is a dark brown color by the time I get home. I go straight to the bathroom to shower. I run the water as hot as it will go and just let the steam suffocate me. I take off my clothes and stare at myself in the mirror.

"Are you okay?" Jaselle surprises me. She doesn't usually get up when I come home anymore, just waits for me. I guess she's worried about us still.

"I'm fine." My voice is croaky. Jaselle comes in and closes the door. She walks over and wraps her arms around my waist and kisses my shoulder.

"Is this blood?" she asks. I nod. "Are you okay?" I nod again. She takes off her clothes and gently pulls me toward the shower. "It's going to get cold soon," she says. I let her pull me inside. She starts washing the caked blood off me. I watch the colored water disappear down the drain.

"You're not high," I whisper. It takes me until now to realize I'm surprised by that.

"No." She kisses my collarbone. The water is still all the way on hot. I wonder if her skin is tingling from it the way mine is. "You know what I hate the most about doing crank?" she asks.

"Uh, withdrawing when you don't have it?"

"No."

"Not having enough money for it?"

"No."

"Waiting for drug dealers?"

"No."

"Fighting with me about it?"

"No." We both start laughing a little.

"Okay, okay. What?"

"It makes me forget how fucking beautiful you are." Part of me melts. The other part sarcastically remarks that it's a wonder she's still with me then, since she's been high for the majority of our relationship. I'm trying to say that out loud, to remain hard to her, to protect myself for once, but she kisses me and I just can't. The fireworks don't go off in my chest like they used to, but I just can't hate her.

She touches my face, and I give in to the kiss. She's so different when she's not high. She's gentle. I can feel the love, not just the lust. I want to want more. I try to want more. I hold her, running my hands down her back and kiss her deeper. She moves her hand down and touches me.

I close my eyes and grab her hand. She parts the kiss. I can see the pain in her face. I don't think I've ever stopped her before, no matter what was going on, no matter how mad I was. When she started touching me, I forgot. She thinks this means it's over, that I've shut off completely and forever.

I touch her face, make her look at me, and kiss her again. "Not yet," I say. It hurts too much still. I see you with him still. She nods like she understands. I think she actually does. Even though I'm saying no, I feel like we have a better chance of moving past this, legitimately. I'm dealing with it. And she's dealing with it. It's not just being shoved aside out of fear of losing her. And she's not high. She's feeling it.

"I love you," I say. I figure telling her that will go a long way. Let's face it, this beautiful, sweet Jaselle who remembers she loves me may not be here tomorrow. She could be sick again tomorrow. She could tell me she's dying again tomorrow. She needs to know she's not alone.

"I love you," she says.

We get out of the shower and go to bed. I hold her as I'm drifting off. I know I'll only get a little sleep. She squeezes my hand every few minutes, or pulls so that my arm is around her tighter. I haven't felt her so aware and concerned about me since the beginning.

❖

A thunderous crash makes me jump a foot off the bed. Through the window I can see it's still dark, middle of the night type dark. I hear footsteps. Someone is in the house. Jaselle is awake but frozen stiff. I grab an iron fire poker Jaselle has by the bed. They don't even have a fireplace, so I guess it's here for this exact reason.

I go to the bedroom door and start to shut it, intending to lock it, but Ice is a second too fast. He kicks the door before I can get it to latch. It slams into me and knocks me over. He walks right past me, followed by Metal Mouth and Short Shit. None of them even look at me. Ice and Metal Mouth grab Jaselle's arms. She tries to swat them away, but she's nowhere near strong enough. Short Shit goes to grab her feet. She kicks him in the face. Ice slaps her and Short Shit wrangles her legs in. They pick her up.

I shake off the hit from the door and stand up. I don't bother saying anything, just swing the fire iron at Short Shit as hard as I can, fully aware that if I connect with his head it will probably kill him.

He has to drop Jaselle's feet to dodge it. I swing again, intending for Metal Mouth this time, but Short Shit tackles me. He punches me and pins my arms beneath his knees. He's a lot stronger than he looks. He hits me repeatedly. I taste blood in my mouth.

"Knock her out, man," Ice yells.

"I'm trying." He keeps punching me. I'm determined I'll stay conscious, but every time I lift my head he hits me and I'm getting weak, so when he does, the back of my head smacks down against the floor. I can't move my arms. I have absolutely no way to defend myself.

A flash of colors knocks Short Shit off of me. I look over and Noah, clad in his bathrobe as always, is fighting with Short Shit. I turn over and spit a mouthful of blood out and grab the fire iron again. Ice finally pulls out his gun.

"That's enough!"

Noah doesn't notice and punches Short Shit again. "Hey!" Ice screams and points the gun at Jaselle. "I said that's enough." Noah looks over and sees the gun finally. He reluctantly gets off of Short Shit.

"Put it down," Ice yells at me. I drop the fire iron. "In the living room."

We all file out obediently. Ice stays glued to Jaselle, keeping the gun against her head. I cringe at him touching her. The long cut across his face from where I took a crowbar to it is cleaned up now, sewn shut with stitches. Is this revenge?

"Sit down," Ice says and pushes Jaselle into the chair. "You two don't move," he says to Noah and me. He looks back at Jaselle. "You got two minutes to give me the money."

"What the fuck is this about?" I ask, realizing it's clearly not about me after all.

"Shut the fuck up, bitch," Short Shit yells. He bounds forward and slaps me.

I push him back. "Do I look scared of you?" I scream. Now that I know this is about money I know Ice won't shoot. Not yet. "Do I look scared of you?" I say again.

He grabs my throat and comes closer to my face. "You better get scared, little girl, or I'll make you mine again to remind you."

"Hey," Ice yells. "Get back over here, stupid." Short Shit releases my throat and does as he's told. "You got it or what? Time's up. Derek won't wait anymore."

I can barely hear Jaselle answer. "I don't have it."

"What does she owe?" I ask.

"I said shut up. This ain't about you," Short Shit yells.

"Five thousand," Ice says. My breath stops in my chest. How did she get so far in debt? I busted my ass to get her what she needed. I guess she was always asking for more money, but beyond what I could find in the streets, I didn't want to hear it. There were plenty of times she asked and I couldn't provide, and when she didn't press I certainly didn't. It went away. That's what I wanted, right?

All the different times are pouring into my mind now. She'd go out, and she'd come back feeling better. And I thought…what? What did I think? That she got some from friends? That she stole things and sold them? Traded them? That she just waited it out until I could give her some money again? Who am I kidding? And when they cut her off? When they wouldn't front her any more, that's when she sold herself to Ice?

"Five thousand dollars?" I repeat.

"Five thousand," Ice says.

"I need time," I whisper.

"Time's up, baby girl," Short Shit says.

"I need some time. I'll find it. I'll figure it out." I'm already searching my brain for how to do this. Beg Benny and the guys? They hate her. They won't do it. Lie to them? Steal? Sell *my*self? Throw myself before my mother? Nothing is too absurd to consider with Jaselle looking down a barrel.

"Oh, look at her think," Short Shit says. "I think we got some free blowjobs comin', fellas."

"I'm sure there's something we can figure out," I say, sick to my stomach. "I need time. Tell me what I have to do to get you guys to give me time."

"Rainn, no," Jaselle says.

"Time's up," Ice says.

"Tell me what you want!" I scream.

"She's had her warning," Ice says.

"What?"

"There's nothing you can do. She's had her warning," Ice says quietly. "It's too late." I see him pistol whipping Jaselle, demanding the money. I see her black eye. I feel her shaking by the door, thinking they'd come. Ice cocks the gun. I jump in front of Jaselle, putting myself between her and the gun, and I push Ice's arm away.

"Wait!" I scream and start crying, knowing I have nothing to offer them. I have nothing. I am nothing.

"You got to get out of the way," Ice says.

"No, fuck you. You can give me time. I know you can."

"I can't. I'm sorry."

"Rainn," Jaselle says. I turn and look at her. She looks so calm. "Rainn, move," she says. I go and kneel in front of her and kiss her.

"No."

"This isn't your fault. I'm so sorry, Rainn," she says. "I love you."

I can tell that was meant to be her good-bye "I love you." I refuse to participate in that. "I'm not moving."

"Then we'll just shoot you both, stupid," Short Shit says. It was supposed to be a threat, but if they end up shooting Jaselle in front of me tonight I *do* want to go with her. What will I have if she's gone? Who will I be if I fail to protect the person I love most again? If my everything dies in my arms *again*. It can't happen. No. An idea finally clicks.

"I want to talk to Derek."

"Mann, nawboddy talks uh Derk," Metal Mouth says.

"He wants his money, right?"

"'Course he does," Ice says.

"I imagine he wants his money more than he wants a body."

"Yeah, but you ain't got it," Short Shit says.

"I can get it. I know how to get it."

"I told you you're out of time."

"Get him on the phone," I say. "You're not going to be allowed to make this decision. I need him on the phone."

"Man, you trying to get my ass kicked? I can't go calling Derek over nothing 'cause some chick is in love. That's why he sends us to do this shit, okay? He doesn't want to hear the nonsense. Everybody says they'll figure it out. No one does," Ice says.

"It's not nonsense. You get him on the phone, and I swear to you I will make this interesting enough you won't get in trouble."

I can see Ice debating it out in his head. I know Derek wants his money. I know he wants it bad. I know Ice probably already got in trouble for letting Jaselle get so far into debt. He should have cut her off a long time ago. He'd rather have the money than a body too.

"Get him on the phone," I say. "Please." That word tastes so bad. How many times will I have to beg these assholes? "Please!"

"All right, man. But I swear to God if you're trying to set me up I'll kill you both."

"You're still the one with the gun."

He reaches in his pocket and pulls out his phone.

"Man, what are you doing?" Short Shit complains.

"Derek," Ice says into the phone. "I'm at the house—" He's interrupted. "No, everything is fine. We got her here. But there's a chick here says she has an interesting offer for you." My heart pounds while I wait to see if Derek will even be interested enough to talk to me. "No, man, I said everything is fine. I can blow her away any time you want. She just—"

Ice nods and hands me the phone. I put the phone to my ear, and like Derek knows the second I can hear him he says, "This better be good."

"I have an antique Baldwin grand piano."

He starts laughing. "You think it'll look good next to my stripper pole?"

"It's worth eight grand, minimum. You give me a week to sell it, and you can have it all."

He pauses for a second. "You're going to overpay me?"

"Yes. I'm going to overpay you for the time you've already waited and for the week I'll need to sell it."

"That's a pretty good offer. Almost makes me think you're up to something."

"The piano is here. You can have your boys look at it if you want."

"I'm sure the piano is there, but even if my boys did know a goddamn thing about pricing antique pianos it wouldn't mean you're planning on selling it. How do I know you aren't going to run?"

"Isn't that what you do, sir? Track down people who rip you off and kill them?"

"It's what I'm doing right now, as a matter of fact," he says.

"Then with all due respect, I don't know what you're worried about. Either I do what I say and you come out of this with a lot more money, or you come kill us and it all works out the same."

"Give the phone back to Gerard." I figure that's Ice's real name and hand the phone back, making an internal note to laugh about that when this is over.

"Yes, sir," Ice says and clicks the flip phone shut. "Let's go."

Noah looks stunned. I smile and take a deep breath.

"What the fuck, dude?" Short Shit screams.

"I said let's go," Ice says.

"Ah, man, you are such a pussy. You shouldn't have even called him. Let's at least have some fun with them first." He starts walking toward me. Out of nowhere, Ice's fist connects and sends Short Shit to the ground. He looks at me deliberately, like he's trying to tell me something. That he really is sorry, maybe? That's he's not such a bad guy? Do guys like Ice have those kinds of awakenings?

He writes something on a piece of paper and hands it to me. "Call me when you have the money." He turns around. "Get up," he says to Short Shit, and they leave. Jaselle, Noah, and I all stay exactly where we are, like we're frozen here until we hear the door close. Then we take a collective breath. Jaselle gets out of the chair and comes over to me. She wipes tears away from her eyes. "I'm sorry." I just wrap my arms around her and kiss her head.

"It's just a piano. And then we're done with them."

I look at Noah. I'm waiting for him to go off, but he doesn't. "You okay?" he asks us both. We nod.

"You?" I ask.

He examines his bloody knuckles and shrugs. "Yeah, pretty much."

I smile. "Savage."

Chapter Twenty-seven

It's not just a piano. It's the most beautiful piano ever made. It is my soul mate. It is my companion. It is the only thing that knows my every secret. It is my doorway to the past. It is my window to the future. It is the language of angels. It is worth $9,459 to a guy named Travis who owns a restoration shop. Thinking about Travis "restoring" my piano makes me want to eat battery acid for breakfast.

But Jaselle is safe. That's what matters. And she still hasn't used. I think she knows she can't now, not after what just happened. So even though I cry when I watch Travis take the piano, I really am happy. Even though I have to see Ice one more time to give him the money, I know this is over.

I figure I should make the most of the positive energy that's going around, so I take a walk down to the Cuff Link. My stomach twists as I stare at the building. Do I have what it takes to show my face here and convince this man to give the band I'm not even an official member of anymore another chance? He doesn't need to know they kicked me out. When I set this right, they'll take me back. They'll remember who I am. I can be her again. I take a deep breath and open the door.

"Hello," Jimmy says from behind the bar. "I'm Jimmy."

"I know who you are, Jimmy. We've spoken several times."

His eyes roll up in his head while he tries to remember me. "Water?"

I smile. It's so good to be recognized. "That's right."

"Brad, water girl is here," Jimmy says.

"Who?" Brad calls from the back.

Jimmy turns back to me. "I'm sorry, sweetie, I don't know your real name."

"Rainn." I half consider giving a fake name. I don't know how mad Brad is I wasn't at the Chapel on the fifteenth.

"It's Rainn," Jimmy says.

Brad comes out in a huff. "You got some nerve," he says.

"Hear me out."

"Standing me up after the way you begged me to come see you."

"I'm sorry," I say. "I'm not going to lie to you; I didn't think you were coming."

"Did we or did we not make an appointment?"

"Yes, we did."

"Here's the thing, Rainn, even if you are as good as you say you are, I can't have unreliable people working for me. I need a band in here when they're scheduled. I make posters and shit. I advertise on the radio. I can't tell everyone to come and see the Suicidal Angels and then not provide the Suicidal Angels. You get what I'm saying?"

I'm just impressed he remembers my band's name. "Yes, I get you, Brad."

"So, what are you doing here, then? You know I can't possibly hire you now, right?"

"Brad, come on, you have to be kidding. How many times did you stand me up?" I ask.

"I'm a busy man."

"Then don't make appointments you can't keep."

"I was trying to do you a favor, kid. I was trying to work you in. Shit happens." Brad turns to Jimmy and asks for a shot.

"Exactly. Shit happens. You've told me that at least ten times. You stood me up and you kept saying 'shit happens, shit happens.' Well, shit happened to me, Brad. I need another chance."

"Shit happens to managers, not to musicians."

"No, shit happens every week to managers and once to musicians. Come on, Brad, you know I'm good. I know you know I'm good. Just come down and see us. Any night of the week, you name it. It doesn't have to be a weekend. I know Saturdays are hard for you."

"Saturdays are a real bitch," Brad says.

"Yeah, so come down during the week, whenever you can."

"I'll be there tonight."

"What?"

"Or do you have shit that needs to happen tonight?"

"No! No, tonight is good. Zero shit happening. I'll see you tonight, Brad." I jump on him and kiss his cheek before he can stop me, then run out the door. I call Jaselle from a pay phone.

"He's coming to see us tonight!"

"That's great, baby."

"So, I have to go get my band back, and then I pretty much have to go set up. Can you come down?" What if it isn't as easy as just getting them back? What if they have another singer? I don't let myself dwell on it.

"I don't know, babe. I'm not really feeling well." I can hear that in her voice the second I calm down enough to listen.

"Are you okay?"

"I'll be fine."

She's been sick off and on ever since she's been clean. Mostly exhaustion, headaches, and depression. Her body is still trying to recover. I always get super nervous when she's going through bad spurts of it. I know it breaks people all the time. "Are you sure? The guys can probably set up. I can come home for a little while at least." That's a dangerous idea. If I go home and she gets into a bad episode, it will be almost impossible to leave, but I'll have to. I can't miss this again. But I can't let her relapse either, not now.

"Rainn, I'm not going to use. I promise. I want you to go have fun and don't worry about me. I'm just going to bed."

It's exactly what I need to hear. I soak in the relief. Things are different, finally. "Okay, but if it gets bad call me at the bar, okay? Or call Noah. Just, call someone."

"Okay."

"I love you so much."

"I love you, Rainn."

The walk to the guys' apartment feels longer than usual. I don't know if it's because I'm not used to walking so much anymore or if it's because I'm excited to tell them about Brad, and terrified to show my face. Finally, the right thing to do comes to me. If they have another singer already and they don't want me back, then the new Suicidal Angels, the one without Rainn, will still perform tonight for Brad. I owe them that whether I get to be part of it or not. I'll be closer to earning back friends at least, if not my band. That's what matters.

Shiloh answers the door. The edges of his mouth twitch when he sees me. "Hey," I say. It's a little hard not to smile. Even if he hates me I can't wait to see him happy.

"Hey."

"Can I come in?"

He turns around and walks away. I guess that means yes. I come in and lock the door. Alex is lying on the couch upside down twirling a drumstick. Shiloh and Jayden were playing video games, but it's paused from Shiloh answering the door. Alex tilts his head a little to look at me. It almost looks like he's interested in what I'm doing here, almost.

"Can I talk to you guys for a minute?" No one answers. "Come on, please?"

"Talk," Jayden says.

"Okay. Could you sit together or something? At least turn off the game?"

Jayden turns off the entire TV and spins around so he's looking at me. Shiloh turns around too but looks like he's only doing it because Jayden did. Alex lets his feet flop down on the couch so now he's sideways instead of upside down. It's an improvement, I guess.

"I know I fucked up, guys," I say.

"Yeah, you really did," Alex blurts.

"I know I hurt your feelings."

"Hella bad, dude," Alex says.

"I know it probably seems like I don't give a shit."

"That's exactly what it seems like."

"Dude, shut up for a minute," Shiloh says to Alex.

"I just want you guys to know that I really love you. I guess our friendship is just so solid I knew you would always be there, and maybe I took advantage of that. I didn't realize how much of an ass I was being until it was way too late."

"You haven't been yourself. I mean, you never, ever used to blow off band practice," Shiloh says.

"I know. And I just want to let you guys know how proud I am of you for throwing me out of the band."

They all blink at me vacantly. "Proud of us?" Alex finally says.

"Yeah. I'm proud of you for stepping up when I wasn't there for you. I'm glad you care enough about the band not to let it fail, to protect it, even from me. I know it sounds weird, but once I thought about it for a while it made me realize you guys are in this as much as I was. I know this is your dream too, not just mine, and I'm so sorry I blew an opportunity for you."

Alex is obviously melting. He was always the quickest to forgive. I search Shiloh's face. It's lost the marble texture it had when he opened the door. I can't bring myself to look at Jayden. We have so much more to settle than this.

"You know," Alex says. "To be fair, you did *get* us the opportunity to begin with. We're pretty massive screwups too. We put it all on you for so long. I just didn't know what you did for us until you weren't there doing it anymore, you know?"

"I love you guys," I say. "I know you'll probably never trust me like you did, but I want to try to make up for it. Brad is going to be at the Chapel tonight to see the Suicidal Angels." A twinge of dread that that doesn't include me anymore flutters through me, but they miss it in their bewilderment.

"Are you being real right now?" Alex asks.

All I can do is smile and nod. Alex and Shiloh start running around the room picking up everything they'll need, too excited for their own good. Alex kisses me on the cheek and hugs me. It's driving me nuts that no one will give me a hint as to whether or not they have a singer, but I remind myself the hug is enough. They're back in my life. Jayden is still on the couch, so I go sit next to him.

"How did you get Brad?" he asks.

I shrug. "Ask and you shall receive."

"It took a year of asking last time."

"I guess I asked better this time," I say. He stays quiet. I can see he wants to say something, but he can't seem to get it out. I just keep hearing my own voice echoing, that awful fight. Can we get past this? Will Jayden and I ever be okay? Can he forget the kiss? Can he forget the way I pulled back? Can he see me and not see her attached to me and all the things he hates? Can he get past what I said? Can he forgive me for telling him he put my brother in the ground? His friend? Why do I always forget how close they were? Is it easier for me to think I'm the only one who feels it? "I'm sorry, Jay. I shouldn't have said it."

"You were right. It was my fault."

"It doesn't do us any good to blame each other. It doesn't bring him back. I don't know why it felt so important to include you in my guilt."

"I loved him, Rainn. I didn't mean to hurt him."

"I know. Of course, you didn't."

"I'm so sorry."

"Me too."

"Hey! Quit with the love fest in there. We have to go!" Alex yells.

I can't stand waiting in limbo any longer. "Do you have a singer or what?"

"Yeah, stupid," Alex says. "You."

I look to Shiloh and Jayden, feeling like I need to verify this with everyone.

"You do want back in, right?" Jayden asks.

"Of course, I do. I just, I don't know, I didn't know what was going on. You said you were finding someone else and I…" I choke up. The guys gather around me and give me a group hug.

"We're not the Suicidal Angels without you."

Chapter Twenty-eight

Benny has no qualms about bumping Travesty for us when we explain what's going on. The singer comes over and pushes me jokingly. "Good to have you back. I was getting irritated with actually playing when we were supposed to all the time."

"Sorry. I won't let it happen again." I wink, and we help them tear down their set so we can get our own up. It's a mad dash of passing cymbals and cords and amps around. We have plenty of time before the show, but we could use some practice after our hiatus, and the window for that is closing fast. Just as we're closing in on being set up, Jayden rests his chin on my shoulder. He gets bad stage fright episodes, but it's a little early for that.

"You okay?"

"I didn't get to do my hair," he says.

I laugh. "Too late now. It looks good. Don't worry about it." I actually like it black for once instead of some ridiculous color.

"Rainn!" he says. "You know I can't go on without my Mohawk!"

"What are you, thirteen? You can't be serious."

"It makes me feel better," he says. "I'm someone who can handle this when I have my Mohawk."

"Well, what the hell do you want me to do?"

"Got any glue?"

"Oh yes, I keep some with me at all times."

"You're not taking me seriously," he says.

"Of course I'm not," I hiss back and keep helping Alex with his drums.

"Rainnnnn," he starts whining. I can't deal with whining.

"Fine, go to the store and get some fucking gel or Gorilla Glue or whatever the hell you need. We'll finish setting up." He leans over and kisses my cheek and runs out the door.

Finishing up in time without Jayden is easy enough. I play with Alex and Shiloh a little, warming up my voice, debating over which songs to include or to ditch. Jayden stays locked in the bathroom, perfecting his hair. I always thought it was vanity more than anything. I feel like I know him a little better realizing how important the ritual is to him. Then again, I kind of just want to smack him.

Too many people start coming in, and we have to stop playing until it's time. We don't get any time to refresh ourselves as a complete group, which makes me nervous. We sit at the bar watching the door and wait. It's painful.

"Rainn." Benny taps my shoulder. I spin. "There's a guy on the phone for you."

"What? Who?" Fuck. My heart sinks as I anticipate Brad canceling. Even if he does, I guess it's a slight improvement that he's going to actually tell us.

Benny shrugs. "Want me to ask?"

"No." I sigh and look at each of the guys. I know they're thinking the same thing. They're trying to be good sports, but I can't stand the disappointment that's filling their eyes. "No, I'll just take it."

I circle the bar and go to the cord phone attached to the wall. I pick the receiver off the bar and take a breath before I answer. "Hello?"

"Rainn? It's Noah."

"Noah? What..." My brain short-circuits. I can't put together a sentence. The relief it isn't Brad drains to be replaced with fear. My stomach twists, and I break into a cold sweat. "What's wrong?"

"I just got a call on my cell. Jaselle's in jail."

"What?" I ask way louder than I mean to. "What are you talking about? I just talked to her a couple hours ago. She wasn't feeling well. She was in bed. What…" My head is spinning. "What?"

"She got picked up buying drugs. She called begging me to bail her out."

"That can't be right." My ears are ringing as my brain starts to catch up. "She…" I can't bring myself to say she promised. It sounds so juvenile at this point, so naïve.

"Sounds like she got caught up in a sting or something," he goes on. "She wasn't making a ton of sense. She was kind of hysterical, crying. Said she was scared."

"Scared? Of what?"

"I don't know. Jail isn't exactly a fun place."

My heart drops. The image of Jaselle in jail is crippling. The idea of her fear is suffocating. Everything in me screams to drop everything and go bail her out, though I don't even know how I would manage it. I know Noah won't do it. I can't seem to move. This doesn't feel real. I look around the bar in a kind of shell shock. The guys and Benny are all staring at me trying to figure out if the show is still on, frozen in anticipation.

It feels like an emergency. Jaselle crying, Jaselle's fear, it's always triggered a fight-or-flight response in me, but I look at the guys, and I can't break their hearts. I won't. "I can't," I say into the phone.

"Can't what?"

"Bail her out. I can't right now."

"You don't—"

"I can't. She lied to me. She lied to me again." The adrenaline is changing shape from dread and fear. The knot in my throat turns to anger. "I have a show tonight. This is the biggest night of my career, and she used it to sneak off and buy drugs. I'm not leaving. This is fucking bullshit. I shouldn't—"

"Rainn," Noah cuts in. "You're right. For God's sake, do your show. I never would have called you there if I'd known. Let her sit in jail. She'll be fine."

It goes against every instinct in my body, leaving me thrashing against the current of my mind. Again, there's that damn connection between us, an invisible circuitry that leaves me feeling everything she feels as vividly as if it were me, but I've had enough. My feelings matter too. My life matters too, and she can't have this night. I can't fix her life by torching mine.

"Noah, I have to go. I have to talk to you about this later. I can't."

"Forget it, Savage. She's safer in jail than the streets anyway. Put it out of your mind and kick some ass."

Put it out of my mind. Right. I hang up and turn to the guys.

"You okay?" Jayden asks. I'm not. I'm walking through the timeline. She would have had to start this little misadventure the moment she got off the phone with me. She promised me she wouldn't use in one breath and started looking for dealers in the next. I don't want to believe that, but there's no way around it. They move to hug me, but I put up a hand to stop them. Sympathy will send me into a tailspin. I have to shake this off. I have to bury it. For now.

Brad walks in. I smack the guys and point him out. Instead of the smiles I expect, they all turn a pale shade of green.

"Fuck, man, we haven't practiced in months," Shiloh says.

"And you just got hit with some heavy shit," Alex says to me. "Can you get through this?"

Jayden looks like a jittery mess, a sure sign his stage fright fit is kicking in.

"Oh God, and you're falling apart too?" Shiloh asks. "This is going to be a disaster."

"I think I need to puke," Jayden says.

"Hey," I snap. "Stop it. All of you. It's going to be just fine. We've done this a million times. It's just the same old Chapel-rats."

"I can't feel my fingers," Jayden says. "How can I play guitar when I can't feel my fingers? I'm going to suck. We're going to eat shit so hard."

"Stop it. Your fingers are fine. You're the best guitarist in the city. You've got your Mohawk. We are *not* going to eat it."

The lights go out. It's almost time.

"I can't remember the set list," Shiloh says.

"God, our minds are so not in this," Alex says. "Jay's going to puke, Shiloh forgot the songs, you're going to run off to save your girlfriend."

"Look at me," I say. They're so rattled it takes them a minute to do it, but when we do all look at each other it has an instant calming effect. "I am here. I am in this, and we're going to slay. Jay's nerves are going to settle twenty seconds in like they always do. Shiloh, the set list is the same as always, just follow my cues. Alex, you're our Mr. Positivity. Shake this off and have fun. Come on." I hold out my fist. They stare at it for a minute before they finally smile and fist bump me.

"That's what I'm talking about." Alex winks.

We take the stage as Benny is getting to the end of his intro. Ideally, we should have already been up here, but whatever, as long as he says the Suicidal Angels and we start playing it's all good.

"The Suicidal Angels!"

Jayden starts us off. Once he gets past the first few notes he's fine. It happens every time. He's the biggest baby in the world before we start, and by the end he has the best presence up here.

"*I'm calling up the dead. Awakening the sickness in my head.*" The crowd is crazier than usual. They're losing their minds because they haven't seen us in so long. It's like rediscovering your favorite toy after it was lost for six months.

"*I am my own insanity, the reflection of my lies.*" It feels so good to sing. I forgot how liberating it is. Just scream. Scream out what's buried and everyone will listen. For once, everyone will listen.

"Drown me in the blood of yesterday's heartache. I am tomorrow's tragedy." The guys are on it. Alex is hitting every beat. You can't even feel our time apart.

"I am tomorrow's tragedy."

It pulses through me. It vibrates the entire room, and the eyes watching me are a warm blanket. Someone understands. All this anger. The pain. The rawness. You all understand. We're all in cells of the same hell.

"You guys are sick, huh?" I yell. They scream back at me. "You're all fucked too, aren't you?" They scream louder. *"I am tomorrow's tragedy. Why can't you be enough for me? I'm not who I'm supposed to be, someone please come and bury me."*

The applause keeps going long after we end the show. I don't think I've ever heard it go so long. We jump off the stage. We don't make it ten steps before Brad is by us. He has to lean close to my ear and yell for me to hear him.

"You guys really are good," he says. "I had a feeling about you."

"Thanks for coming," I yell.

"Yeah, yeah. Well, look, I have to go, but I've got some nine o'clocks I want to give you. Once you have more of a following we can talk about a better slot."

I think I'm trying to say yes, but nothing is coming out. I'm just smiling. Brad holds out his hand. It takes me a second to realize I'm supposed to shake it.

"See you Friday." He turns and disappears into the crowd like this is just a day in the office for him. When I turn, the guys and Benny are all staring at me again, waiting for the news they couldn't hear in the chaos.

I want to keep them in suspense, but I'm grinning ear to ear. "Friday at nine."

"Yes!" They whoop in unison and jump all over me. I laugh as I endure them bashing into me in excitement. They turn their attention to the row of shots Benny has lined up on the bar. Good ol' Benny. I push past the guys and give him a long hug.

SHADOWS OF A DREAM

"Good to see you again, kid," he says.

"I'm so sorry, Benny. I missed you."

"Hey," he says. "Forget it."

The celebration goes on, but Jaselle slowly creeps back into my thoughts. She's still in jail, and as furious as I am with her, I can't ignore that. My fix of shoving it into the soil of my emotions is temporary at best, and the issue is starting to sprout. Benny was right. Coming back to the Chapel, to my friends, my family, it's air when I've been choking for so long. My thoughts are linear again, free if only for this moment from the spiral they've been trapped in. Even if it's all a mess again later, for a moment, I'm me. For the moment, I am a human being who is separate from Jaselle, and I know I'm not happy. I know this is wrong.

"Benny, you think I could bartend with you tonight?"

He looks puzzled but ecstatic. "Absolutely. Of course, you can."

I pass behind the bar and start taking orders. At first, people are confused. I'm the star of the show, not the help, so I turn it into a proper after-party and use the soda nozzle to shower them all with water. It turns into the best fun I can remember even though it's tainted by the darkness underneath. Soon they're throwing more money at me in tips than I've had collectively in the last year.

Chapter Twenty-nine

Inmates can start making calls again in two minutes. When I got home last night and found out I couldn't talk to Jaselle for seven hours, I about came unglued. The cycle of confusion, desperation, and rage is a storm that's taking everything out of me. The only way I could keep myself sane was to learn more than I ever cared to know about how getting someone out of jail works. Not only will it require more money than I have, but doing it last night as Jaselle wanted wasn't even in the picture. Thank God I didn't run out on the show. The idea I even considered it sends me into fits of anger. After all we've been through, I don't know what she can possibly say to me, but I can't wait to hear it. The clang of the house phone ringing splits my thoughts. I swipe up the receiver and listen to the recording announcing an inmate from the Denver Detention Center is calling. When I accept the call, the line opens.

"What happened?" I demand.

"Rainn, God it's so good to hear your voice. I need you to get me out of here, baby. It's awful. I can't stay in here." Her voice is strangled with tears. This must be how she was with Noah.

"Wha—"

She lowers her voice to a whisper. "I'm so scared. Please, you have to get me out."

I want to grill her about how she ended up in jail a few hours after she said she was going to bed. I want to hold on to this anger like a lifeline, but one of the things that attracted me to Jaselle from the beginning was her solid disposition. Nothing makes her flinch. Bar fights, breakdowns, suicide art, hard drugs, a gun in the face, she's strong, calm, and cool. Anything that can make her act like this has my attention.

"What is it? What's scaring you?"

"This place. The guards, the girls, I'm not safe here. They're fucking crazy. I just want to come home, baby."

"I don't know how much it's going to be," I say. "They set it at your hearing."

"It's this afternoon. You have to be ready to get me out right when it's done, Rainn. I can't stand it here. It won't be more than a grand. Probably less."

"A grand! Where the hell am I supposed to get a grand?"

"I don't know, but you have to find it. Please get me out, Rainn. You have to."

I sigh and rub my eyes. The whole thing is so surreal I can barely engage with it. I feel so far away. "I bartended at the Chapel last night and made a hundred and fifty. If I keep doing that I'll have enough in a week."

"A week!" She breaks down, a complete puddle. "No, baby, please. Ask someone, ask Benny."

"I can't ask Benny," I say, but her panic is contagious. My skin is crawling as I search for another answer.

"The guys? Your mom? Anyone, Rainn."

The idea of asking anyone is repulsive to me. I've hurt them all so much already. If she's even thinking like that it means she's already been turned down by Noah and her mother. "I can try to sell some things. And I'll work. I'll work around the clock until I have it."

"Sell some things?"

"Your paintings. Is that okay?"

She scoffs. "Yeah right, you know how many times I've tried to sell those? They're worthless."

"Jaselle, what happened?"

"There's no time for that, Rainn. I only have ten minutes and it's almost over." She must be watching a clock, because just as she says it the recording kicks in to say we only have thirty seconds left.

"These fucking girls are going to kill me. You have to get me out. We can talk about it as much as you want then, I promise. But please, you have to get me out. Promise me."

"I'm trying, Jaselle."

"You have to, baby. Promise." A woman's voice drifts into the background. I can't make out the words, but the tone is mean. "I won't make it in here."

"I'll figure something out," I say.

"Don't leave me in here." Her shell is gone, her armor soft. She's naked and crying, begging without shame.

"I'm not," I say. "I'll find a way."

The call drops off and returns to a recording I cut off by slamming the phone down. "Goddamn it." I slam my fist on the kitchen counter. I try to play back the woman's voice in the background, seeing if I can pick out any semblance of a word. Were they yelling at her? Is she really in danger? Why would she be? It's just jail. She's not in San Quentin, for God's sake. But she's an oak. She doesn't cry wolf.

Not a single question is answered. Not an ounce of pressure has been released from my chest. I still don't know what she did or who she did it with or what she can possibly plan to say for herself, and yet I know I will do this task she's begged me to do. It's like she threw all her fear at me and I reflexively caught it, and now that I have it I have to handle it. I'll get her out because my sanity depends on it, because this hole in my chest is unbearable, because I need to look her in the eye while she explains her lies, her betrayal. I need to see what that looks like.

Jaselle's keys are on the coffee table, thank God. I'll need her car. It also means that wherever she went to buy, it was close enough to walk, which means it wasn't Ice's place. That's something, I guess. I go into the hallway and run my hand over the paintings. I take them down one by one, stacking them by the door to take downtown. I'll sell them on the corner. I'll spend all night out there if I have to. With the walls empty and the piano room vacant, it's like there's nothing left of us. I'm a ghost coming back to visit home a century later, finding emptiness where all our character has been erased in favor of white plaster. The meth took it all. Everything we were. Every swipe of color. Every tone of heart. Drained.

CHAPTER THIRTY

Selling Jaselle's paintings on 16th Street Mall is a piece of cake. Sure, it takes a while, but I find I can get people to buy them for fifty a piece pretty easily, and two go for seventy-five. Combined with my tips from bartending, I have five hundred and fifty by the time Jaselle's hearing is over. When I call to find out what bail landed at, I find out it's enough. Her bail is five grand, which means I only need five hundred for bond.

I meet the bondsman in the lobby of the jail and give him the money. Getting the paperwork in order that promises Jaselle's car to him if she skips out takes some time, but she obviously agrees, because the bondsman disappears without me even noticing and the pissy woman behind the glass tells me Jaselle will be out in ten to fifteen minutes. Now that it's all done, I'm nervous to see her. Anticipating everything I need to say, everything she'll say back, is making my body run at full speed. I can't believe what I'm about to do.

A heavy door swings open, and she's standing there. She's washed out and looks confused, like she just woke up. She brightens a little when she sees me, but it's not the joy I expected after how dire she claimed her situation was. I hand over her keys and lead her out to where the car is parked. I slide into the passenger seat. The silence is making me sick. It's full of something so foreign. I don't know her. I've never felt that, not even when we met.

"Thank you," she says.

"You're welcome."

"I can't wait to just be at home in bed with you again."

"No." Just that one word is enough to make my voice shake. "This ends here, Jaselle."

"Wha—" She stalls on the directness of it. "I know you're mad. I know I need to explain. I told you as soon as I was out I could explain everything, and now I will."

"I thought I wanted that, but what could you possibly say? You lied to me. After everything that's happened, the second you had a few hours alone you snuck out behind my back to buy meth."

"Look, that's not how it happened."

"Yes, it is."

"No, it's not." She spins in the seat to face me. The sun is starting to really beat through the windshield on the dark interior. Her face has a little color again. "An old friend called saying he was in trouble. I was feeling a little better, so I went to help him out."

"Just stop."

"He said someone was after him, and he just needed me to hold on to it for him for an hour until after the guy could try to shake him down. I was never going to use—"

"Fucking stop. Just stop. What kind of idiot do you take me for?"

"You're really going to just look me in the eye and call me a liar?"

"What choice are you giving me?"

She locks on to my eyes. I can feel her digging through them trying to figure out just how sure I am, trying to figure out the right move. It makes me sick watching her try to manipulate me. Has it always been like this? Have I been this blind?

"You don't know how it feels," she finally whispers.

I nod. "You're right. I don't. But I know how this feels, and I can't do it anymore."

"Oh, so you're just going to punk out and walk away?" She pulls back, as if she needs to be farther away from me. "Don't you think I wish I could just quit? Don't you know I wish it was as easy for me as it is for you?"

"You think this is fucking easy?"

"You're not addicted, Rainn. You don't understand how bad it hurts. My head always hurts. I'm exhausted, but I can't sleep. I am always scared, Rainn. Always. I can't even fucking feel happy without it anymore. My brain won't do it. I swear to God I want to die. It takes everything I have not to do *that* to you. And you want what from me?" She's screaming by the end.

She hits her mark with the mention of suicide. A jolt of adrenaline has me ready to back all the way down this trail I've started with my tail between my legs. I close my eyes and try to center myself. Remember. What happened is so much bigger than this moment right now. It's not one mistake. It's lies, sneaking around, not coming home at night, screaming, cheating, pushing. It's lost dreams and desperation. It's that I haven't laughed in a month. It's that in trying to save her, I've lost me.

"I tried, Jaselle. I tried everything I knew to try, but I'm not helping you. It just…" I pause to try to keep myself from crying. "It just keeps getting worse."

"No, it's not." Jaselle leans forward and grabs my face. She peppers me with kisses. "It's not getting worse. I'm going to quit, baby. I got closer this time. You just have to hold on with me."

I shake my head and pull out of her grip. "I can't believe you anymore. You've broken too many promises."

"It will be different. I can't do it alone. I need you, Rainn. I can do it this time."

I'm defeated by how meaningless her words are to me. I'd love to wrap myself in them and feel better, but they just don't have that effect anymore. They're hollow. We're hollow.

"I can't do it again," I say. "I told you last time that was it. I meant it." Even I didn't realize how much.

"You're going to leave me alone with it? You're going to kill me?"

It hits so hard, so deep. I can't stop myself from falling apart. Everything in me is terrified that's the truth. She'll die without me. She'll have no reason not to use, and she'll barrel down that path until it's over. I gave it everything I had, and I'm still going to lose her.

"Fine, Rainn. Just go. If you're that much of a pussy, do it. If it's all just too *hard* for you, just go. Go to hell!" She clenches her hand into a fist and tightens her jaw. She looks at me with a fury I expect to burn out of her control, but she spins it on her car door and hits it as hard as she can. "You slept in a fucking alley when I met you. Where the hell do you get off forgetting everything I've done for you? Like you haven't had a bed to sleep in because of me. Like you haven't had a shower to use because of me. I guess you're the only one allowed to have hard times. I guess when we said we'd be together forever I was the only one who meant it."

"You fucked my rapist!" I yell. "If our relationship meant anything to you at all that would have been enough to stop you! If you were ever going to stop for me, it would have been then. You do not need me. You do not give a flying fuck about me!"

"It doesn't work like that!"

"Yes, it does!"

"Fine, then just go. You're right. I don't need you. All you ever do is feel sorry for yourself and try to make me feel like shit. Probably do better without you anyway."

"I hope you do." I say it sincerely. I mean it with all my heart, but it's too big a gear shift too fast, and she just scoffs.

"Get the fuck out of my sight, Rainn."

I look at her for an extra second after I open the door, not long enough to get her going again, just enough to try to memorize her. She's looking back at me. I wonder if she's doing the same thing, but I can't tell. I get out and close the door. I expect her to screech off, but she pulls away normally. I watch her car merge into traffic, blending with all the rest. Seeing her become part of the masses, a member of the billions of people who aren't part of my life puts a toxic blend of panic, longing, and horror in me. I sit down in the parking space and fall apart. I don't know what to do with this kind of pain. I can't go back. I know what I did was right, but that means I have to feel this.

Chapter Thirty-one

It's the four-year anniversary of Michael's death. Combined with it being just my second week without Jaselle, I figure it might kill me. I cry over her like a death. As bad as I knew it would be, somehow it still surprises me just how much this can hurt. But it's Wednesday, one of the nights I've told Benny I'll bartend, and I have to move. I have to get up off this cold concrete. I have to pull myself together.

"Hey," he says when I walk in the back door. He says it carefully, like I'll break.

"Hey."

"You up for this?" he asks. I nod. I know my eyes are probably still red and swollen, but that's just my existence right now. I actually enjoy working with Benny.

"Anything I can do?"

"Pass me a rag?" He does, and I start wiping down the bar. Light is coming in from the windows, the kind of light that eventually feels warm if you stand under it long enough. Sun. Warmth. It brings me back to life a little.

"I'm recording the game if you want to watch after work," Benny says. I smile. After work. It's a new phrase in my life. Watching the game with Benny is an old one, though. The invitation sends me grasping for an excuse out, but then I remember I don't need one. I don't need to go back to Jaselle. There's no crisis I have to handle. I can watch the game with Benny. To my surprise, I actually want to. I don't want to go back to the alley. I don't want to wallow.

Band practice is tomorrow. Our first show at Brad's place is the next day. When I used to picture life without Jaselle, all I could see was emptiness. Loneliness. Sadness. It's not like that. I'm not alone. It's not a substitute. The hole is there, but for the first time, I feel like I'll survive. I feel lighter. I feel free.

I still go through attacks of insane urges to run back, to call. I tell myself I'll just be making sure she's okay, and that's not the same as getting back together, but I know that will hurt us both more than it helps. I can't stop her from doing what she's going to do. I can't love her out of this. I can't fix it no matter how much I yell or beg or spy or cry. I've set down that burden, and I'm not picking it back up. The shadows look so much darker now that I'm out of them. My eyes adjusted to such pain. It's a dangerous thing I don't want to get too close to in case it tries to swallow me again. A tingle of something creeps up my spine as I look at Benny. What is it?

"I'd love to watch the game." Happiness. I'm happy. Jesus, why does it feel foreign if I was so happy with Jaselle all this time? I hold on too tight. All this time I've been holding on with everything in me. Holding on to things that aren't mine to control. I have to let go.

"Hey, Ben, do you mind if I use the phone real quick?"

"Of course not."

I pick it up and punch in a collection of numbers I can hardly believe I remember. It rings twice, then picks up. There's a pause before she speaks. "Hello?"

It's jarring to hear my mother's voice after so long. I recognize it, but it's not the same as I remember. I can't seem to get any words out. I should have made more of a plan. What if she doesn't realize what day this is? It wouldn't be good to remind her if she doesn't. But of course she knows. "It wasn't your fault," I say.

Silence stretches for a year. Just when I think she'll probably hang up, she speaks.

"Rainey."

It seems like that's all there will be, but with some sixth sense, I know more is coming. I know she's crying.

"It wasn't yours either, Rainey. I'm so sorry. There's so much I wish I could take back. I just couldn't handle it."

"It's okay. Me either."

I hear music in the background. Rock music. It almost makes me laugh at first it's so out of character, but when it sinks in a lump forms in my throat.

"The Doors," I say.

"What?"

"If you want to listen to something, he loved the Doors."

"Thank you." It barely comes out. She hates crying. "I love you, Rainey."

"I love you too, Mom."

Chapter Thirty-two

It takes me about four paychecks from Brad and Benny to be able to afford a studio apartment. It's small. It's basement level with brick walls and no windows whatsoever, and the front door doesn't stay closed. The latch doesn't quite latch. If I had anything of value, that would bother me a lot more, but since the only thing in here so far is some ramen noodles, a plastic bowl and spoon, my electric keyboard that's still missing the middle A key, and a couple blankets, I'm not too worried. Jayden gave me one of his old heavy amps to use to block the door when I'm home at night. It's not like someone can't get past it if they try, but the idea is that no one will think to try because the door will appear to be closed and locked like a normal place.

Even though I'm not thrilled about the lock, mostly I'm just happy I have a door. To tell you the truth, it bothers everyone else a lot more than it bothers me. Noah keeps going on about how it isn't safe. It sort of cracks me up since I used to sleep outside. No deadbolts there, but I guess the concern is sweet.

"Hello?" Noah waits by the door like a gentleman instead of just walking in.

"Hey."

"I called a locksmith," he says. "They're coming to fix your shit."

"Tonight?"

"Yeah."

"I told you I don't have money for that yet," I say.

"Yeah, yeah. I'm paying for it, calm down. You can pay me back when you have it if you want to be stubborn, but I'm more than happy to take care of it for you. It's not that much anyway."

"You still should have asked me. I play at the Cuff Link tonight. I'm not going to be here."

Noah holds out his arms. "Ta-da! That's why I'm here. You go do your show. I'll stay here and babysit, and when you get home I'll give you the keys, and no one will be able to randomly walk into your place anymore."

"Apparently, I don't have a choice. You're here and I have to go."

"Yeah, that was the idea. Have fun! See you tonight."

I try to drown myself in music. Brad not only lets us play the Cuff Link, he connects us with tons of people in the game, boosting us to an average of three gigs a week with a wave of his hand, and we still make time to go play the Chapel too. It's just fun for us since that's where we came from, and believe it or not, we actually bring Benny business. It's the least we could do for him. We practice almost every single day, and when the guys are tired of me, I go home and practice by myself. I think they know I'm using this as a distraction. There are worse ways I could try to cope with missing and worrying about Jaselle.

We finish up our show around eleven. Usually, I'd stay and hang out with them a little longer, but I know Noah is still sitting around my apartment just waiting for me to get home so he can leave. I wonder how painful it is for him trying to kill five hours in an apartment with no weed, alcohol, or TV.

It takes me about half an hour to walk from the Cuff Link to the apartment, to *my* apartment. I'm still getting used to that. I picked a place close by on purpose. I still don't see a car coming into my life any time soon. I get to the door, and there's a brand-new lock on it, as promised. I knock and wait for Noah to answer. It takes him a while. I wonder if he fell asleep. I knock again.

"I'm coming, I'm coming. Calm down," he says. I hear the new deadbolt slide back and he opens the door. "You like?"

"Very nice," I say. He holds up two keys. One is a spare, I guess. My throat tightens as I immediately wish I could give it to Jaselle. I wonder if moments like this will ever stop happening. I shake it off before he can see. I don't want him to see me being sad while he's being so damn happy.

I close the door and lock it behind me. Noah beams like a little kid when I do that. He turns around and walks the short entryway back toward my one and only room. I guess he's planning to hang out a while. I just want to go to bed. I roll my eyes a little but try to keep the smile face ready to go.

I turn the corner and freeze. My muscles stop moving like I've been sprayed with that liquid nitrogen that makes everything shatter. Taking up basically the entire room is Jaselle's piano. My piano. It looks just the same as the day I had to sell it. The finish is still faded from the years, the strings are still dusty, the ivory keys still have their little chips.

"Oh my God, Noah. What did you do?" I fight the mist forming over my eyes.

"Don't worry, I got it back before he did anything to it."

"How did you…" I can't form a full sentence.

"Don't worry, I didn't steal it or anything. I bought it back from him."

"How?"

"Don't worry about it, Rainn. It's a gift. You're not supposed to ask me how much it was or where I got the money. I promise you it's all legit."

"But shouldn't you give this back to Jaselle?"

"Why? So she can sell it for crank? She gave it to you, Rainn, and that was a good call. You'll take care of it."

That's a twist of the knife. "She isn't any better, then?"

He tilts his head and looks at me with soft, watery eyes. "She's not any worse, either, if it helps. She's doing what she does."

Every time I think the vise grip on my chest is as tight as it can possibly go, something else happens to make it squeeze another notch.

"Hey," Noah says. "Let's not get all sad, okay? That's not why I brought it. If it's too much having it here, I can take it away. I just thought it was the right thing for you to have it."

"Don't take it away."

He smiles. "Good. Then can you look at your piano now? Can you play something?"

I circle around the piano like the first time I saw it. I try to will myself to sit down and play something, but I'm still fighting to stay composed. I know Noah can see it. He's blurry from the layer of tears permanently formed over my eyes. This piano is a piece of her. Of me. A piece of us. What we were before the drug, anyway. It's a version of us that was lost.

"I miss her," I say.

"I know."

"I was so sure I could save her."

"You did, Rainn. You saved her so many times, in so many ways."

"It wasn't enough."

"I don't think it's about 'enough.' You did everything you could, but you can't do it for her."

"You told me that so many times, but I wouldn't believe you. I couldn't."

"Don't beat yourself up about it, Rainn. It took me a long time to get there. I wanted to show you the shortcut, but we all have to walk the path ourselves." Noah's voice is quiet, like he's thinking about all this for the first time.

"Do you think she'll ever get clean?"

He shakes his head. "I don't know."

I run my hand over the strings of the piano as my mind fills with her voice explaining suicidal angels to Shelby. "There's a darkness inside that will never go away. They touch our lives and then they're gone." Was she always only meant to be a visitor in my life?

"I wish we hadn't left off so horribly."

"She knows you love her," Noah says. "She's just in it too deep to love you back the way you deserve."

"I know."

I sit down on the piano bench and hold my hands over the keys, afraid to touch them. I remember her watching me play, the way her stormy eyes went so deep into me I lost my breath. I remember her coming up behind me, interrupting my song to wrap her arms around me, her breath in my hair. I remember her telling me not to look so rigid while I played so she could paint a natural portrait. I remember her lying beneath the piano just listening, her painting to my music in the other room.

I remember Michael's bow crying over violin strings. The way his violin exploded when he swung it like a baseball bat at Mom's dreams. Circles around a bag of spray paint. Screaming in the woods, drumming on rocks. Jumping chain-link and risking everything for art. This is where it's all come.

Maybe they can still hear me. Maybe even through space and time and loss they can still feel our connection as clearly as I can. Maybe now that I've come back to myself, I can be the guardian of the beautiful pieces of them that were lost at sea instead of an echo chamber for their pain. I call up that frozen place in time before things were broken. I reach out for it with the notes of my soul. I take a deep breath and begin Michael's song.

About the Author

Nicole is a lifelong storyteller who loves exploring the hidden corners of the human experience. She lives in Denver, Colorado, where she is a collector of jobs and hobbies that inspire her writing. She has worked as a 911 operator, police dispatcher, and martial arts instructor. Most recently, she and her wife started a music video production company and love working together as producer and director.

Books Available from Bold Strokes Books

Date Night by Raven Sky. Quinn and Riley are celebrating their one-year anniversary. Such an important milestone is bound to result in some extraordinary sexual adventures, but precisely how extraordinary is up to you, dear reader. (978-1-63555-655-1)

Face Off by PJ Trebelhorn. Hockey player Savannah Wells rarely spends more than a night with any one woman, but when photographer Madison Scott buys the house next door, she's forced to rethink what she expects out of life. (978-1-63555-480-9)

Hot Ice by Aurora Rey, Elle Spencer, Erin Zak. Can falling in love melt the hearts of the iciest ice queens? Join Aurora Rey, Elle Spencer, and Erin Zak to find out! (978-1-63555-513-4)

Line of Duty by VK Powell. Dr. Dylan Carlyle's professional and personal life is turned upside down when a tragic event at Fairview Station pits her against ambitious, handsome police officer Finley Masters. (978-1-63555-486-1)

London Undone by Nan Higgins. London Craft reinvents her life after reading a childhood letter to her future self and in doing so finds the love she truly wants. (978-1-63555-562-2)

Lunar Eclipse by Gun Brooke. Moon De Cruz lives alone on an uninhabited planet after being shipwrecked in space. Her life changes forever when Captain Beaux Lestarion's arrival threatens the planet and Moon's freedom. (978-1-63555-460-1)

One Small Step by Michelle Binfield. Iris and Cam discover the meaning of taking chances and following your heart, even if it means getting hurt. (978-1-63555-596-7)

Shadows of a Dream by Nicole Disney. Rainn has the talent to take her rock band all the way, but falling in love is a powerful distraction, and her new girlfriend's meth addiction might just take them both down. (978-1-63555-598-1)

Someone to Love by Jenny Frame. When Davina Trent is given an unexpected family, can she let nanny Wendy Darling teach her to open her heart to the children and to Wendy? (978-1-63555-468-7)

Tinsel by Kris Bryant. Did a sweet kitten show up to help Jessica Raymond and Taylor Mitchell find each other? Or is the holiday spirit to blame for their special connection? (978-1-63555-641-4)

Uncharted by Robyn Nyx. As Rayne Marcellus and Chase Stinsen track the legendary Golden Trinity, they must learn to put their differences aside and depend on one another to survive. (978-1-63555-325-3)

Where We Are by Annie McDonald. Can two women discover a way to walk on the same path together and discover the gift of staying in one spot, in time, in space, and in love? (978-1-63555-581-3)

A Moment in Time by Lisa Moreau. A longstanding family feud separates two women who unexpectedly fall in love at an antique clock shop in a small Louisiana town. (978-1-63555-419-9)

Aspen in Moonlight by Kelly Wacker. When art historian Melissa Warren meets Sula Johansen, director of a local bear conservancy, she discovers that love can come in unexpected and unusual forms. (978-1-63555-470-0)

Back to September by Melissa Brayden. Small bookshop owner Hannah Shepard and famous romance novelist Parker Bristow maneuver the landscape of their two very different worlds to find out if love can win out in the end. (978-1-63555-576-9)

Changing Course by Brey Willows. When the woman of your dreams falls from the sky, you'd better be ready to catch her. (978-1-63555-335-2)

Cost of Honor by Radclyffe. First Daughter Blair Powell and Homeland Security Director Cameron Roberts face adversity when their enemies stop at nothing to prevent President Andrew Powell's reelection. (978-1-63555-582-0)

Fearless by Tina Michele. Determined to overcome her debilitating fear through exposure therapy, Laura Carter all but fails before she's even begun until dolphin trainer Jillian Marshall dedicates herself to helping Laura defeat the nightmares of her past. (978-1-63555-495-3)

Not Dead Enough by J.M. Redmann. A woman who may or may not be dead drags Micky Knight into a messy con game. (978-1-63555-543-1)

Not Since You by Fiona Riley. When Charlotte boards her honeymoon cruise single and comes face-to-face with Lexi, the high school love she left behind, she questions every decision she has ever made. (978-1-63555-474-8)

Not Your Average Love Spell by Barbara Ann Wright. Four women struggle with who to love and who to hate while fighting to rid a kingdom of an evil invading force. (978-1-63555-327-7)

Tennessee Whiskey by Donna K. Ford. Dane Foster wants to put her life on pause and ask for a redo, a chance for something that matters. Emma Reynolds is that chance. (978-1-63555-556-1)

30 Dates in 30 Days by Elle Spencer. A busy lawyer tries to find love the fast way—thirty dates in thirty days. (978-1-63555-498-4)

Finding Sky by Cass Sellars. Skylar Addison's search for a career intersects with her new boss's search for butterflies, but Skylar can't forgive Jess's intrusion into her life. (978-1-63555-521-9)

Hammers, Strings, and Beautiful Things by Morgan Lee Miller. While on tour with the biggest pop star in the world, rising musician Blair Bennett falls in love for the first time while coping with loss and depression. (978-1-63555-538-7)

Heart of a Killer by Yolanda Wallace. Contract killer Santana Masters's only interest is her next assignment—until a chance meeting with a beautiful stranger tempts her to change her ways. (978-1-63555-547-9)

Leading the Witness by Carsen Taite. When defense attorney Catherine Landauer reluctantly becomes the key witness in prosecutor Starr Rio's latest criminal trial, their hearts, careers, and lives may be at risk. (978-1-63555-512-7)

No Experience Required by Kimberly Cooper Griffin. Izzy Treadway has resigned herself to a life without romance because of her bipolar illness but wonders what she's gotten herself into when she agrees to write a book about love. (978-1-63555-561-5)

One Walk in Winter by Georgia Beers. Olivia Santini and Hayley Boyd Markham might be rivals at work, but they discover that lonely hearts often find company in the most unexpected of places. (978-1-63555-541-7)

The Inn at Netherfield Green by Aurora Rey. Advertising executive Lauren Montgomery and gin distiller Camden Crawley don't agree on anything except saving the Rose & Crown, the old English pub that's brought them together. (978-1-63555-445-8)

Top of Her Game by M. Ullrich. When it comes to life on the field and matters of the heart, losing isn't an option for pro athletes Kenzie Shaw and Sutton Flores. (978-1-63555-500-4)

Vanished by Eden Darry. A storm is coming, and Ellery and Loveday must find the chosen one or humanity won't survive it. (978-1-63555-437-3)

All She Wants by Larkin Rose. Marci Jones and Tessa Dalton get more than they bargained for when their plans for a one-night stand turn into an opportunity for love. (978-1-63555-476-2)

Beautiful Accidents by Erin Zak. Stevie Adams and Bernadette Thompson discover that sometimes the best things in life happen purely by accident. (978-1-63555-497-7)

Before Now by Joy Argento. Can Delany and Jade overcome the betrayal that spans the centuries to reignite a love that can't be broken? (978-1-63555-525-7)

Breathe by Cari Hunter. Paramedic Jemima Pardon's chronic bad luck seems to be improving when she meets police officer Rosie Jones. But they face a battle to survive before they can find love. (978-1-63555-523-3)

Double-Crossed by Ali Vali. Hired thief and killer Reed Gable finds something in her scope that will change her life forever when she gets a contract to end casino accountant Brinley Myers's life. (978-1-63555-302-4)

False Horizons by CJ Birch. Jordan and Ash struggle with different views on the alien agenda and must find their way back to each other before they're swallowed up by a centuries-old war. (978-1-63555-519-6)

Legacy by Charlotte Greene. When five women hike to a remote cabin deep inside a national park, unsettling events suggest that they should have stayed home. (978-1-63555-490-8)

Royal Street Reveillon by Greg Herren. Someone is killing the stars of a reality show, and it's up to Scotty Bradley and the boys to find out who. (978-1-63555-545-5)

Somewhere Along the Way by Kathleen Knowles. When Maxine Cooper moves to San Francisco during the summer of 1981, she learns that wherever you run, you cannot escape yourself. (978-1-63555-383-3)

Blood of the Pack by Jenny Frame. When Alpha of the Scottish pack Kenrick Wulver visits the Wolfgangs, she falls for Zaria Lupa, a wolf on the run. (978-1-63555-431-1)

Cause of Death by Sheri Lewis Wohl. Medical student Vi Akiak and K9 Search and Rescue officer Kate Renard must work together to find a killer before they end up the next targets. In the race for survival, they discover that love may be the biggest risk of all. (978-1-63555-441-0)

Chasing Sunset by Missouri Vaun. Hijinks and mishaps ensue as Iris and Finn set off on a road trip adventure, chasing the sunset, and falling in love along the way. (978-1-63555-454-0)

Double Down by MB Austin. When an unlikely friendship with Spanish pop star Erlea turns deeper, Celeste, in-house physician for the hotel hosting Erlea's show, has a choice to make—run or double down on love. (978-1-63555-423-6)

Party of Three by Sandy Lowe. Three friends are in for a wild night at billionaire heiress Eleanor McGregor's twenty-fifth birthday party. Love, lust, and doing the right thing, even when it hurts, turn the evening into one that will change their lives forever. (978-1-63555-246-1)

Sit. Stay. Love. by Karis Walsh. City girl Alana Brendt and country vet Tegan Evans both know they don't belong together. Only problem is, they're falling in love. (978-1-63555-439-7)

Where the Lies Hide by Renee Roman. As P.I. Camdyn Stark gets closer to solving the case, will her dark secrets and the lies she's buried jeopardize her future with the quietly beautiful Sarah Peters? (978-1-63555-371-0)